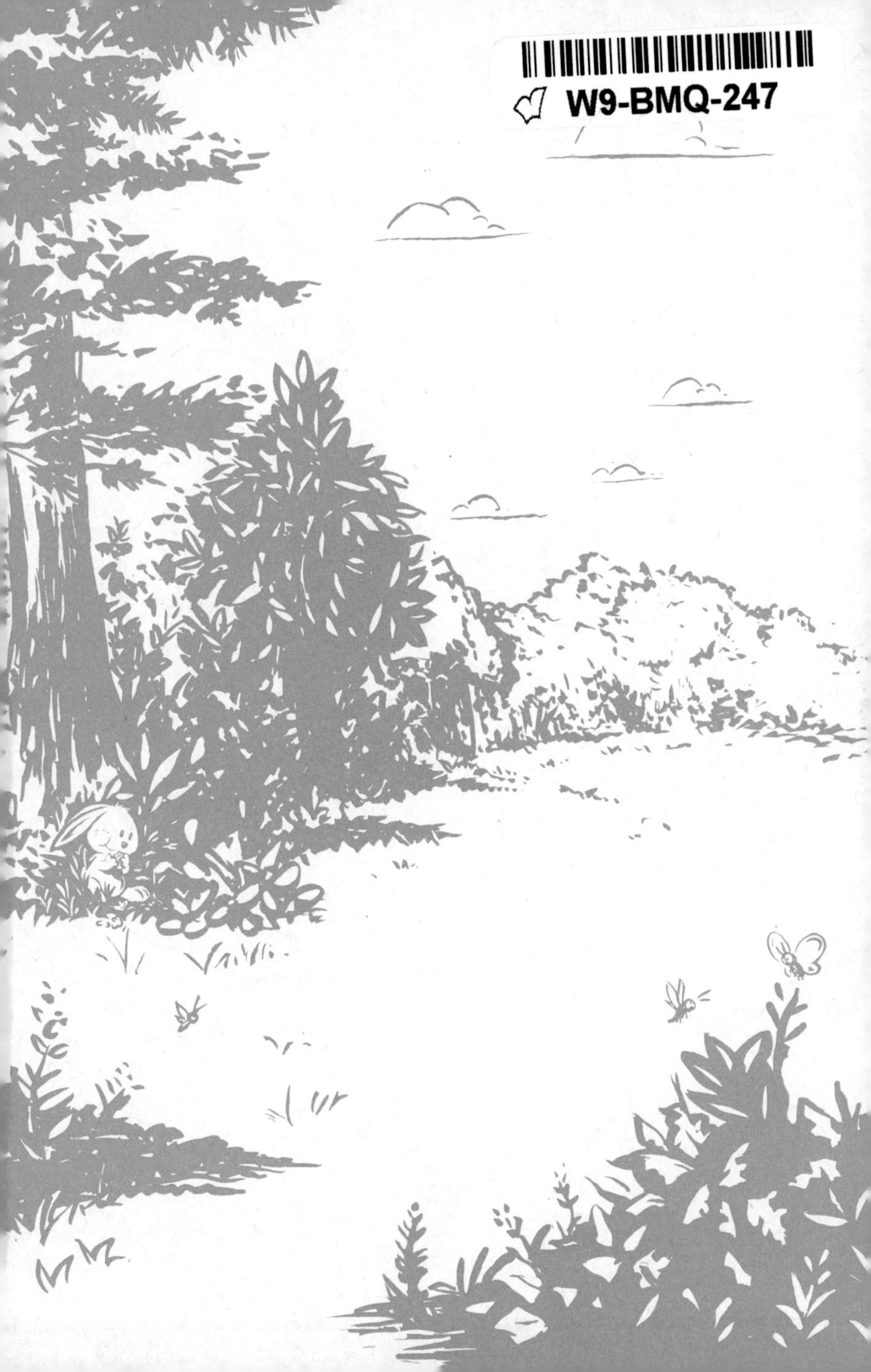

OWLY®

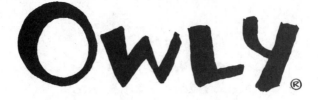

TINY TALES

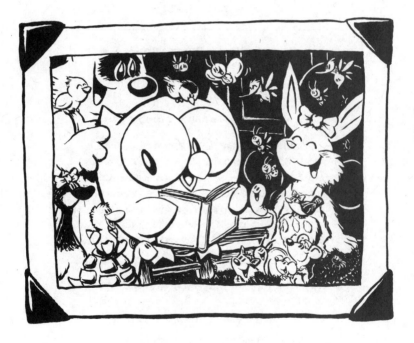

ANDY RUNTON

OWLY:
VOLUME FIVE, TINY TALES

© 2003-2008 ANDY RUNTON

OWLY is © & ® 2003-2012 ANDY RUNTON

ISBN: 978-1-60309-019-3

1. ALL-AGES
2. ORNITHOLOGY
3. GRAPHIC NOVELS

TOP SHELF PRODUCTIONS
P.O. BOX 1282
MARIETTA, GA 30061-1282
U.S.A.

WWW.TOPSHELFCOMIX.COM / OWLY

PUBLISHED BY TOP SHELF PRODUCTIONS, INC.
PUBLISHERS: CHRIS STAROS AND BRETT WARNOCK.
TOP SHELF PRODUCTIONS ® AND THE TOP SHELF LOGO ARE
REGISTERED TRADEMARKS OF TOP SHELF PRODUCTIONS, INC.
ALL RIGHTS RESERVED. NO PART OF THIS PUBLICATION MAY
BE REPRODUCED WITHOUT PERMISSION, EXCEPT FOR
SMALL EXCERPTS FOR PURPOSES OF REVIEW.

EDITED BY CHRIS STAROS & ROBERT VENDITTI

TREE FRIENDLY!
PRINTED ON RECYCLED PAPER

SECOND PRINTING, FEBRUARY 2012
PRINTED IN CANADA

WWW.ANDYRUNTON.COM

CONTENTS

THIS BOOK COLLECTS MANY NEVER BEFORE PUBLISHED STORIES, THE OWLY FREE COMIC BOOK DAY COMICS, AND STORIES THAT ORIGINALLY APPEARED IN:

WIDE AWAKE #5
COMICS ANTHOLOGY
(GONE SWIMMIN')
WWW.WIDEAWAKEPRESS.COM

MOO COW FAN CLUB
CHILDREN'S MAGAZINE, SPRING 2004
(LET'S GO FLY A KITE)
WWW.MOOCOWFANCLUB.COM

BALTIMORE COMIC-CON
2004 CONVENTION PROGRAM
(AW NUTS!)
2006 CONVENTION PROGRAM
(MISSIN' YOU)
WWW.COMICON.COM/BALTIMORE

WIZARD #174
COMICS MAGAZINE, APRIL 2006
(HANGIN' UP TO DRY)
WWW.WIZARDUNIVERSE.COM

SPECIAL THANKS TO ALL OF THESE PUBLICATIONS AND TO CHRIS, DUANE, HOLLI, ANGELA, JUSTIN, BECKY, RYAN, MARC, AND STEVE, AND, OF COURSE, TO MY MOM, GALE, CHRIS, BRETT, ROB, AND ALL OF THE OWLY FANS FOR THEIR OVERWHELMING SUPPORT. ☺

SPLASHIN' AROUND

MAY, 2005

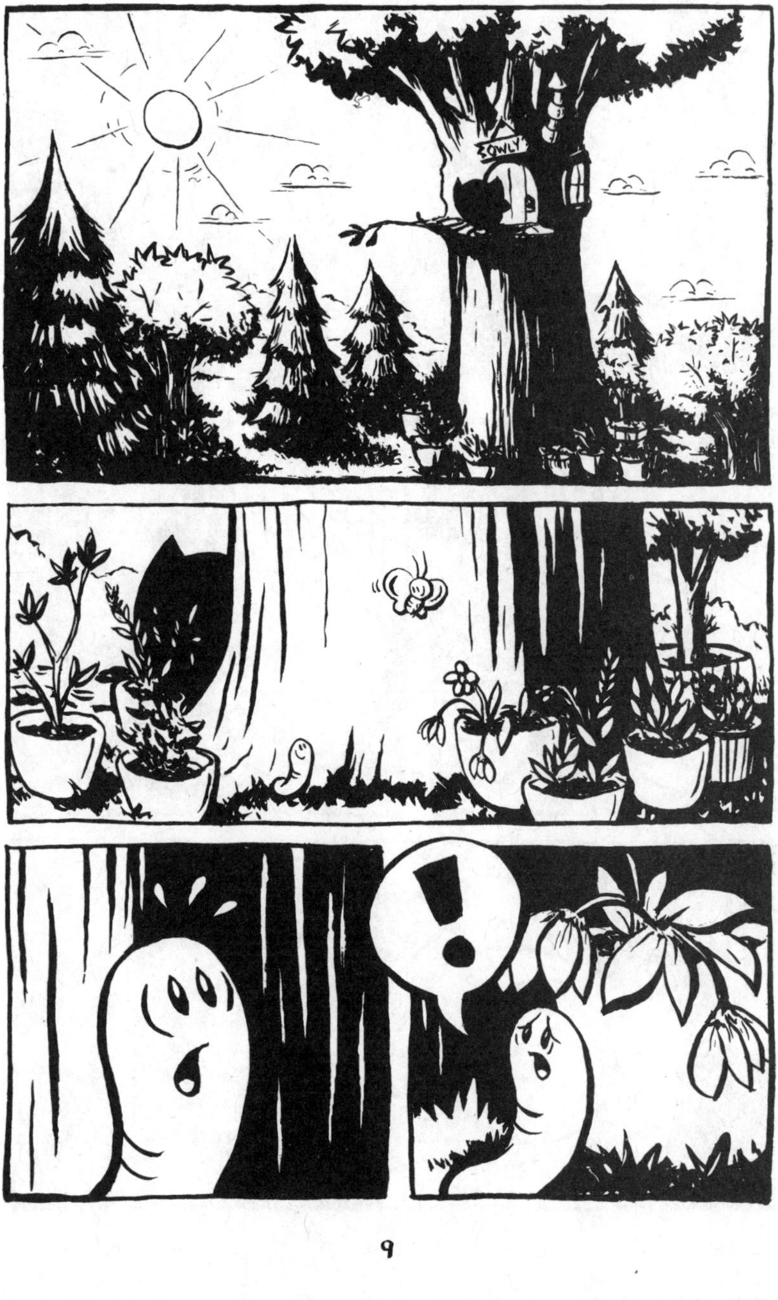

OWLY
!

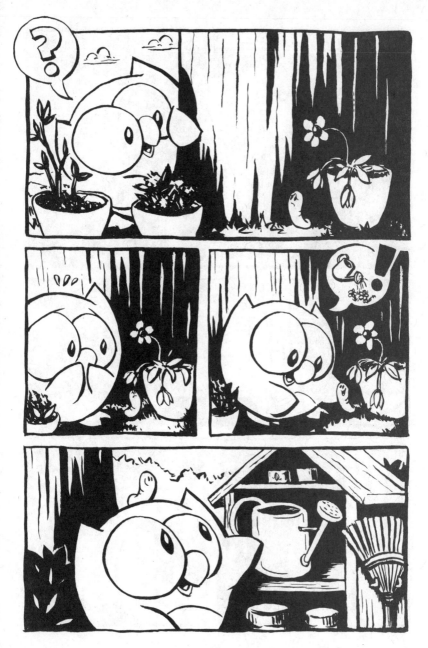

10

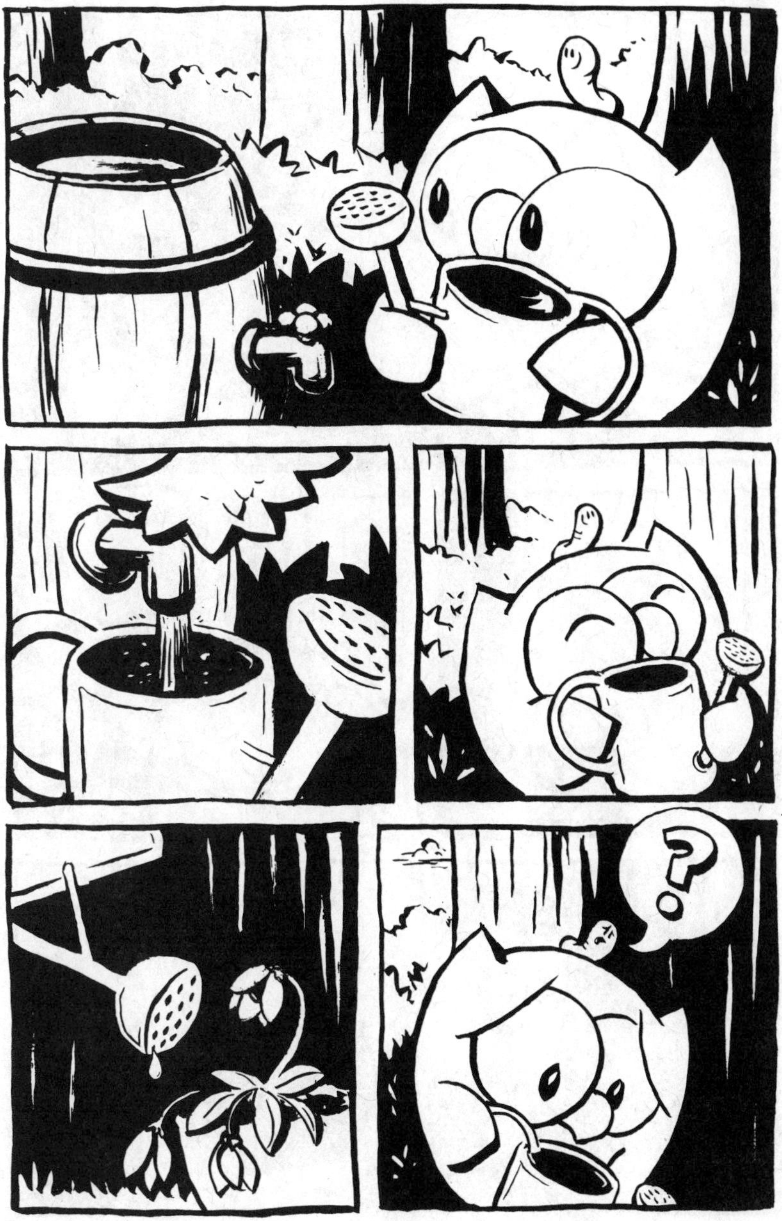
?

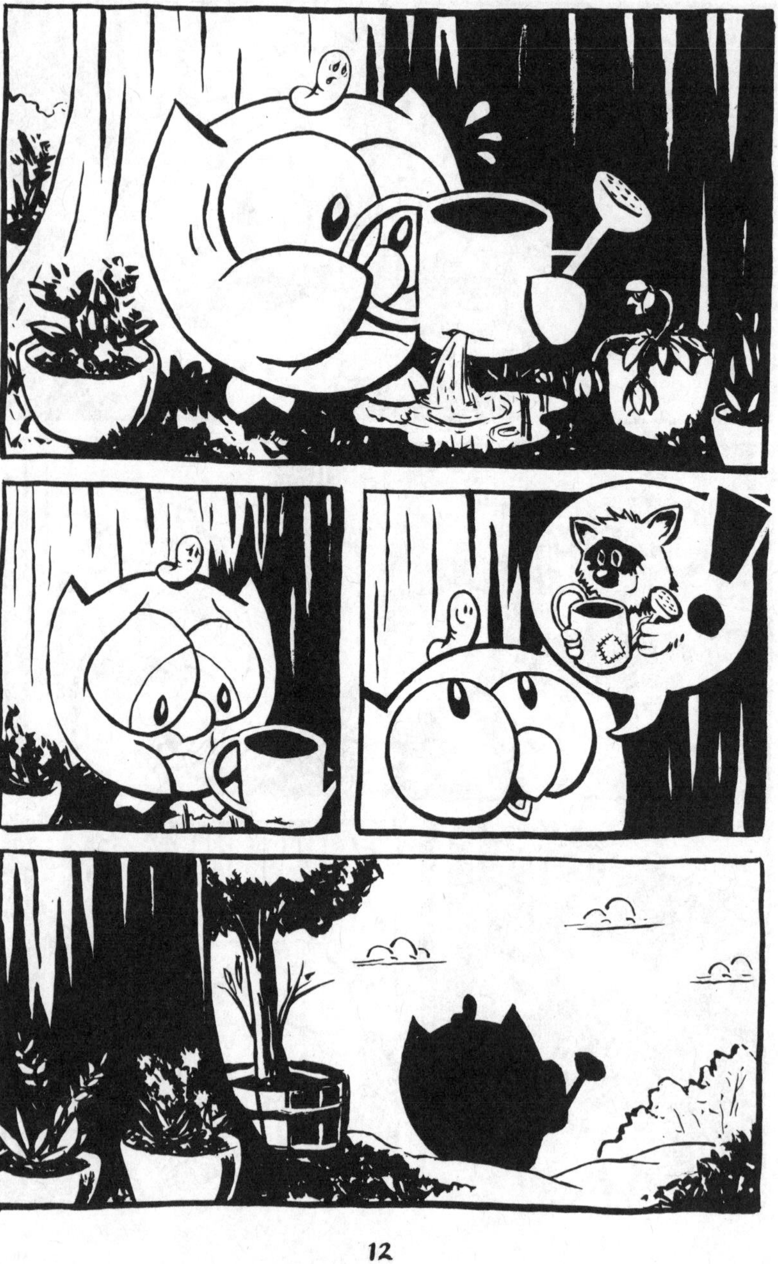

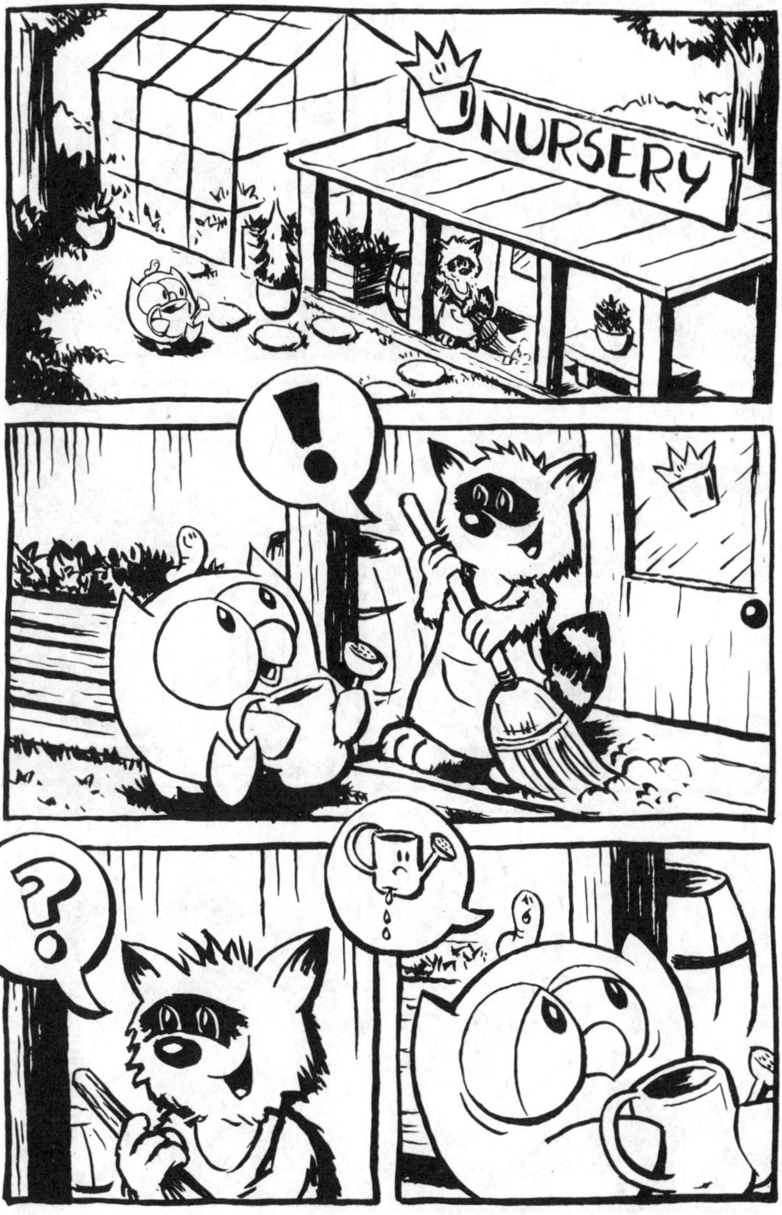
NURSERY
!
?

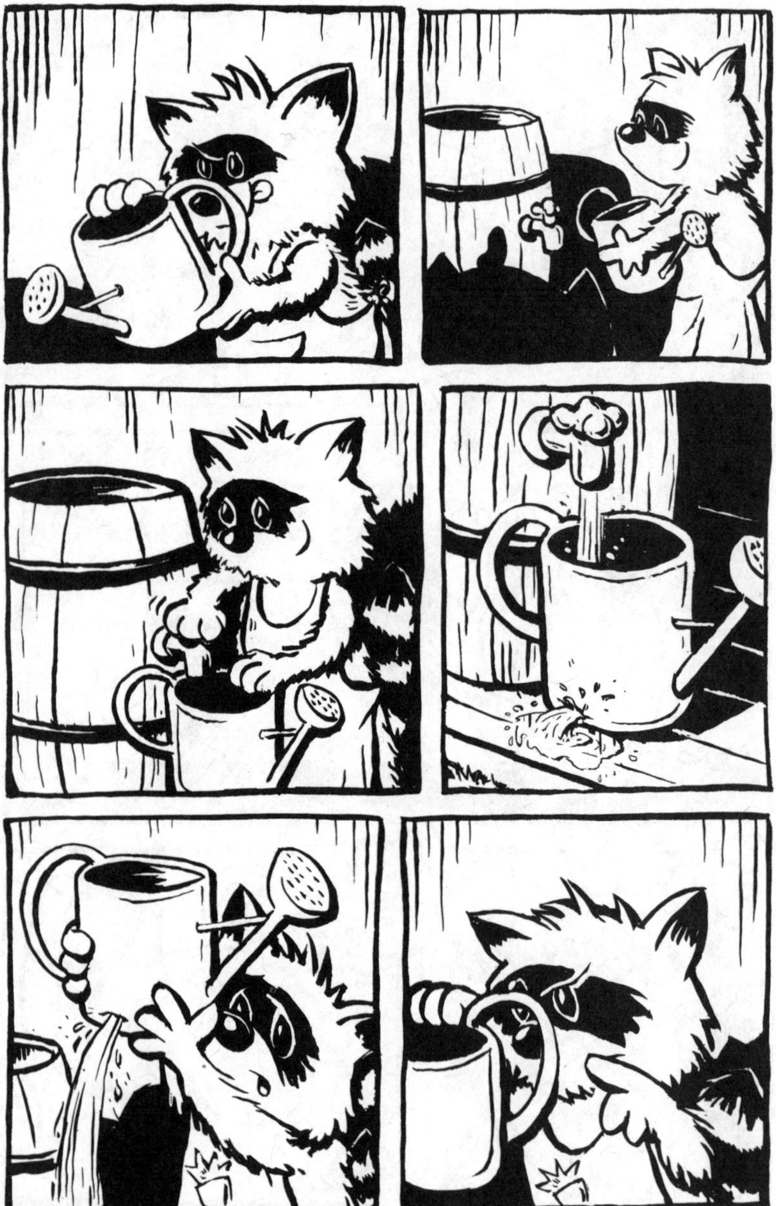

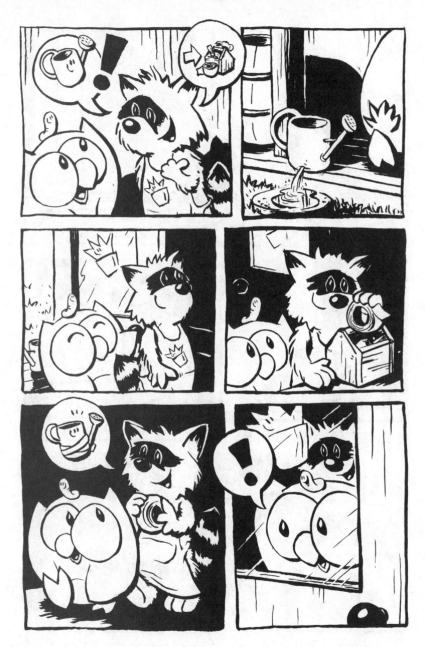

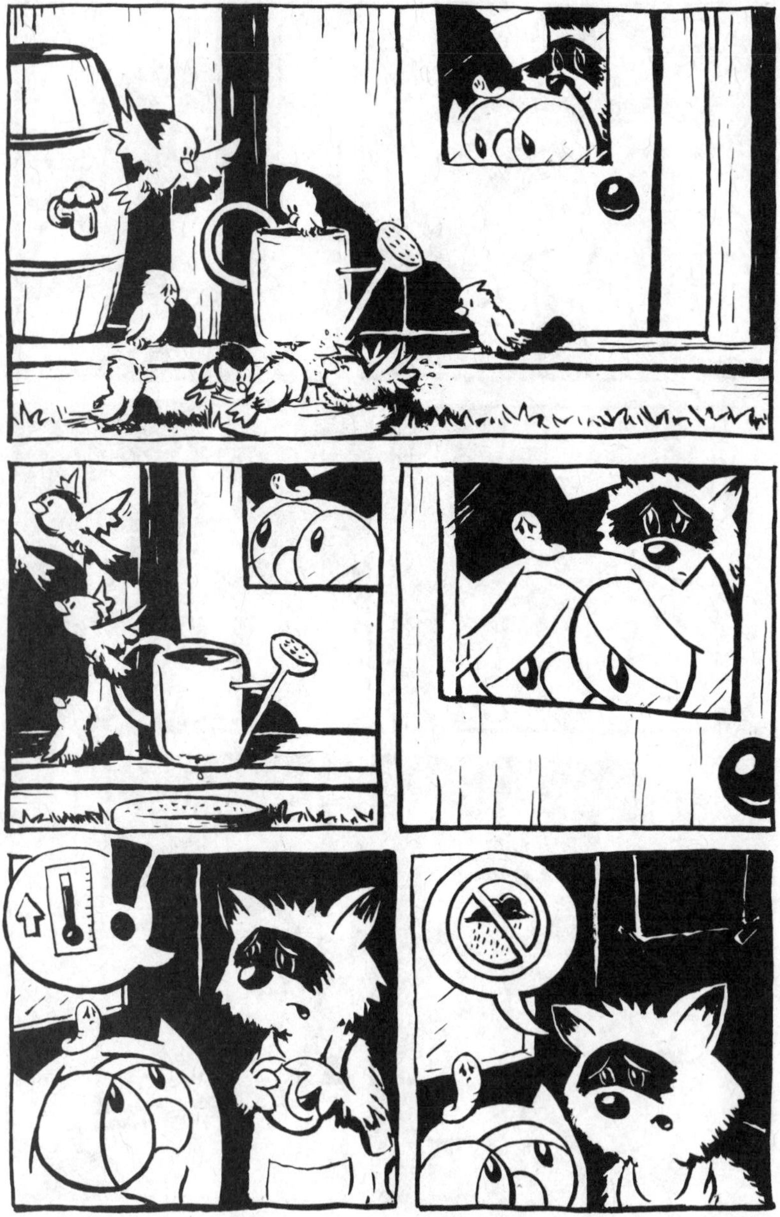

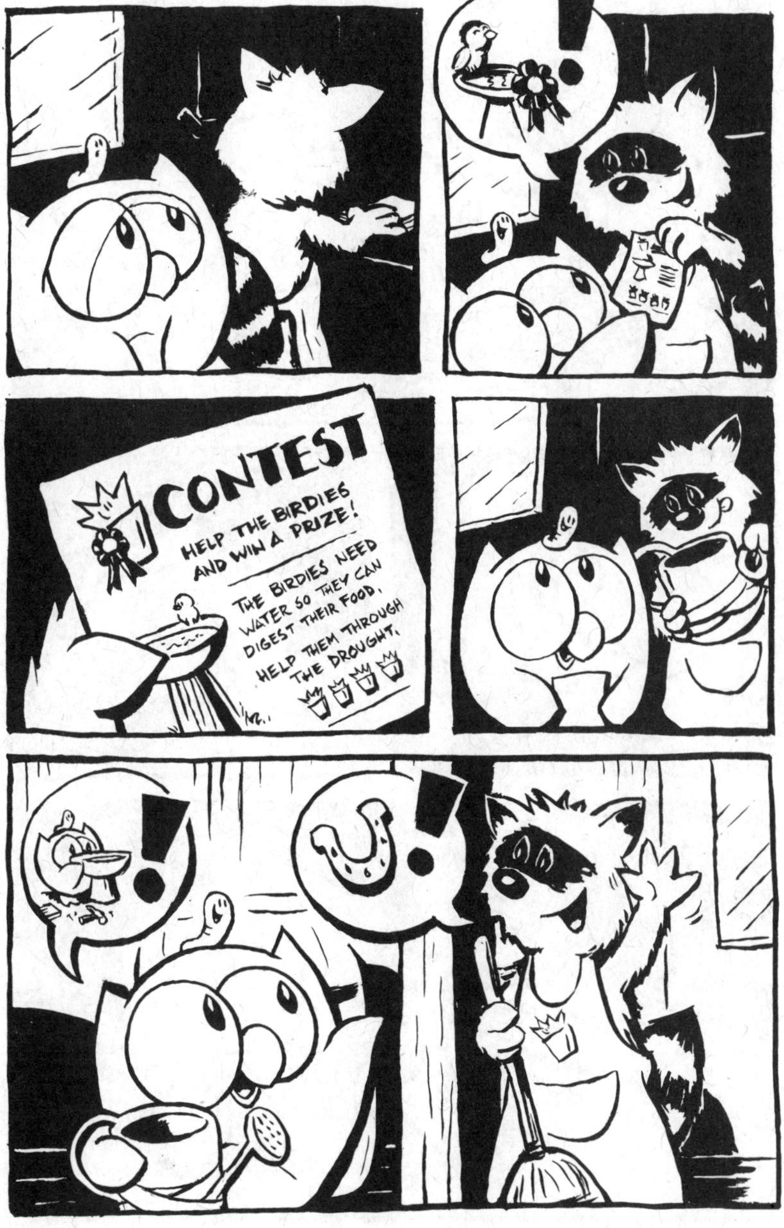

!
CONTEST
HELP THE BIRDIES AND WIN A PRIZE!
THE BIRDIES NEED WATER SO THEY CAN DIGEST THEIR FOOD.
HELP THEM THROUGH THE DROUGHT.
!
!

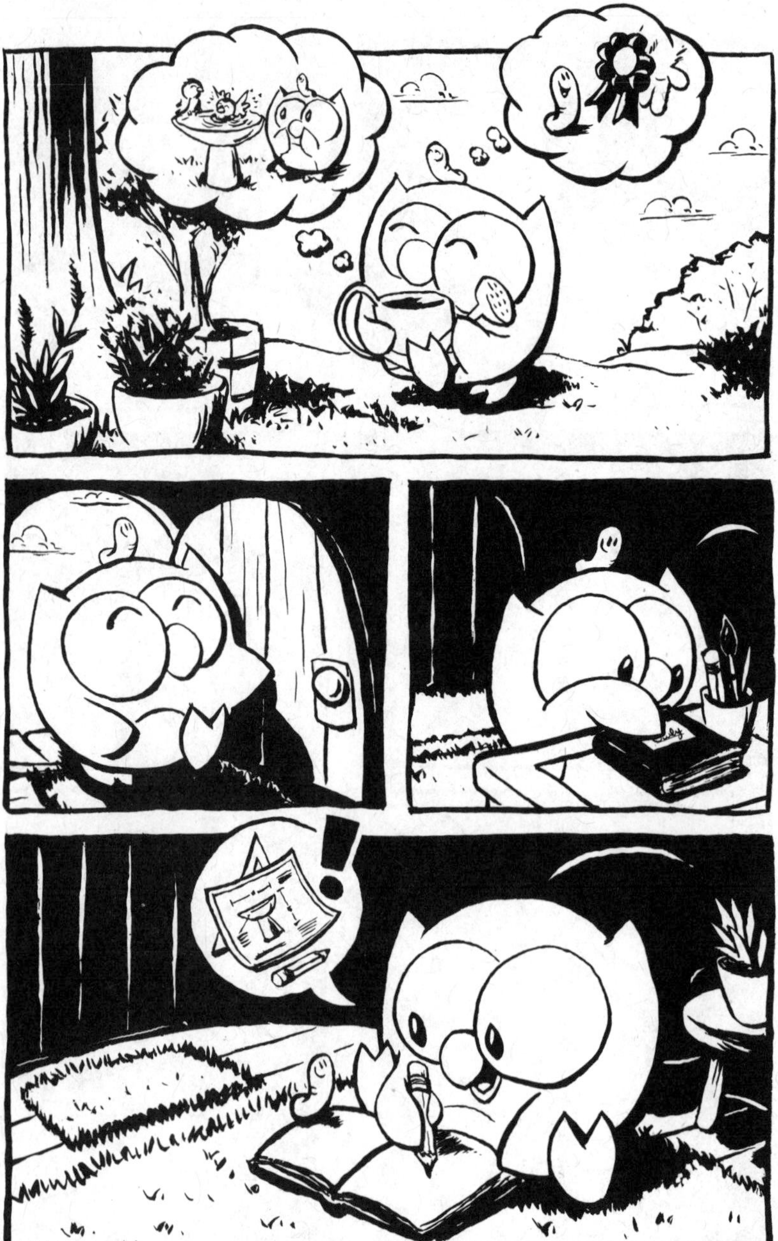

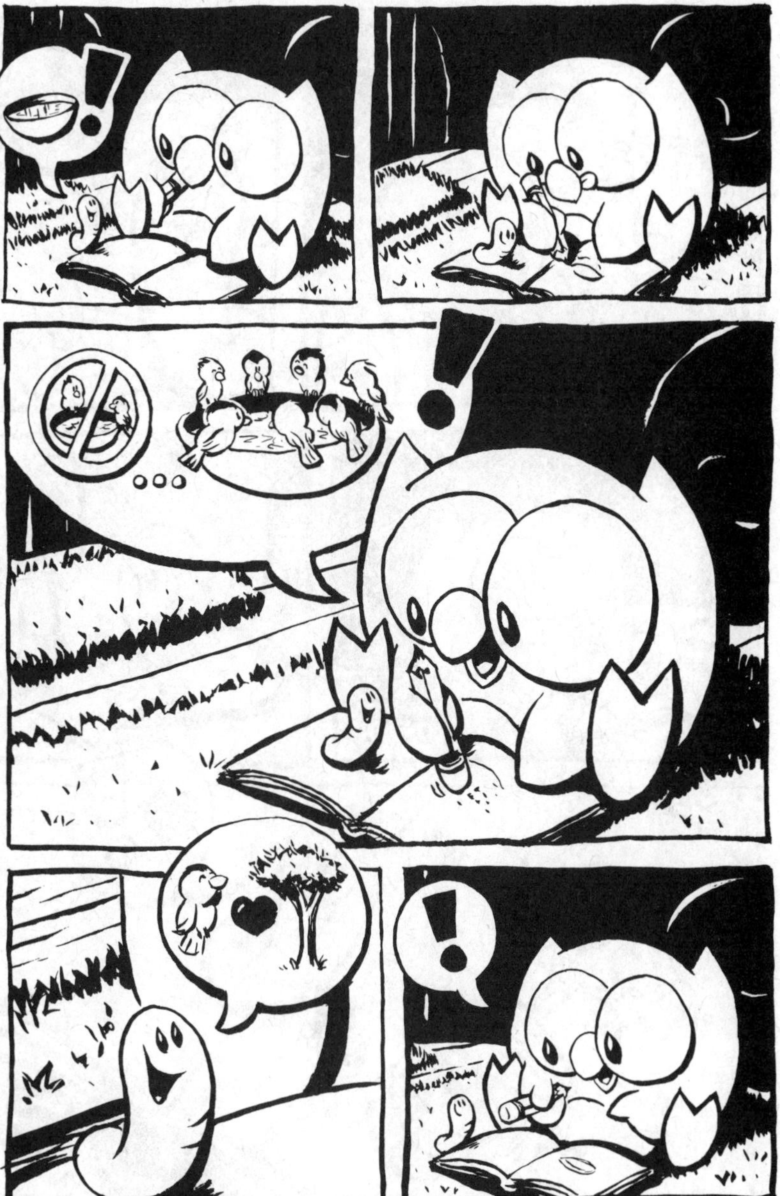

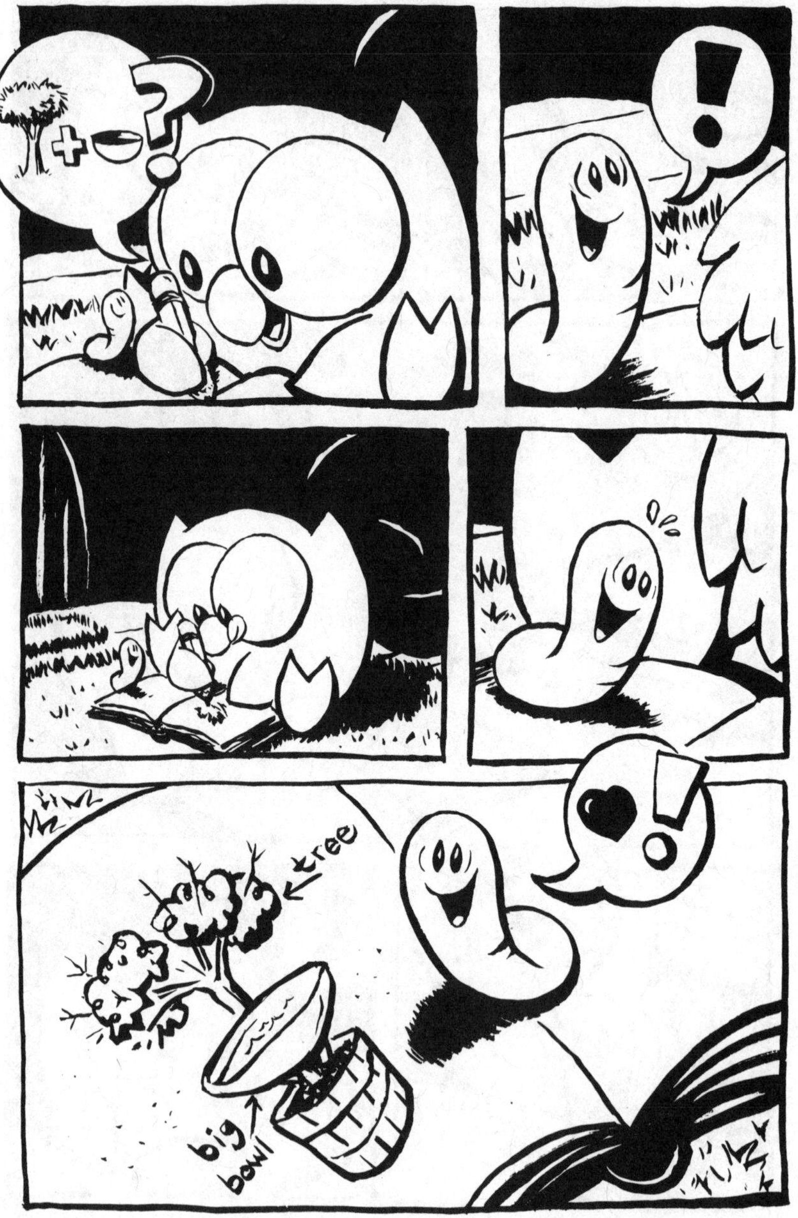
tree
big bowl

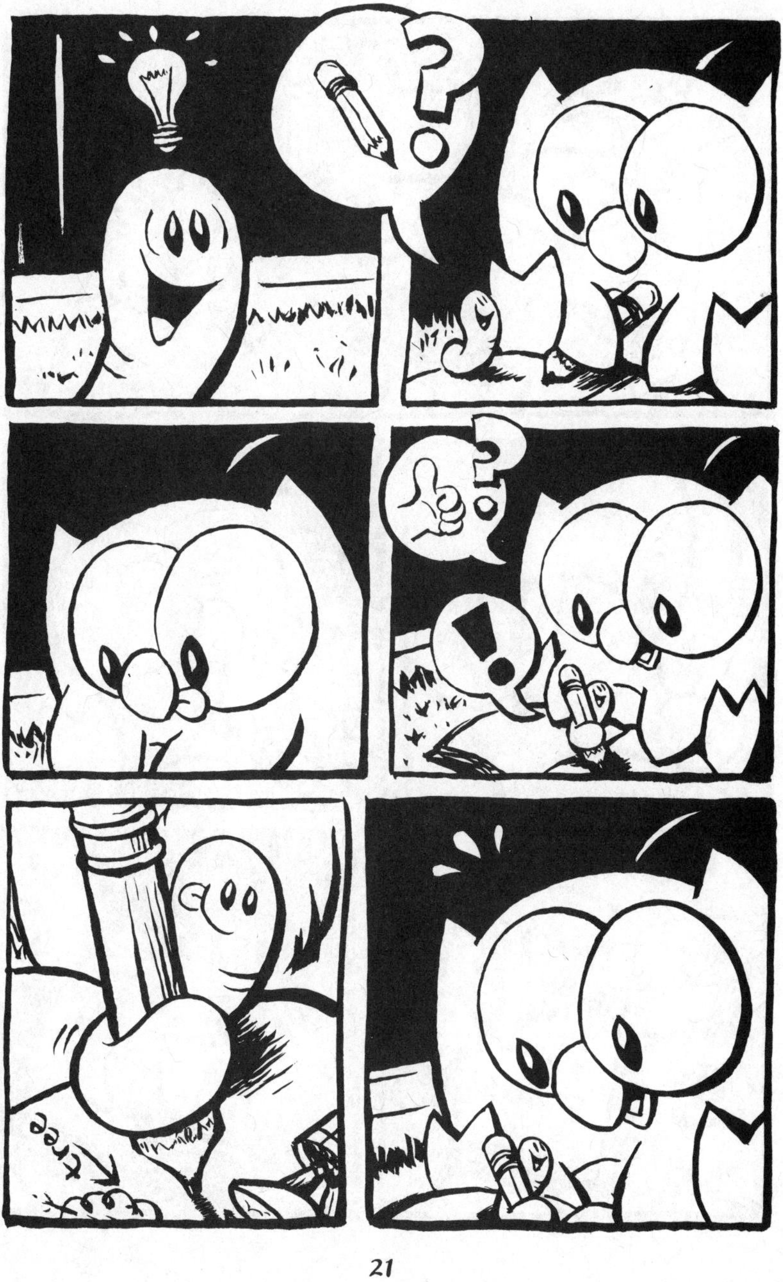
tree

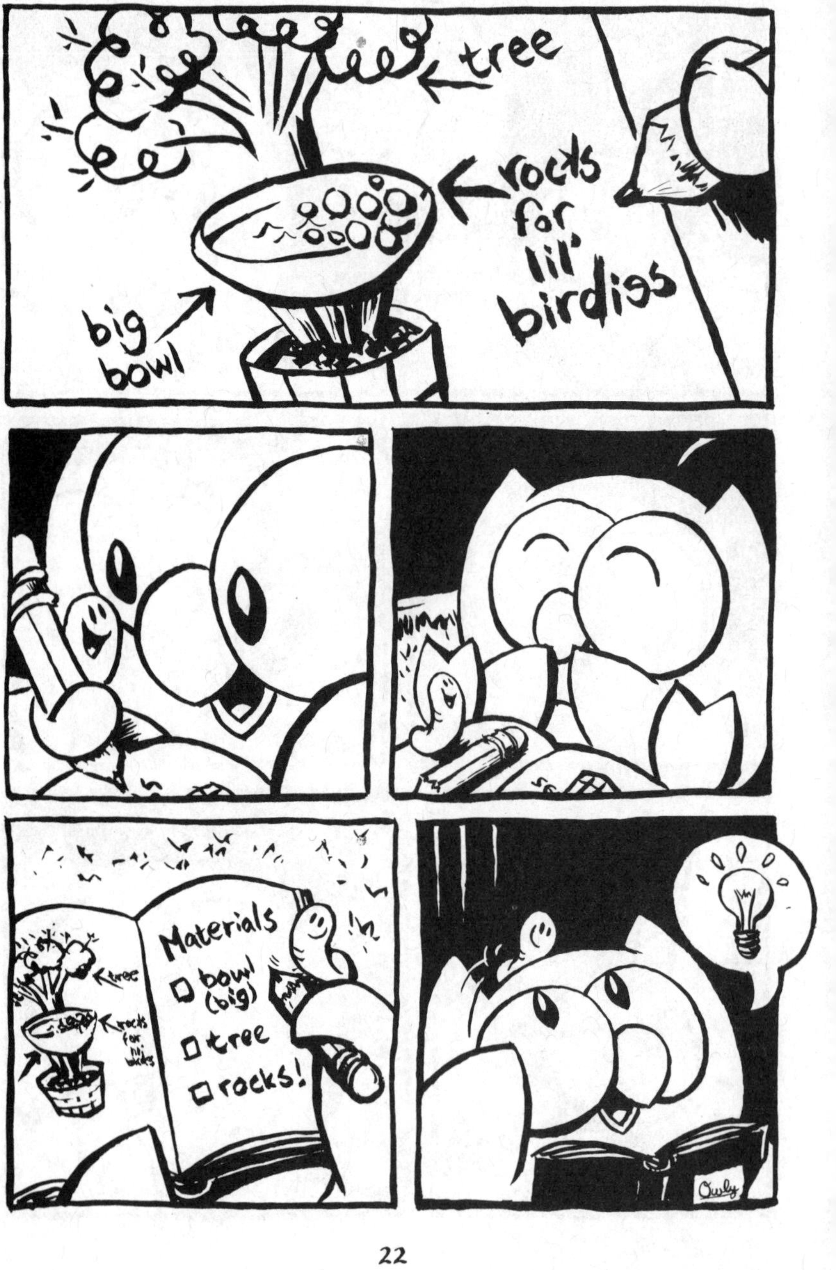
tree
rocks for lil' birdies
big bowl
Materials
bowl (big)
tree
rocks!
Owly

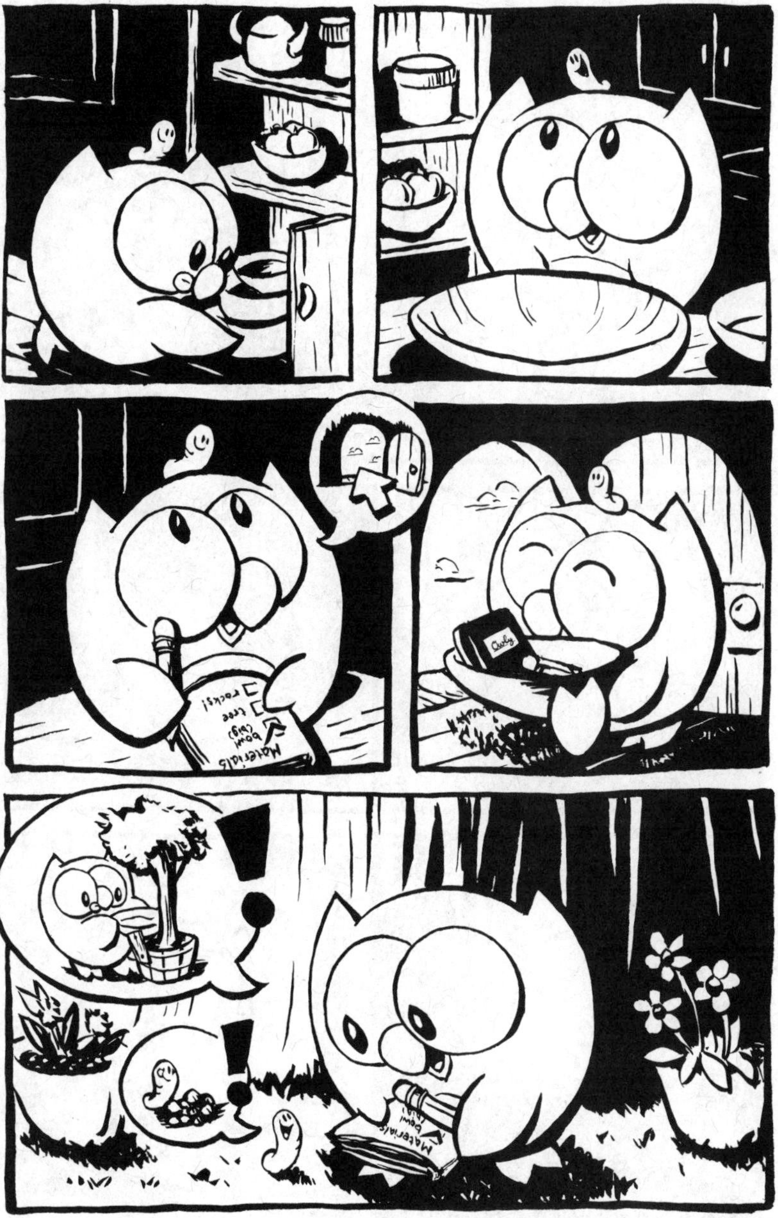
Materials
bowl (big)
tree
rocks!
Owly
Materials
bowl
(big)

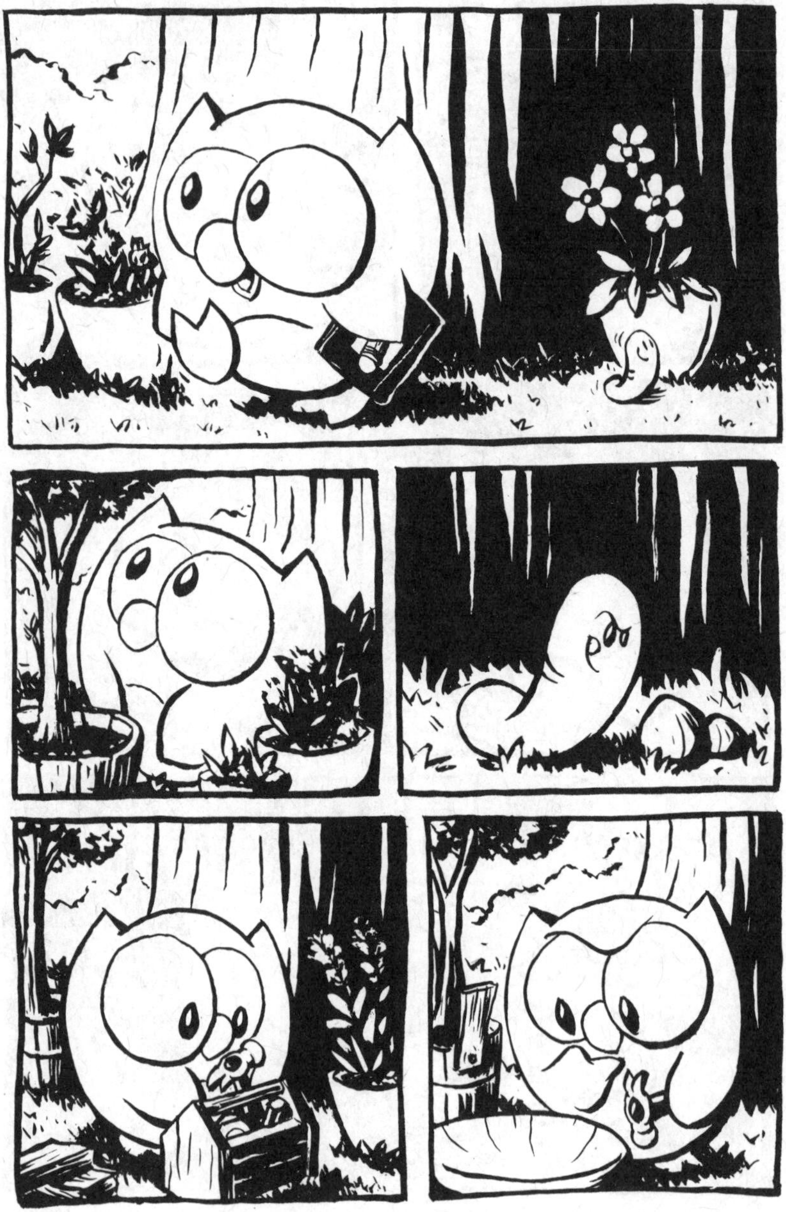

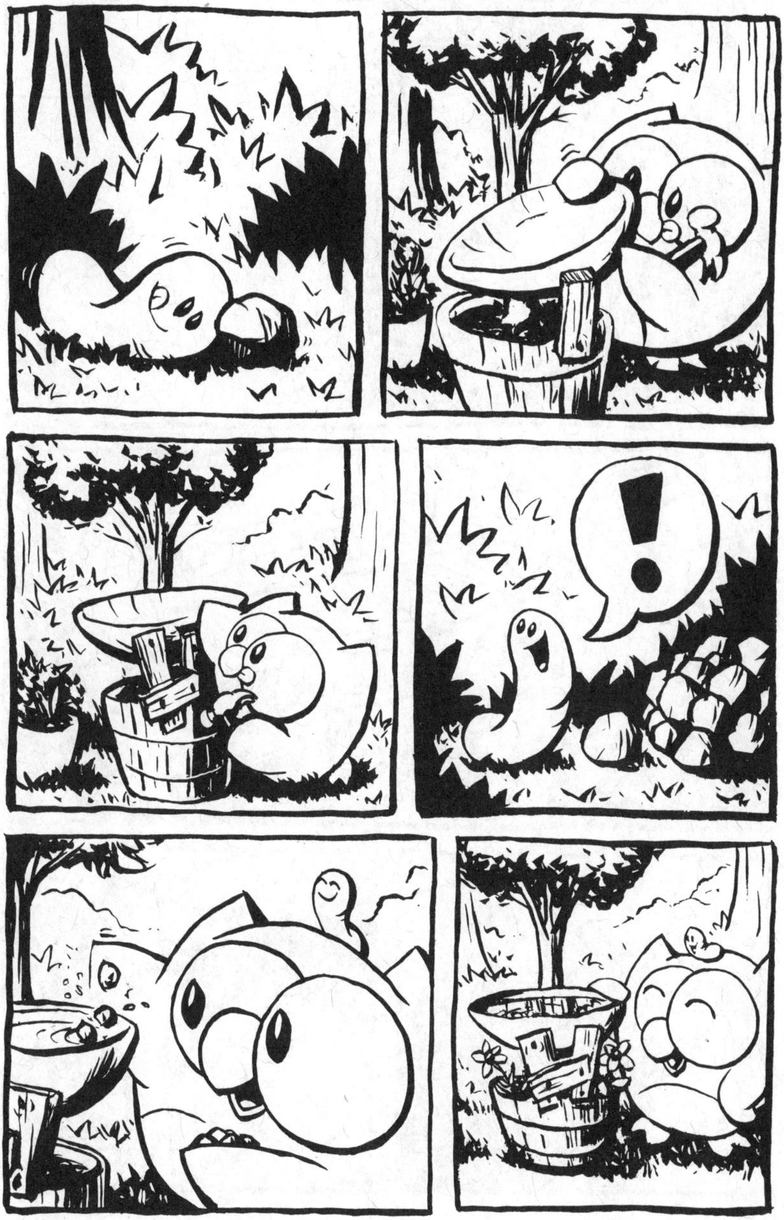
!

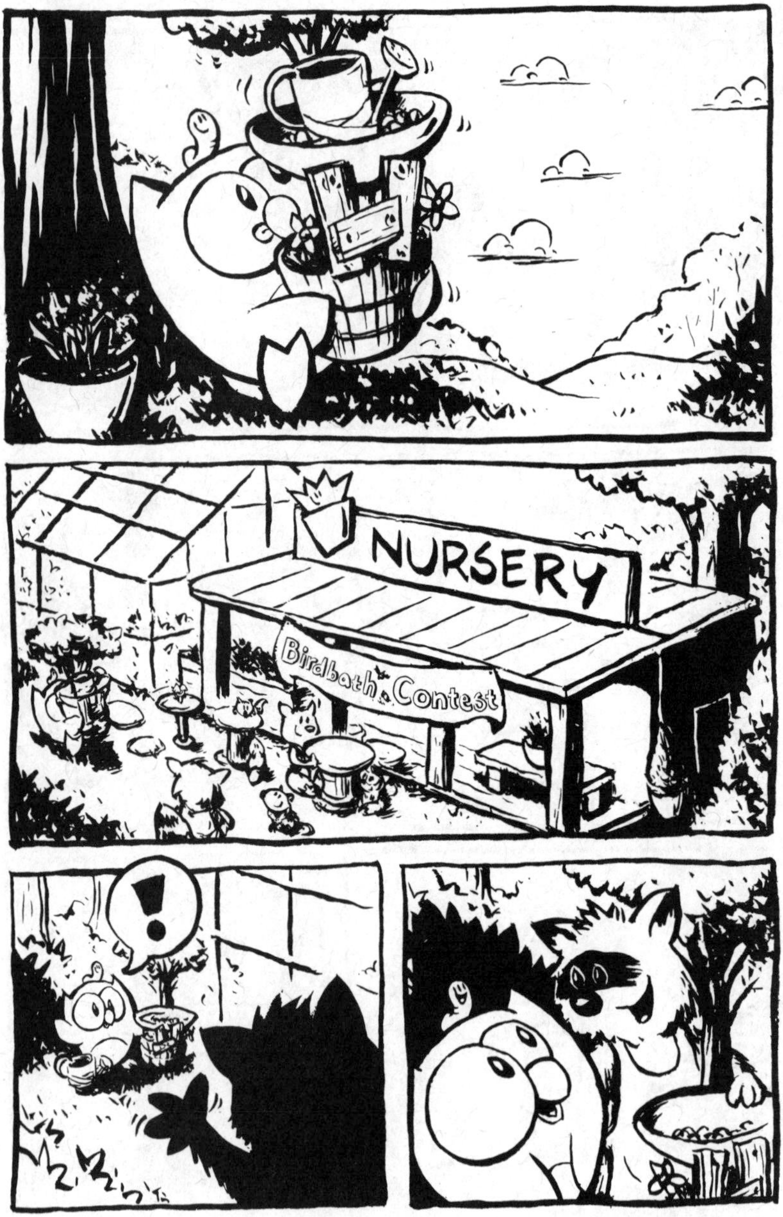
NURSERY
Birdbath Contest
!

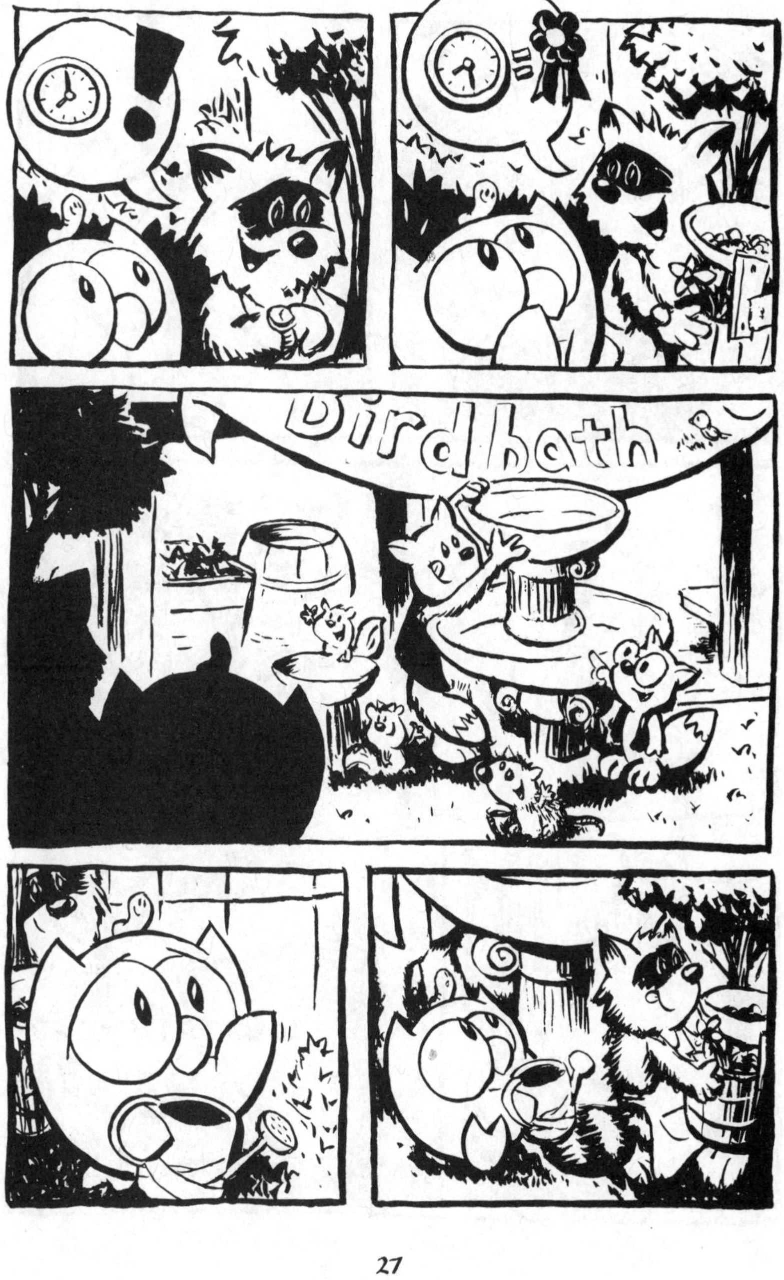
Birdbath

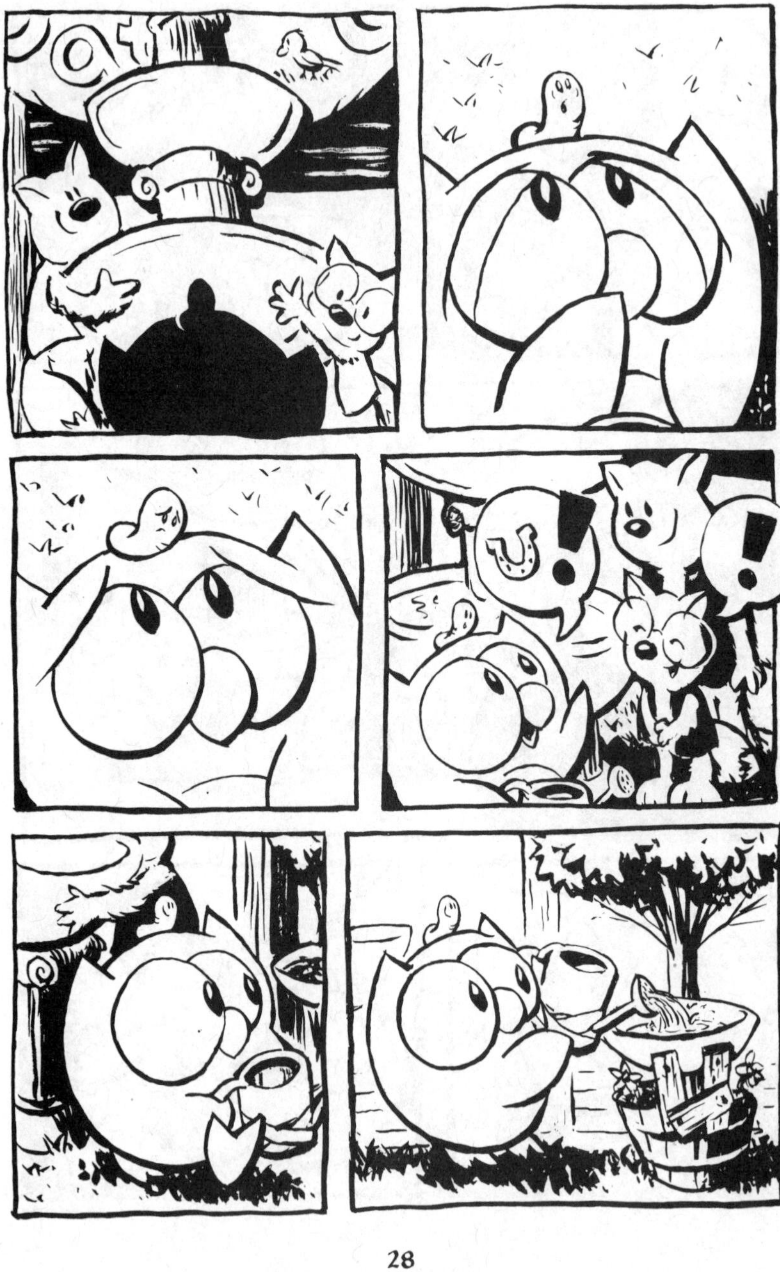
!
!

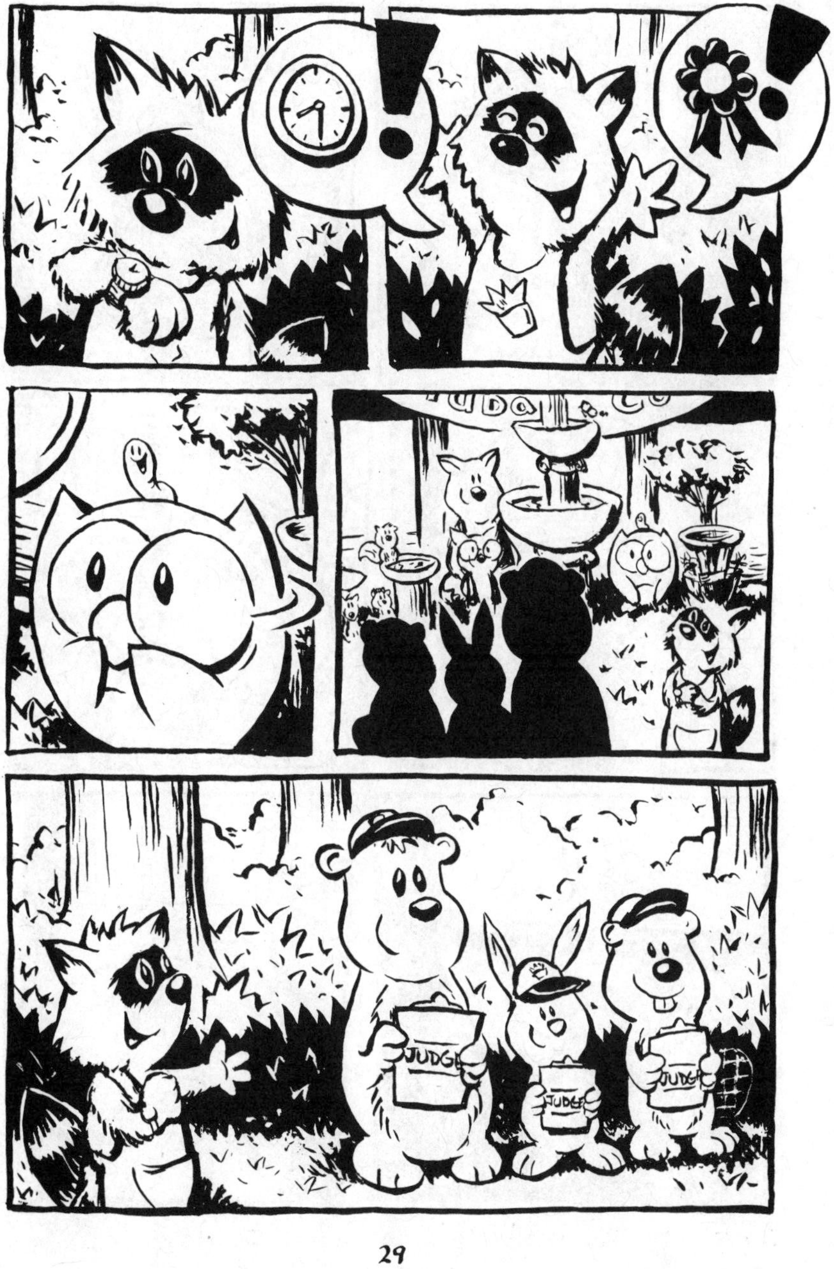
JUDGE
JUDGE
JUDGE

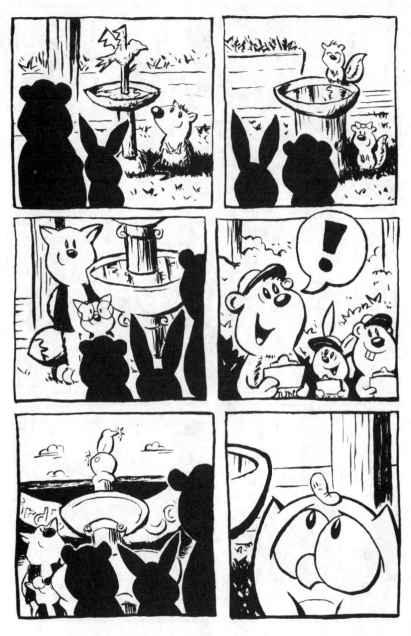

30

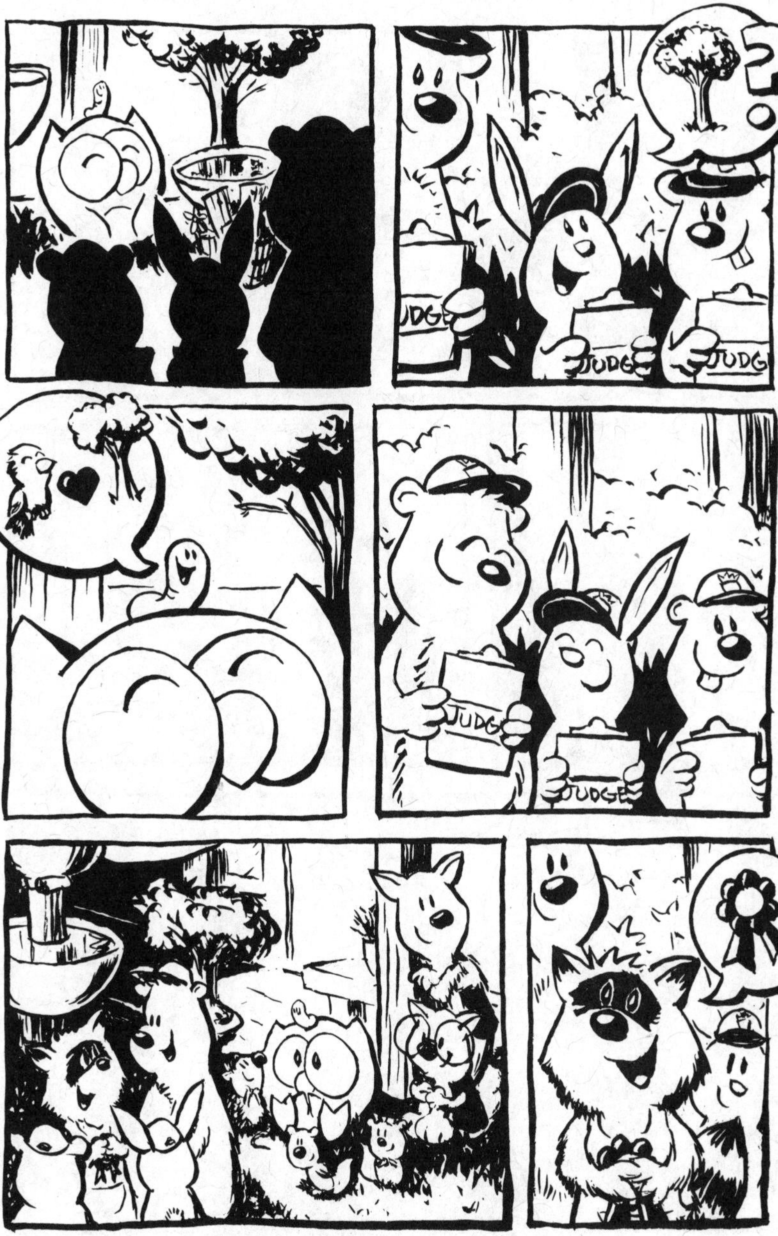
JUDGE

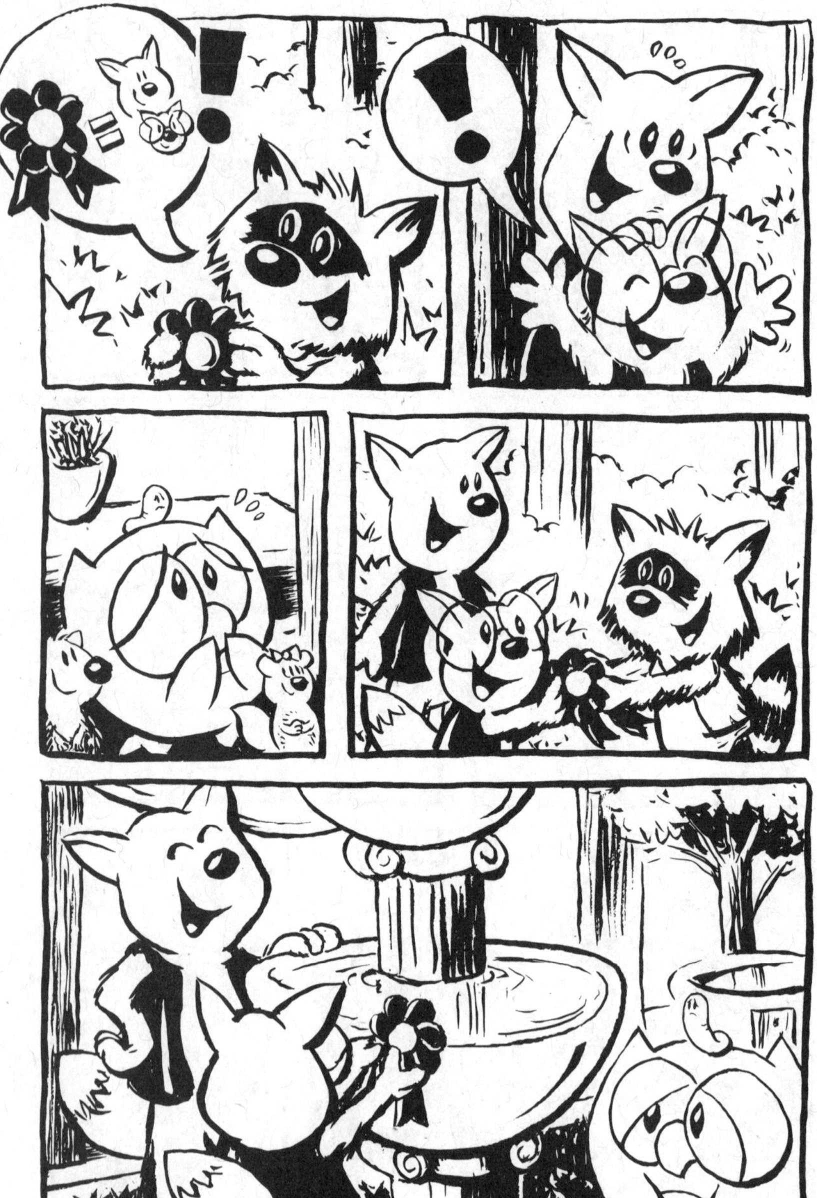
!
!

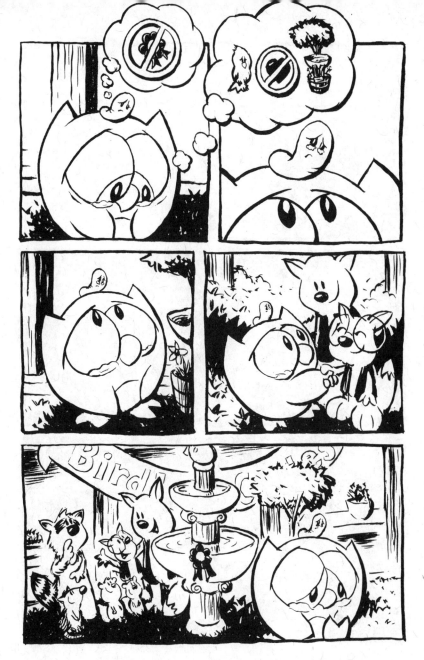

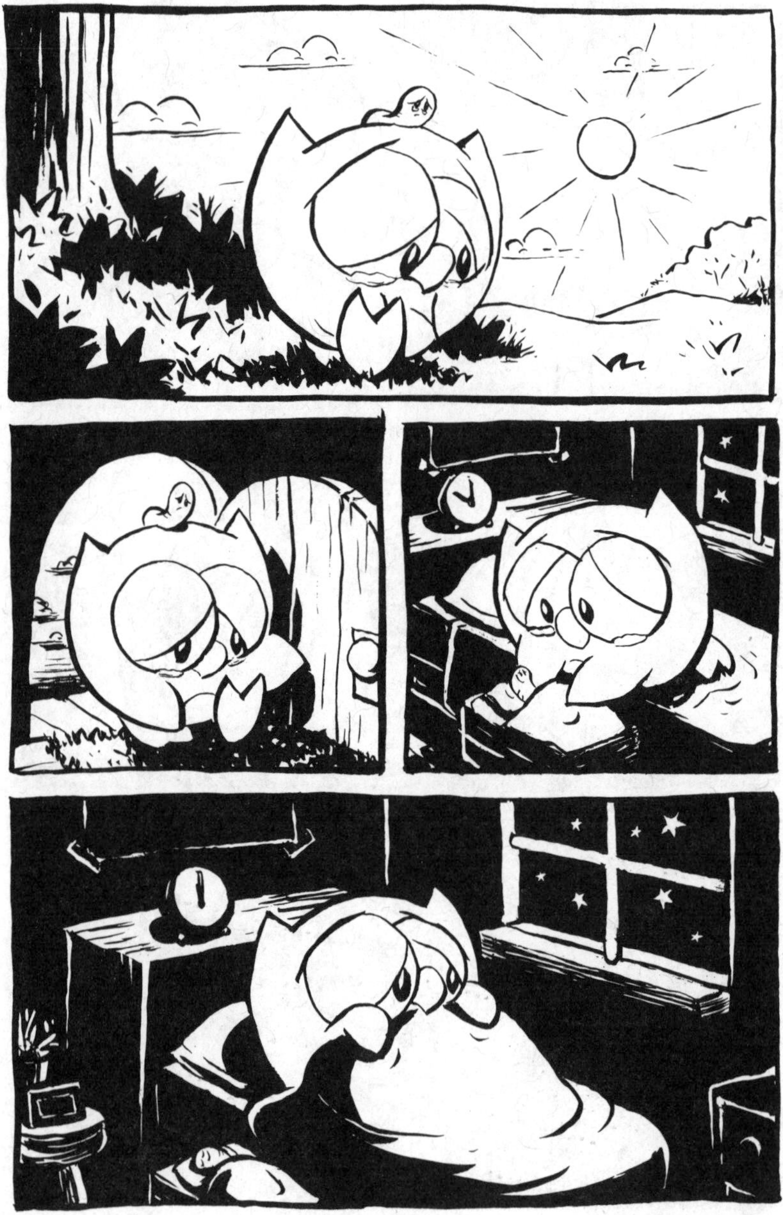

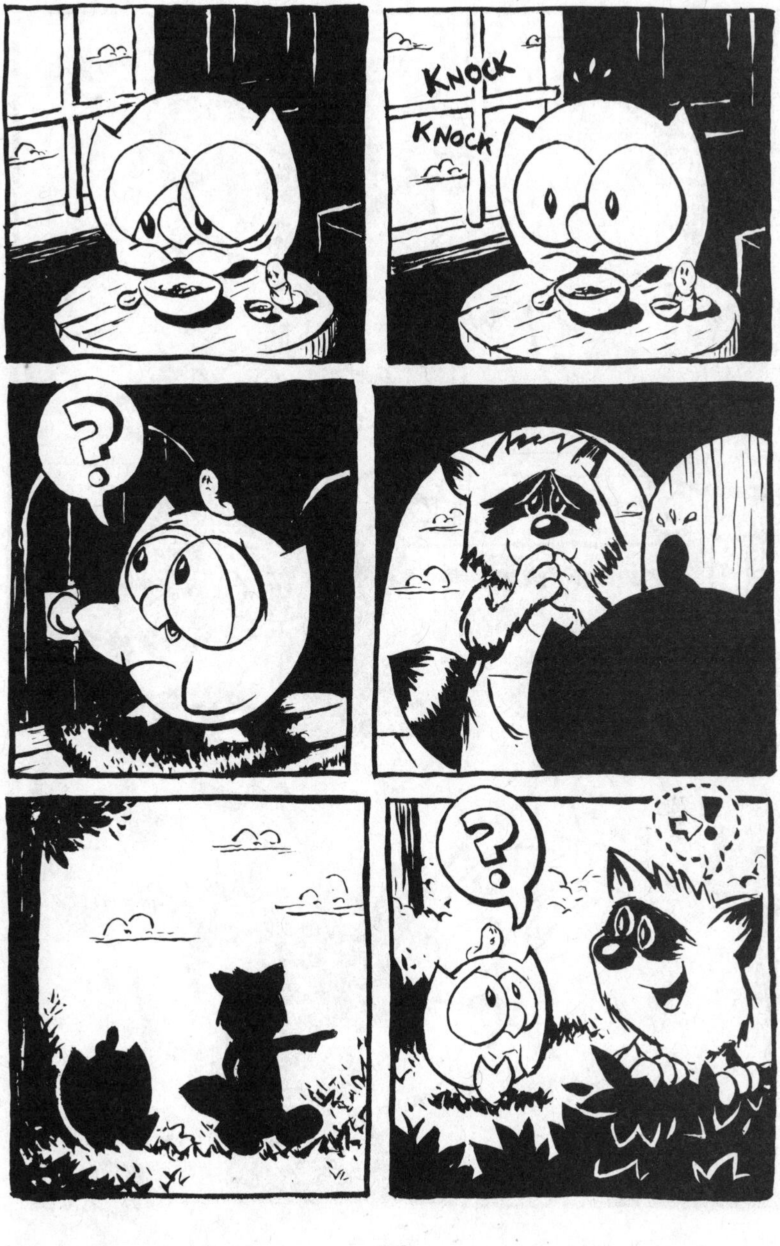
KNOCK
KNOCK
?
?
!

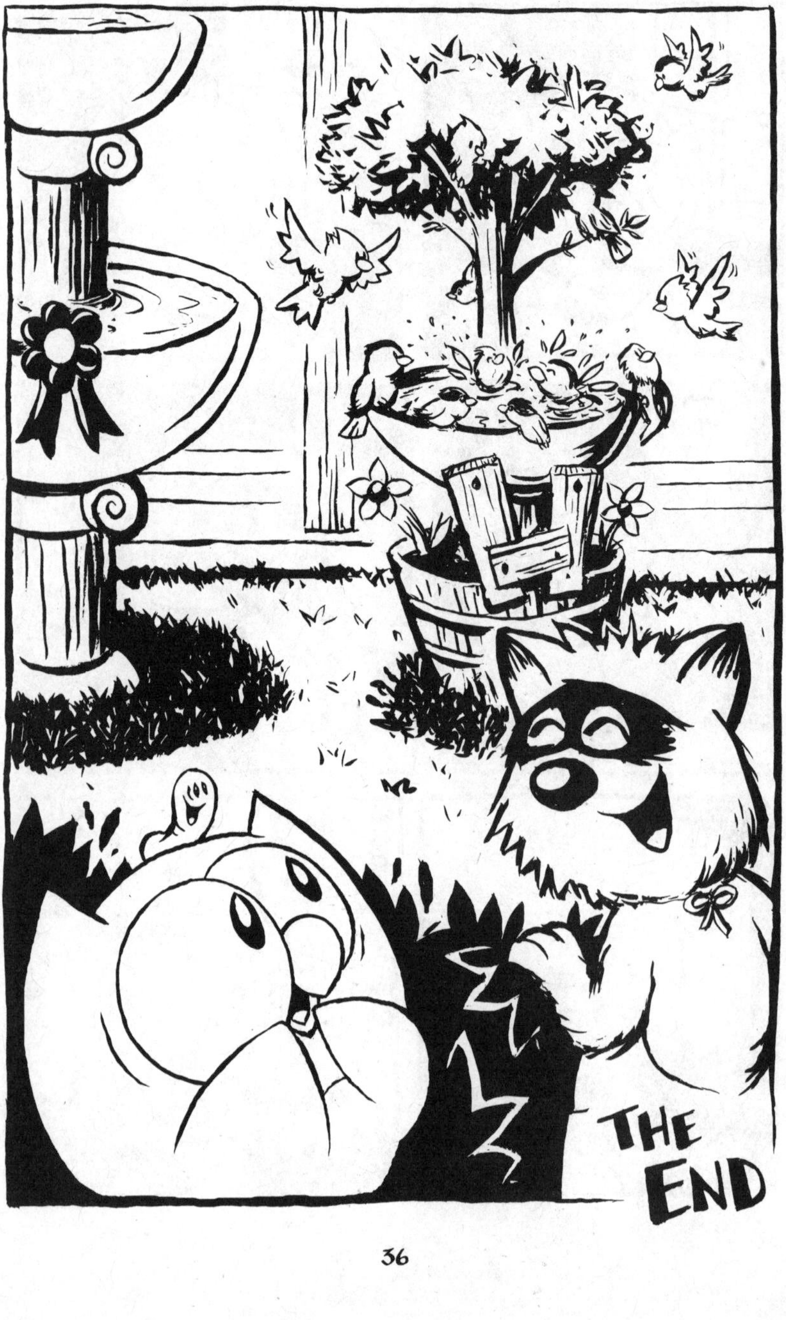
THE END

AW NUTS!

AUGUST, 2004

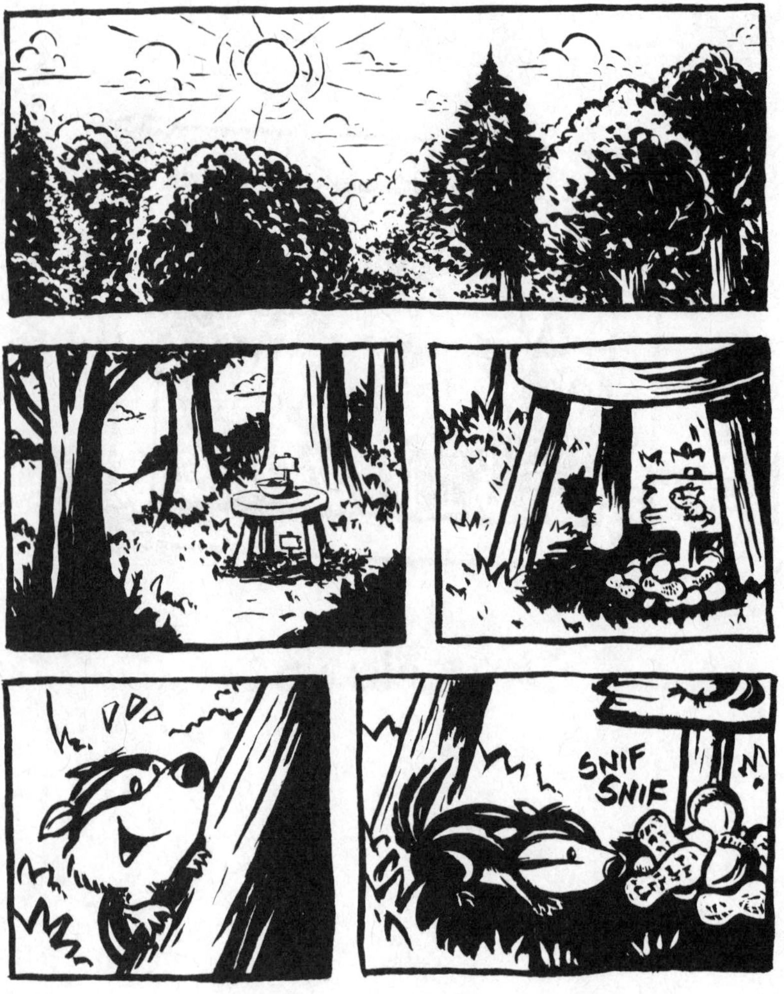
SNIF
SNIF

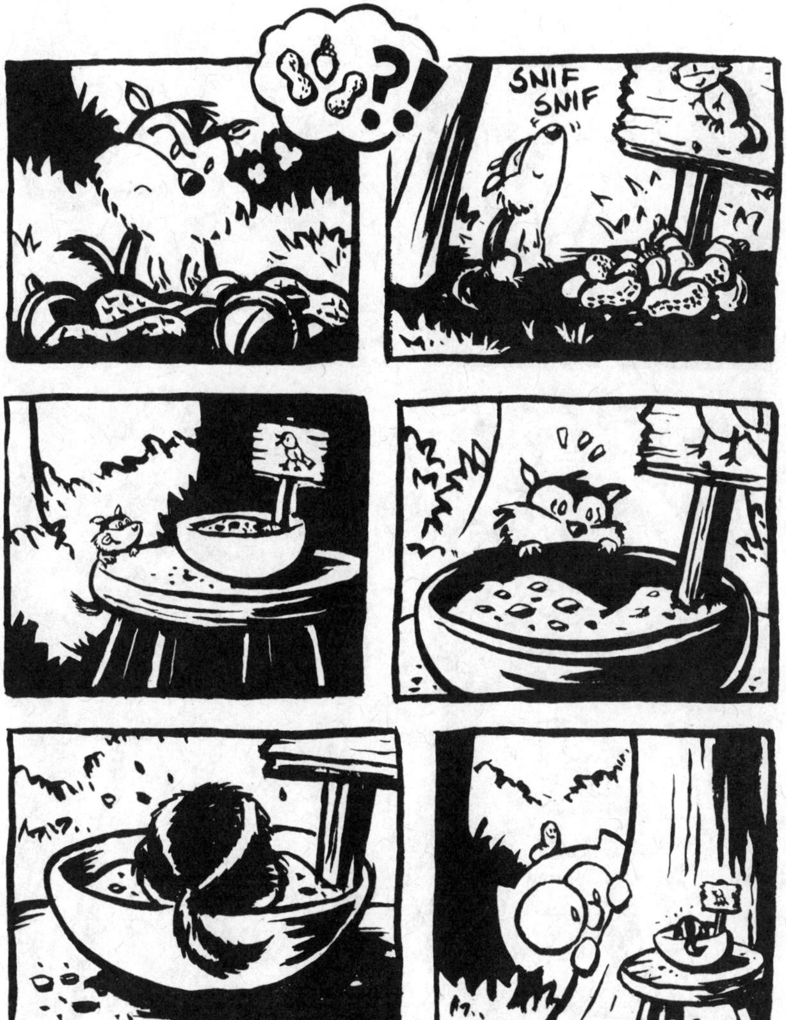
?!
SNIF
SNIF

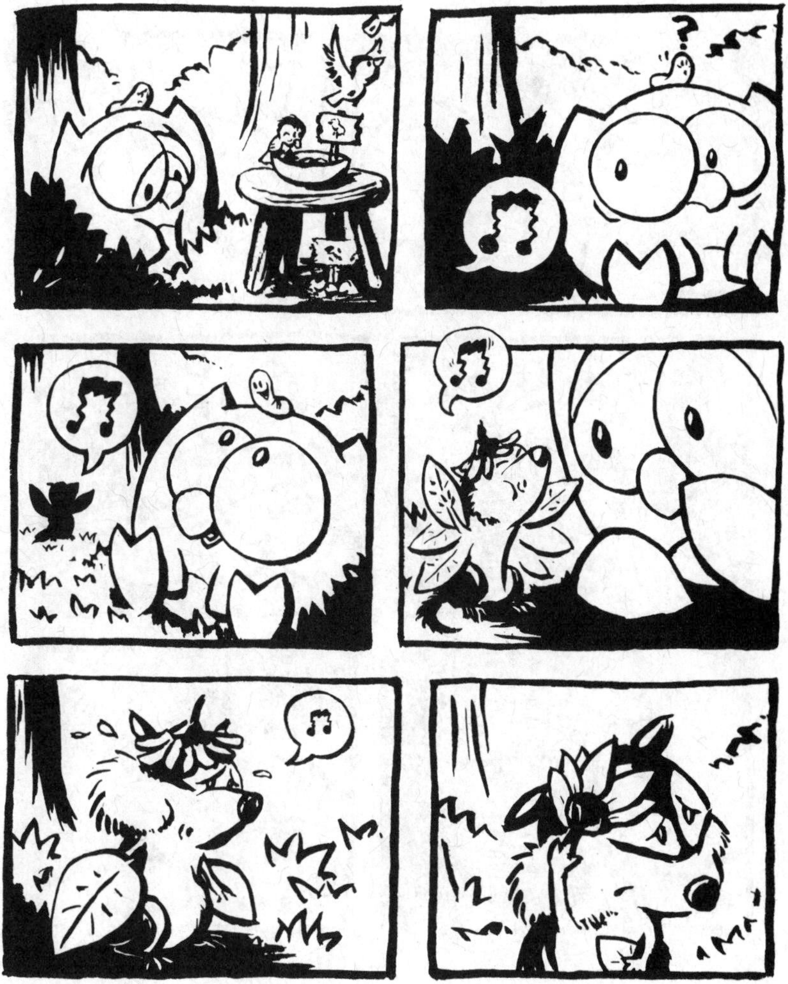

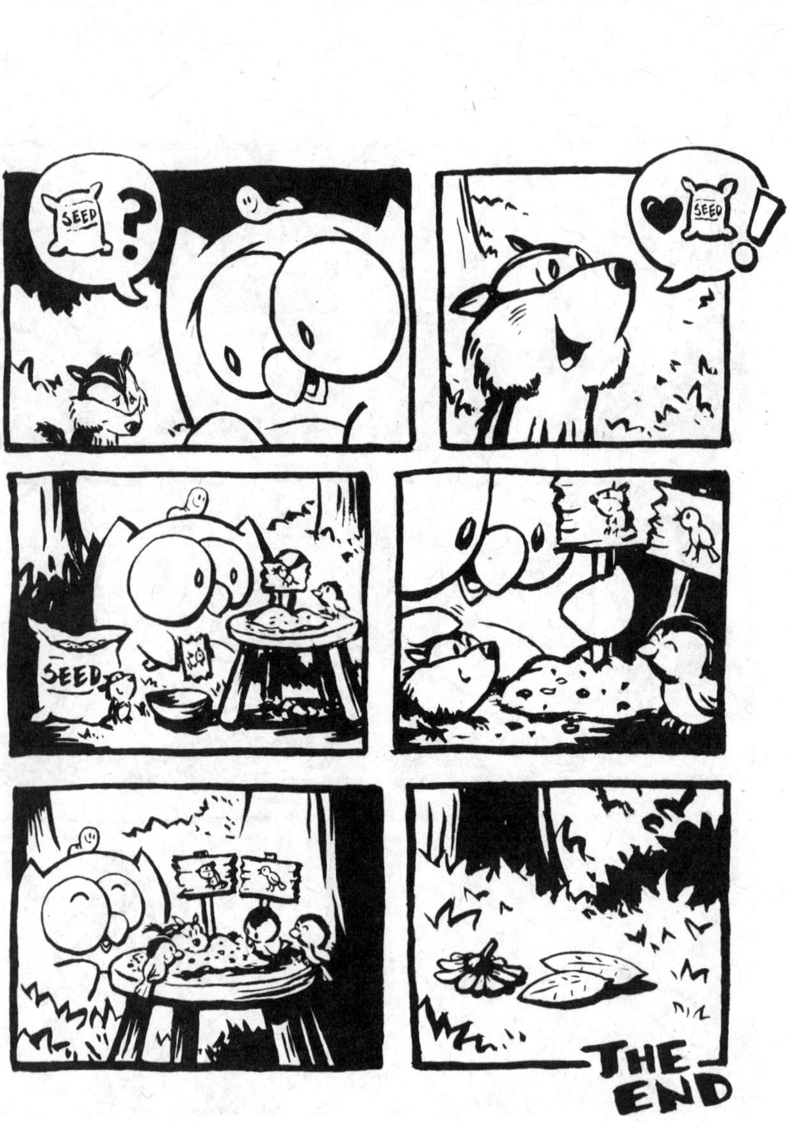
SEED ?
SEED !
SEED
THE END

BREAKIN' THE ICE

APRIL, 2006

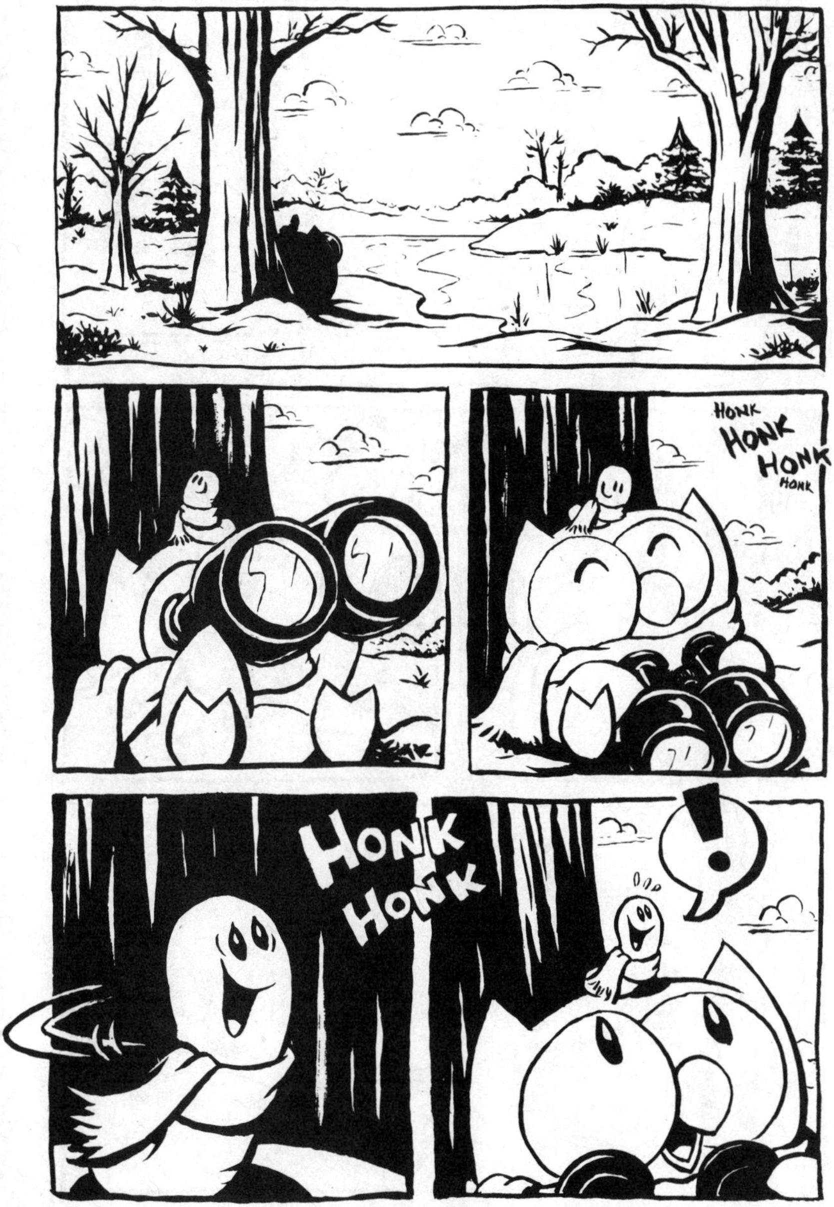
HONK
HONK
HONK
HONK
HONK
HONK
!

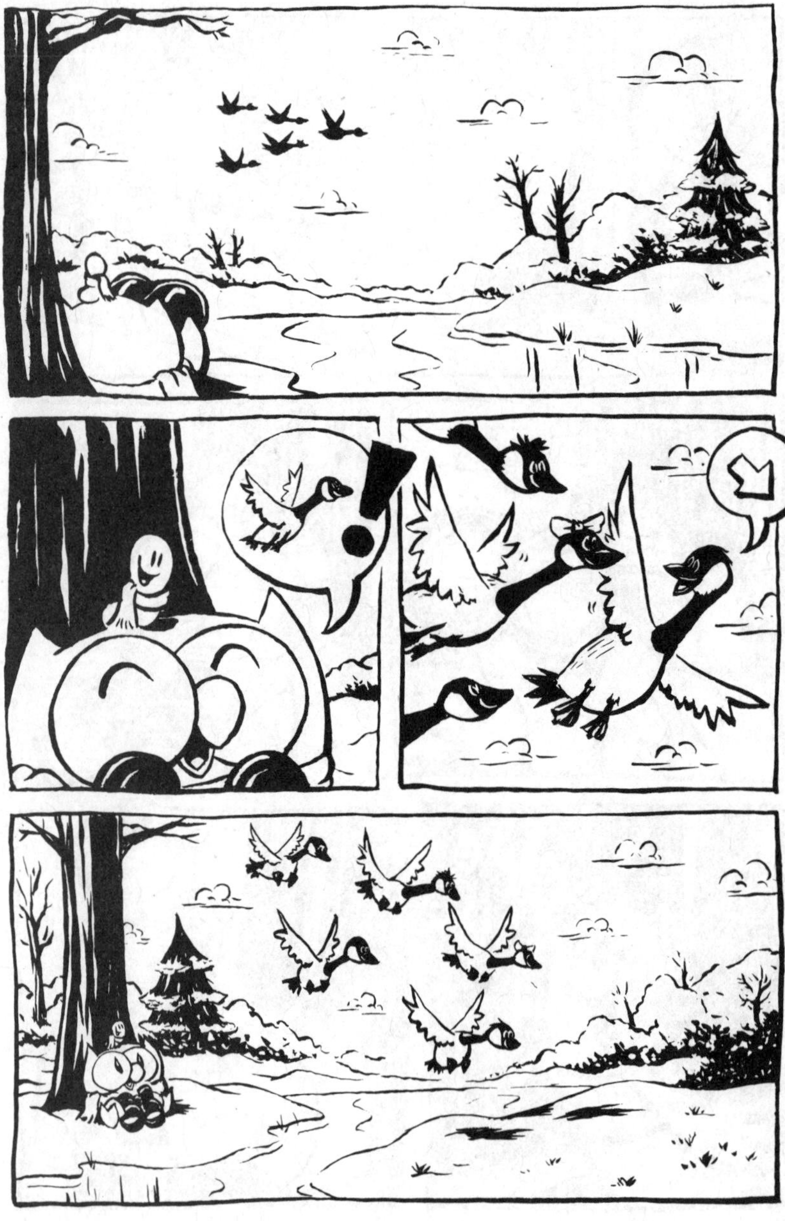
!

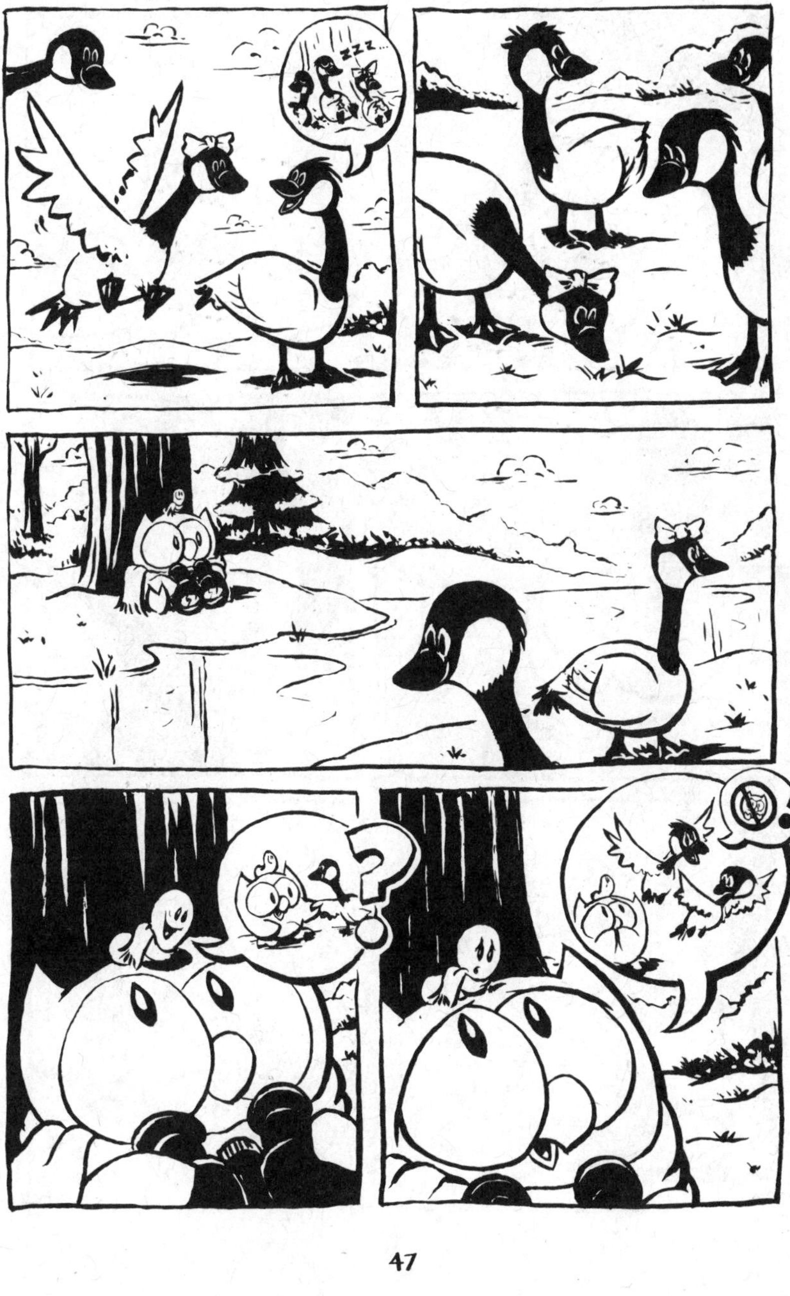
zzz...
?
!

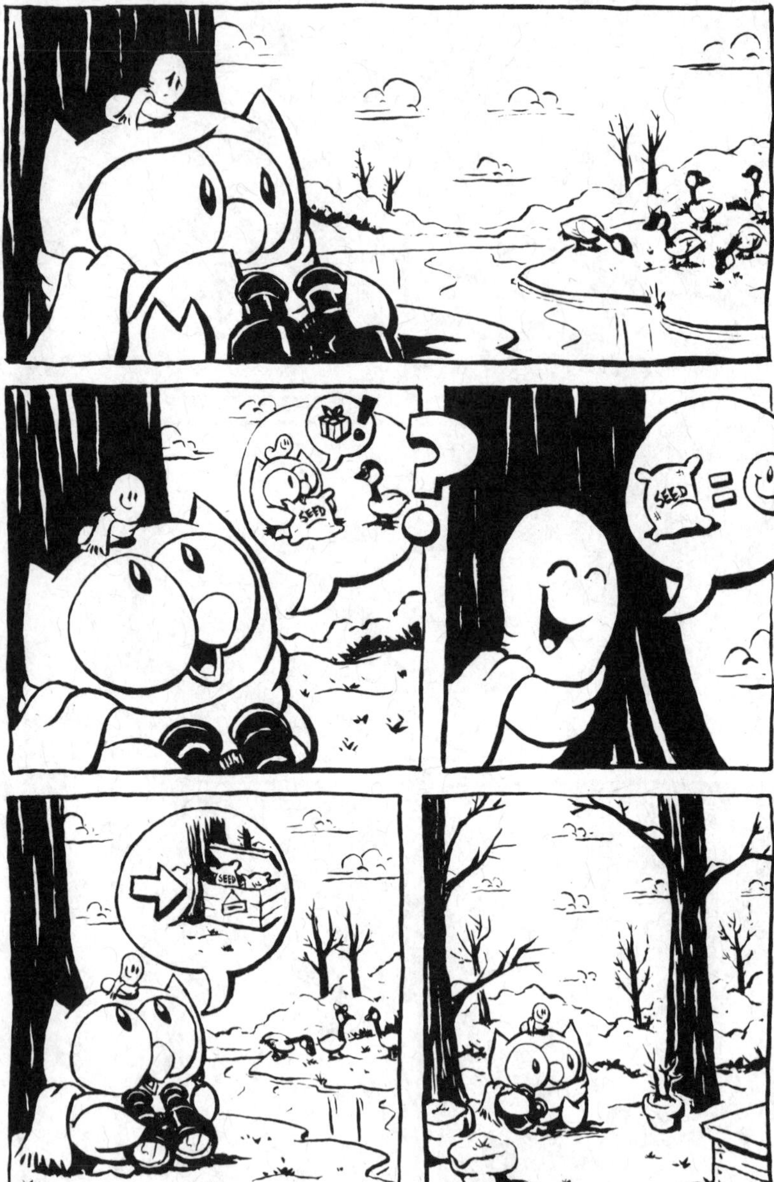
SEED
SEED
SEED

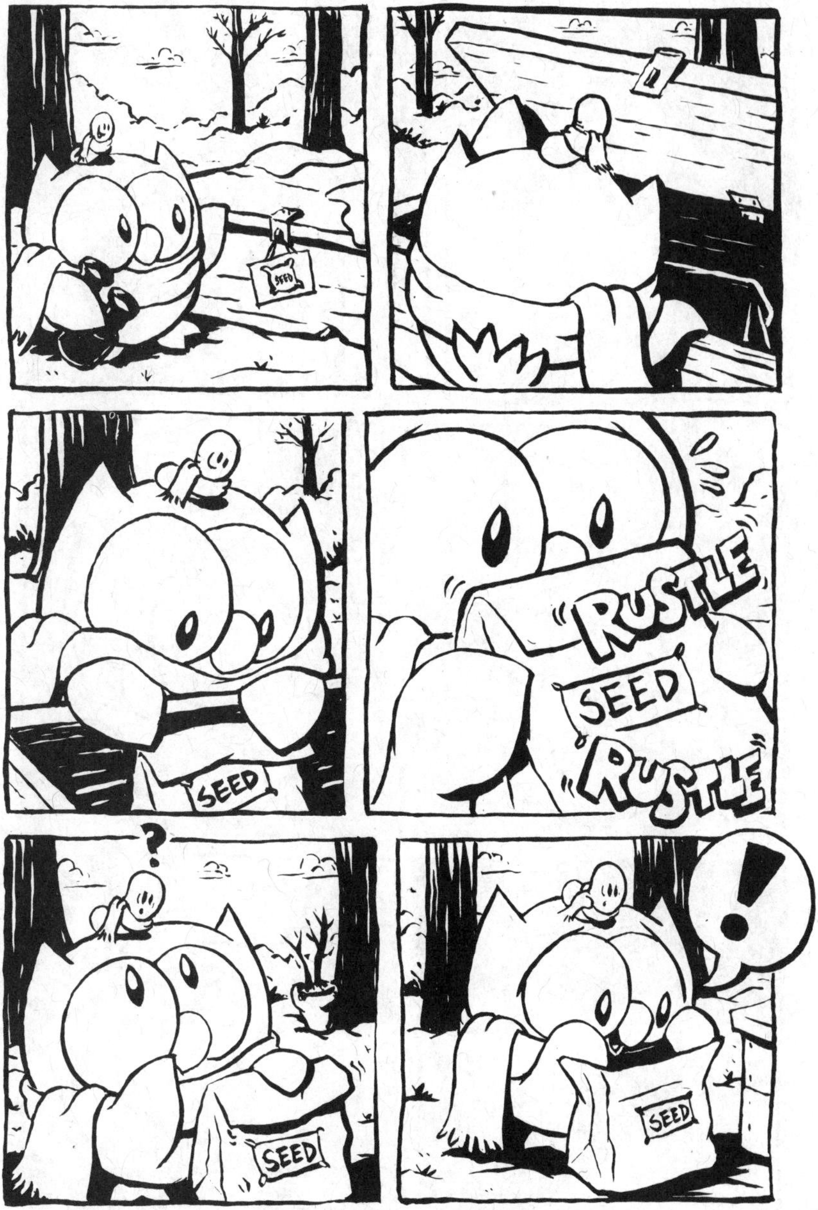
SEED
SEED
RUSTLE
SEED
RUSTLE
?
SEED
!
SEED

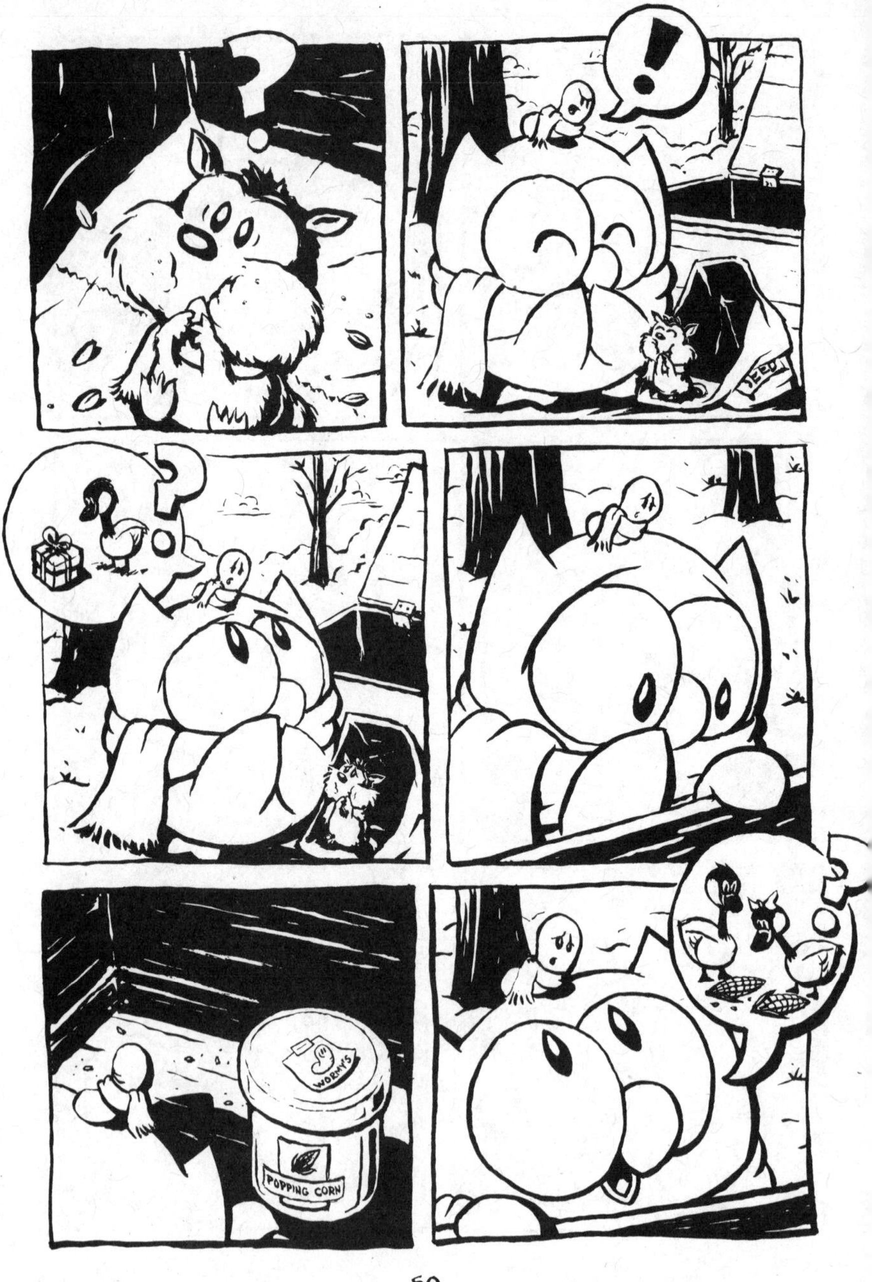
?
!
?
WORMY'S
POPPING CORN
?

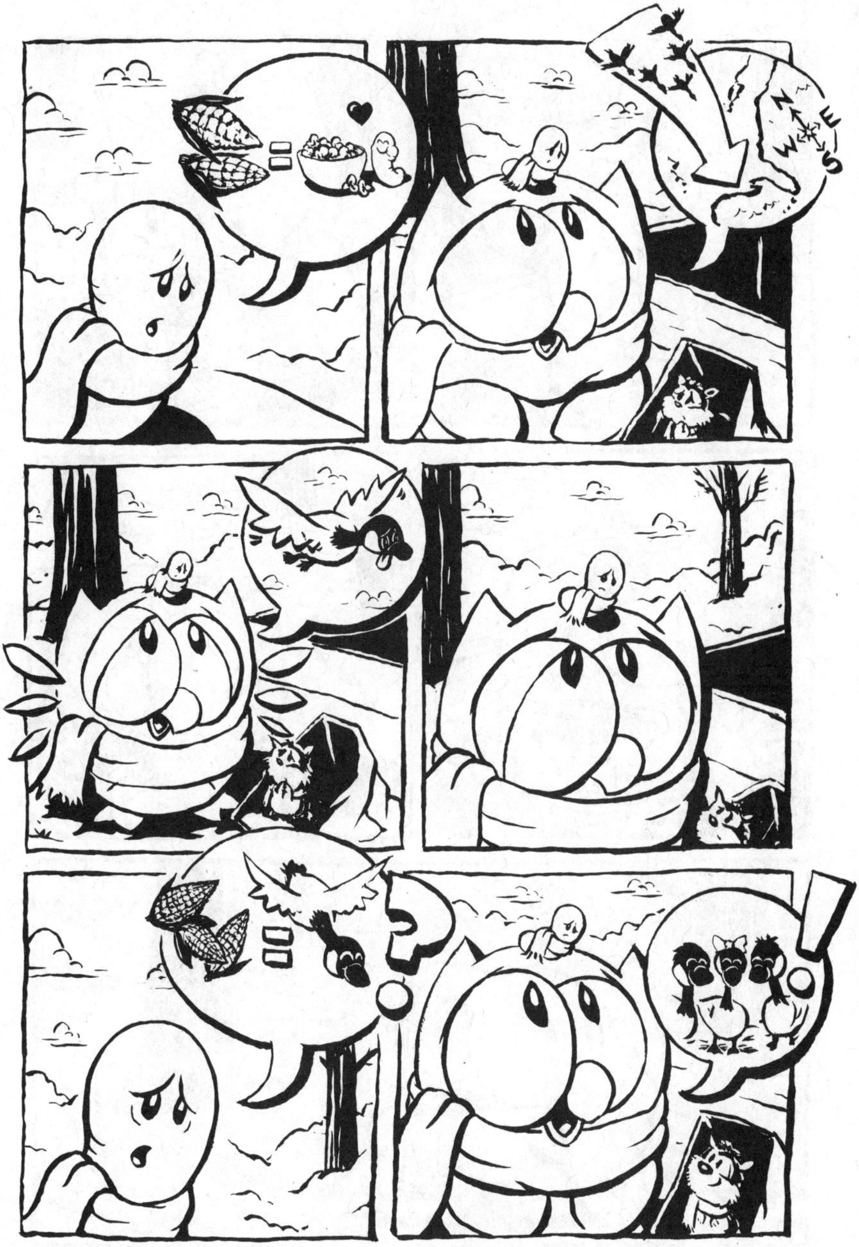
N
E
W
S

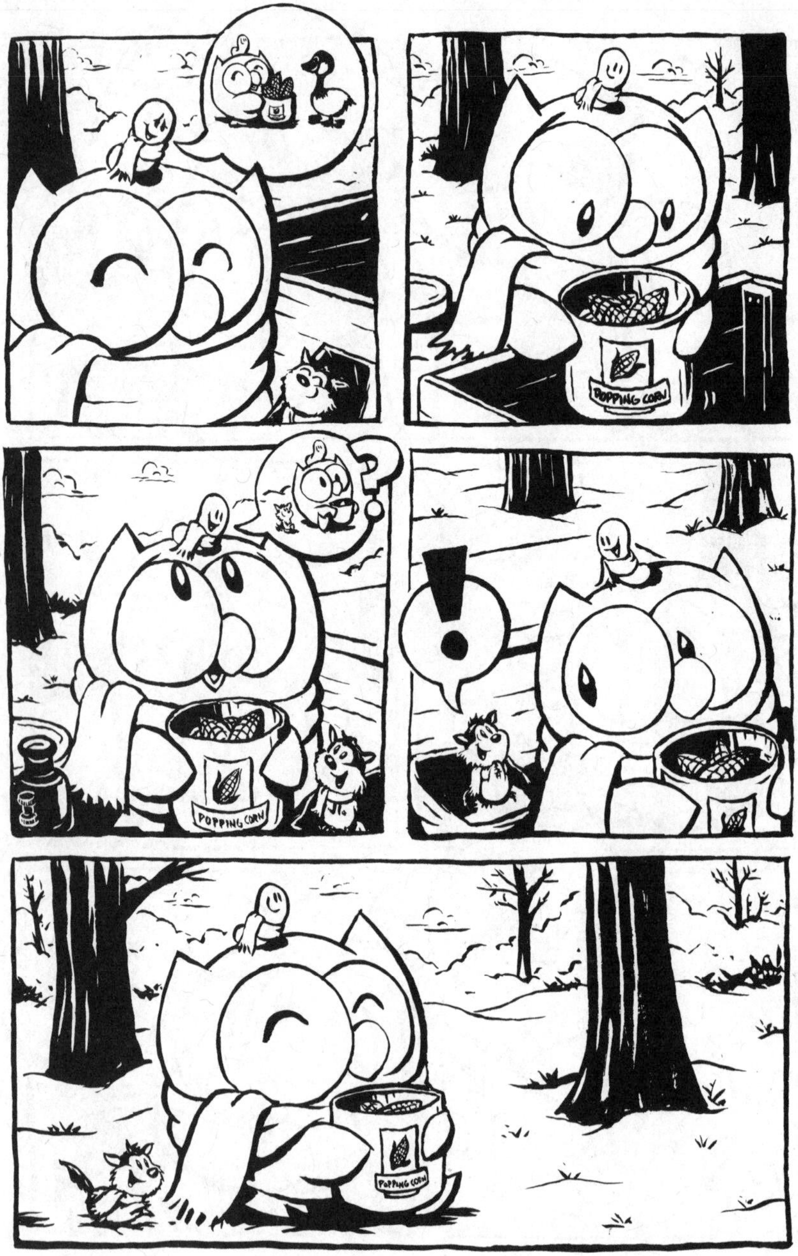
POPPING CORN
!
POPPING CORN
POPPING CORN

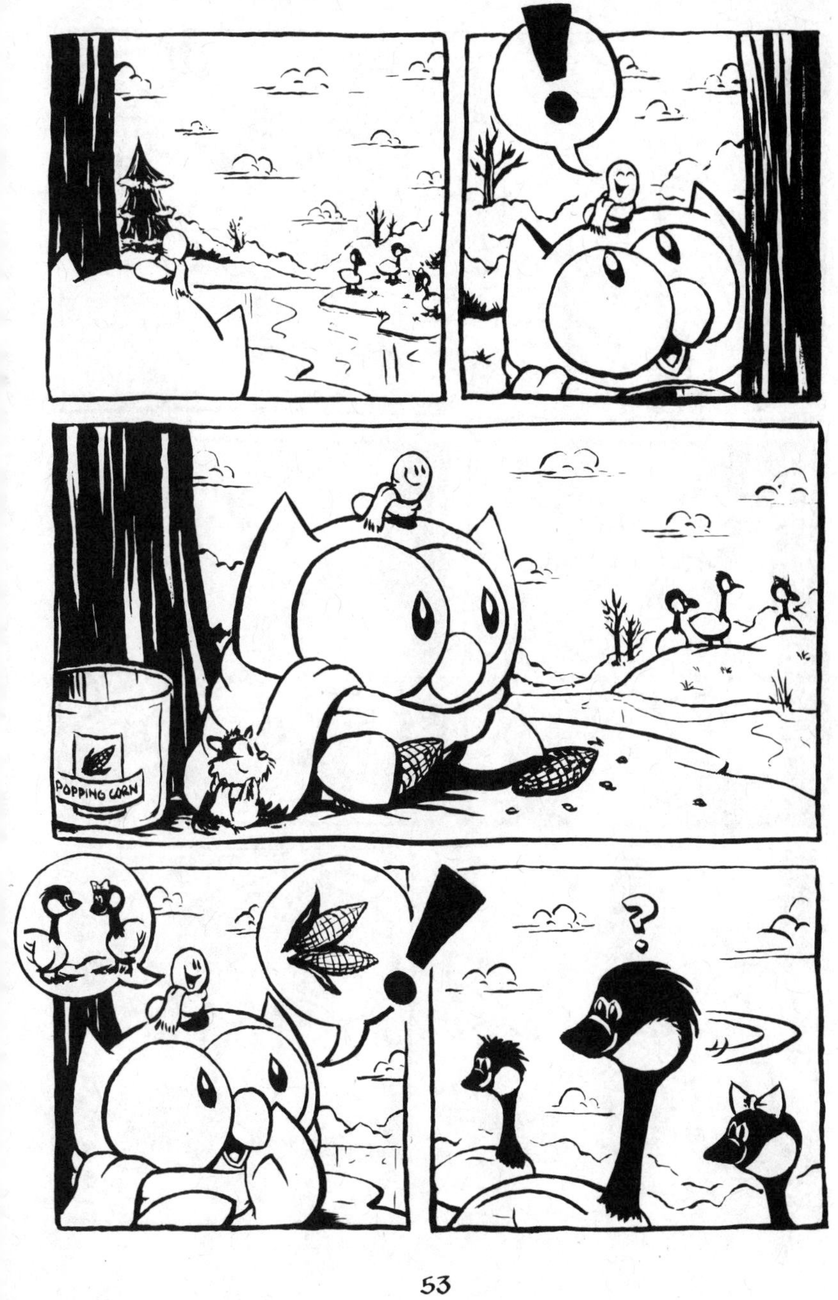
!
POPPING CORN
!
?

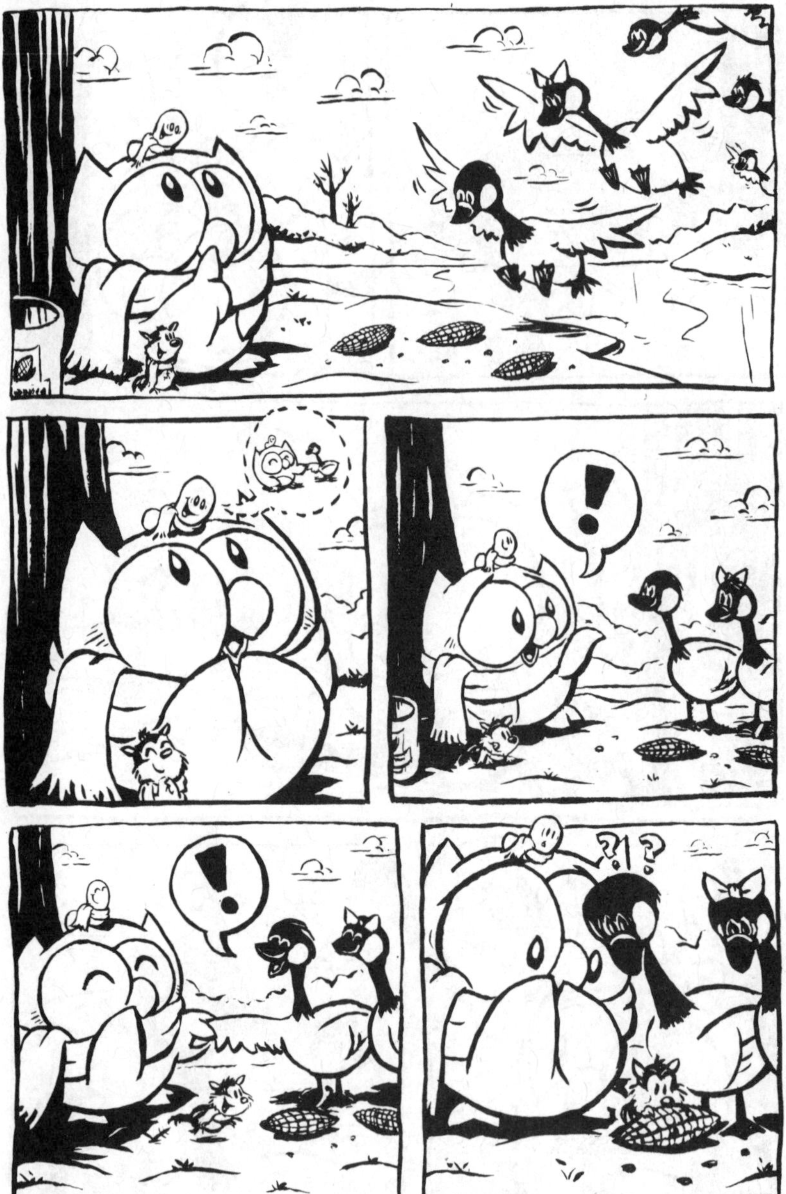
!
!
?!?

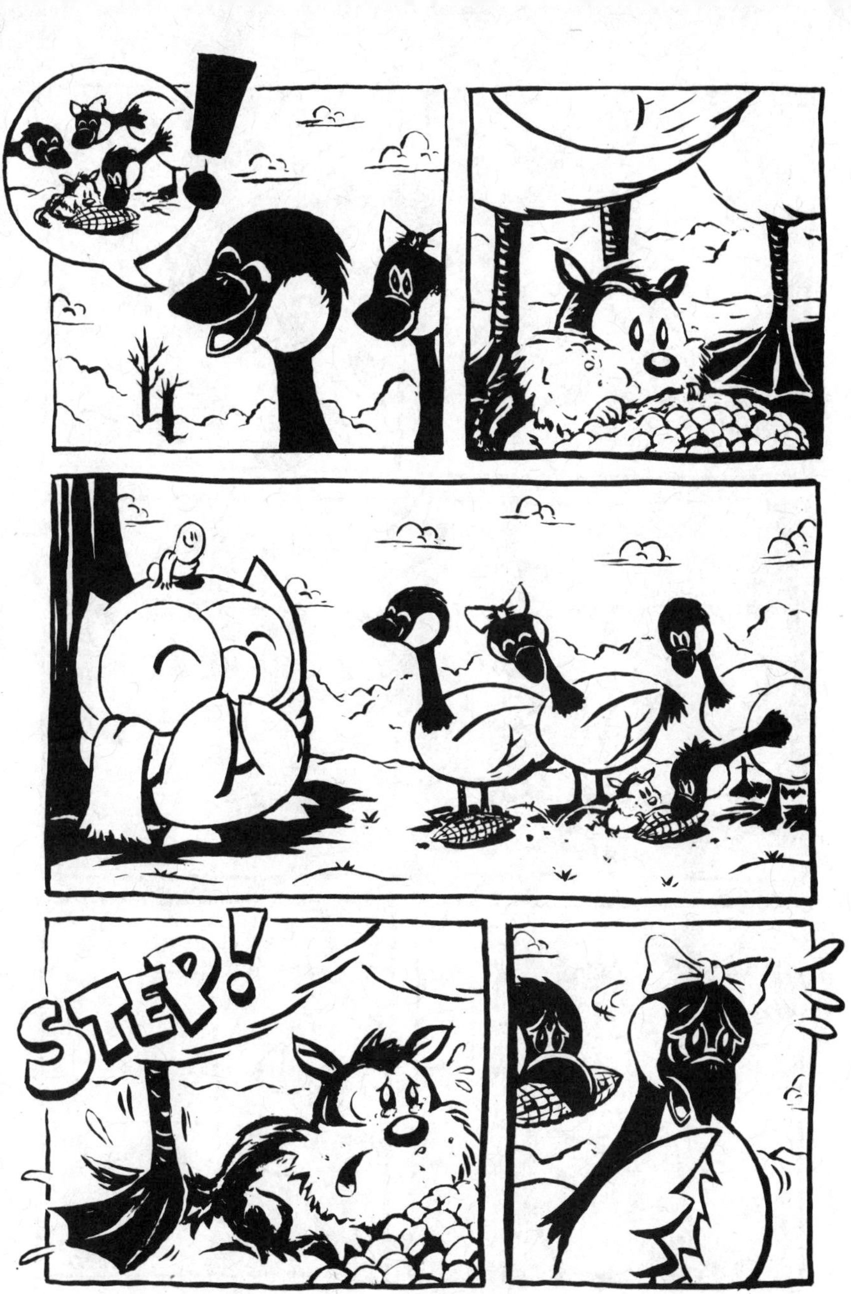
STEP!

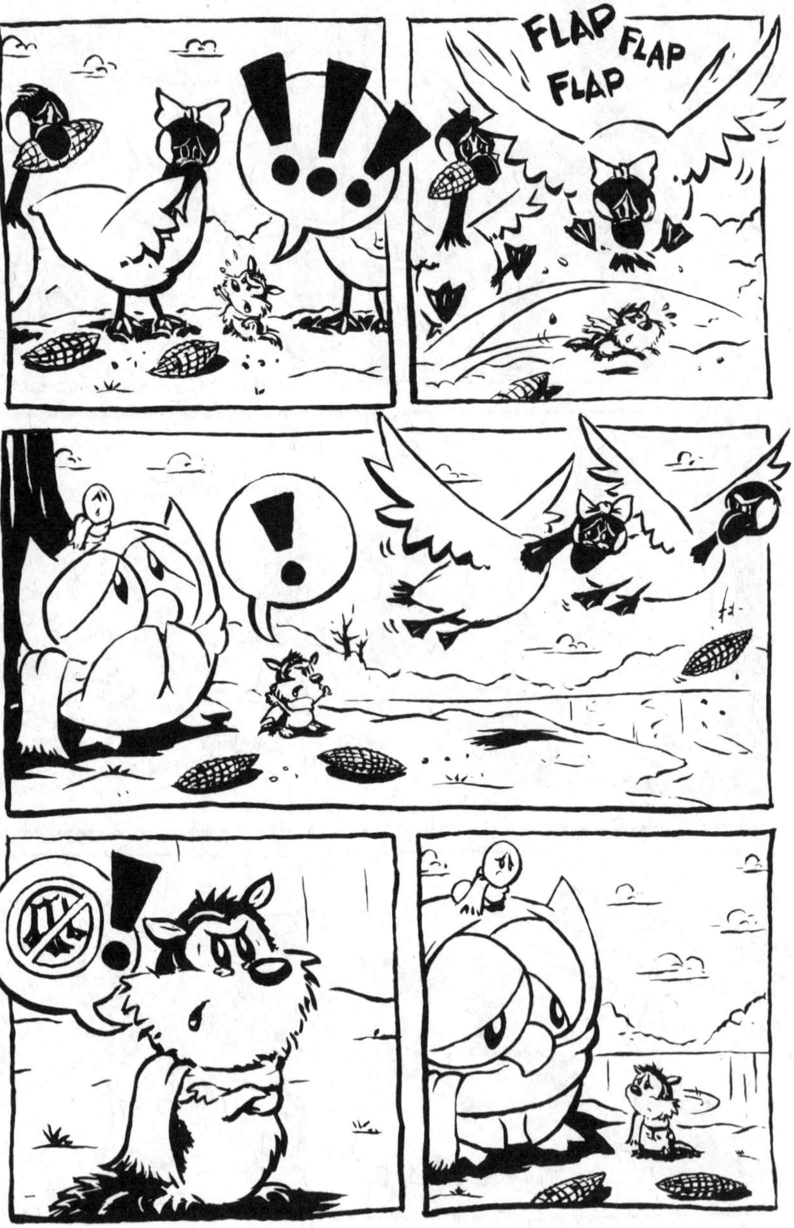
FLAP FLAP
FLAP

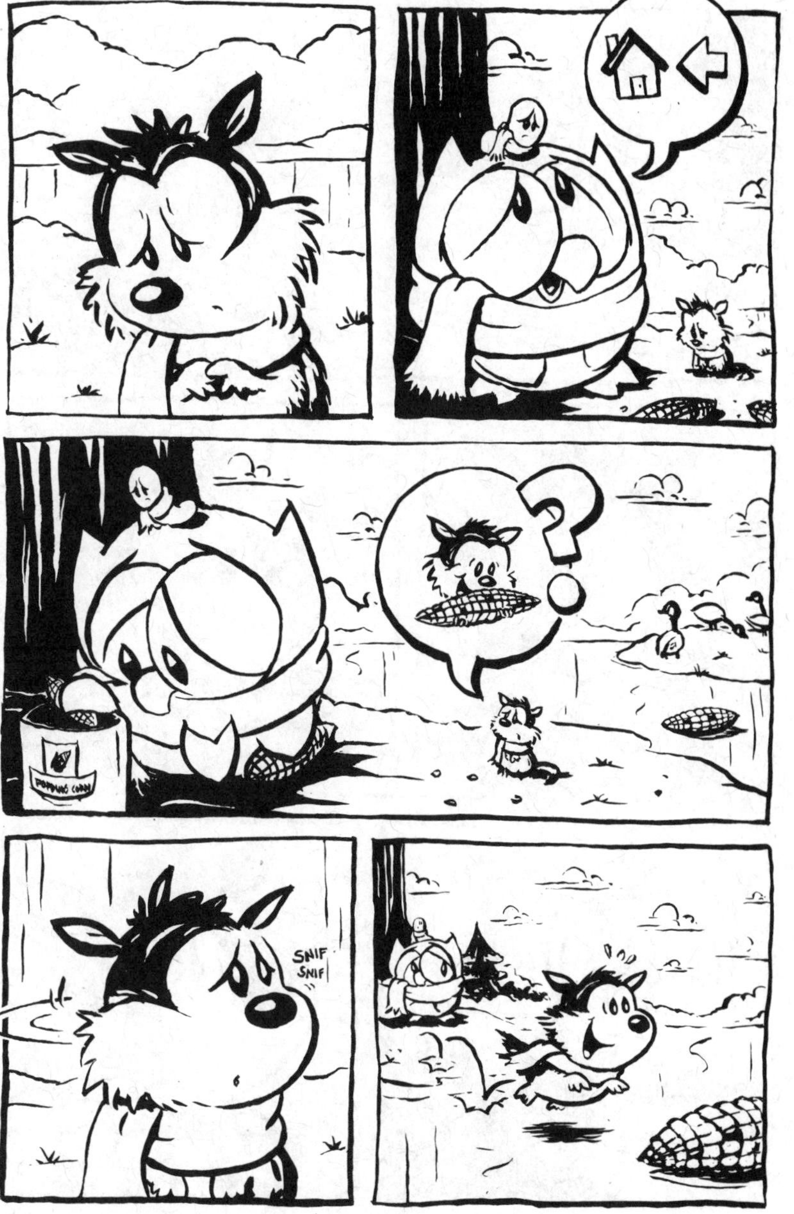
SNIF
SNIF

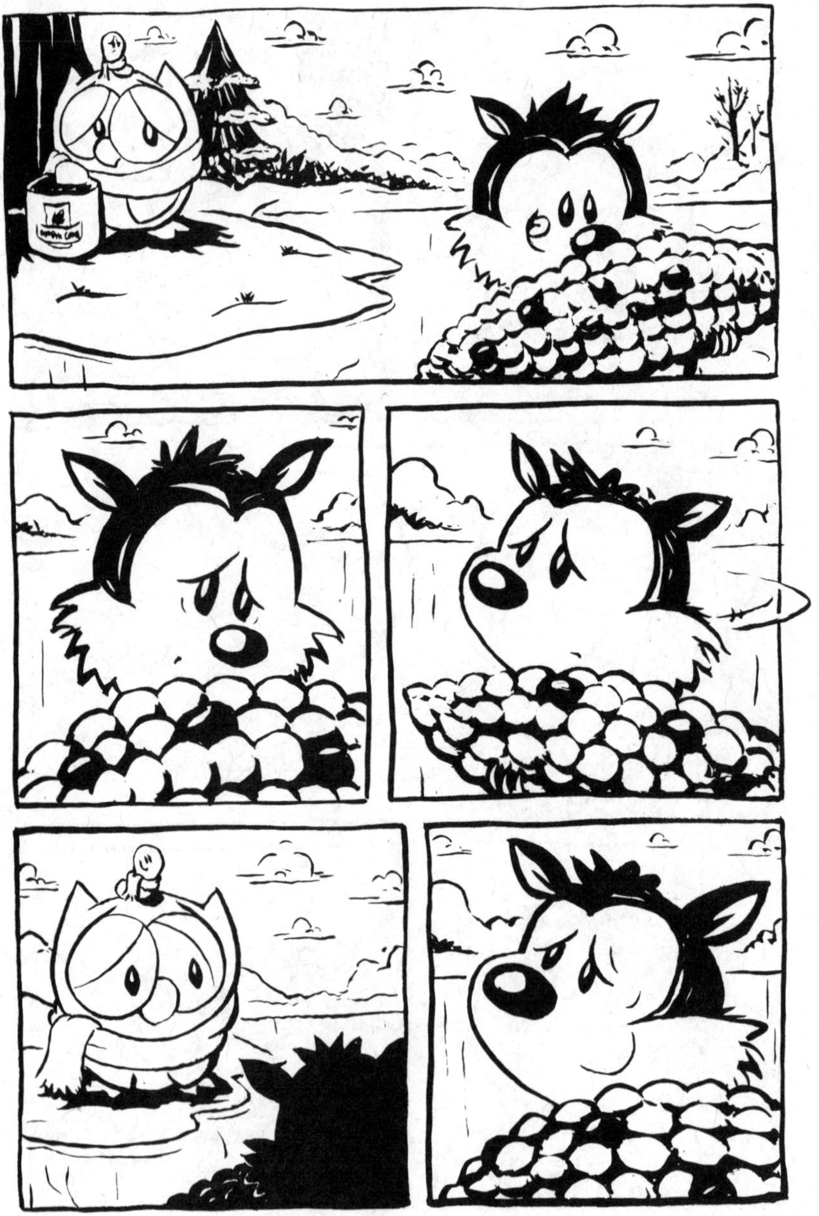

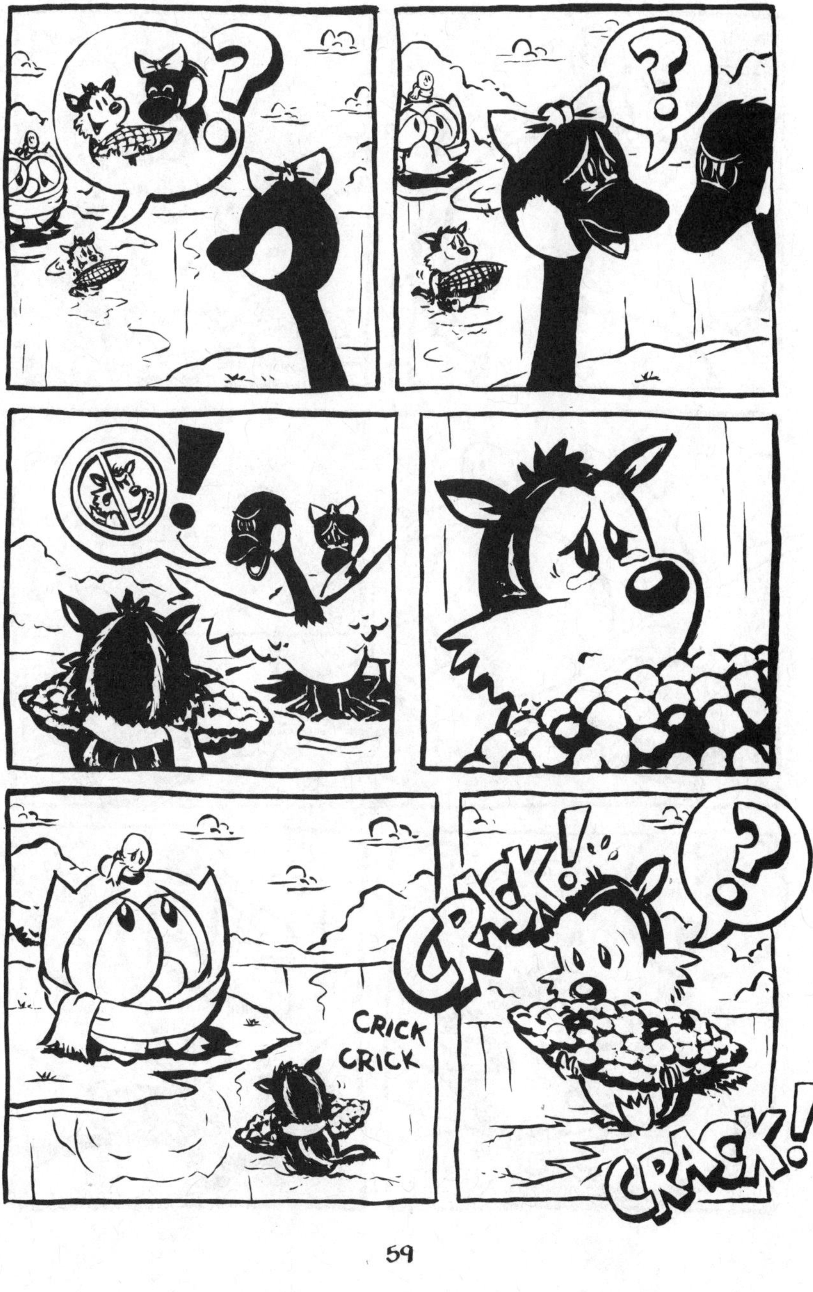
?
?
!
CRICK
CRICK
CRACK!
?
CRACK!

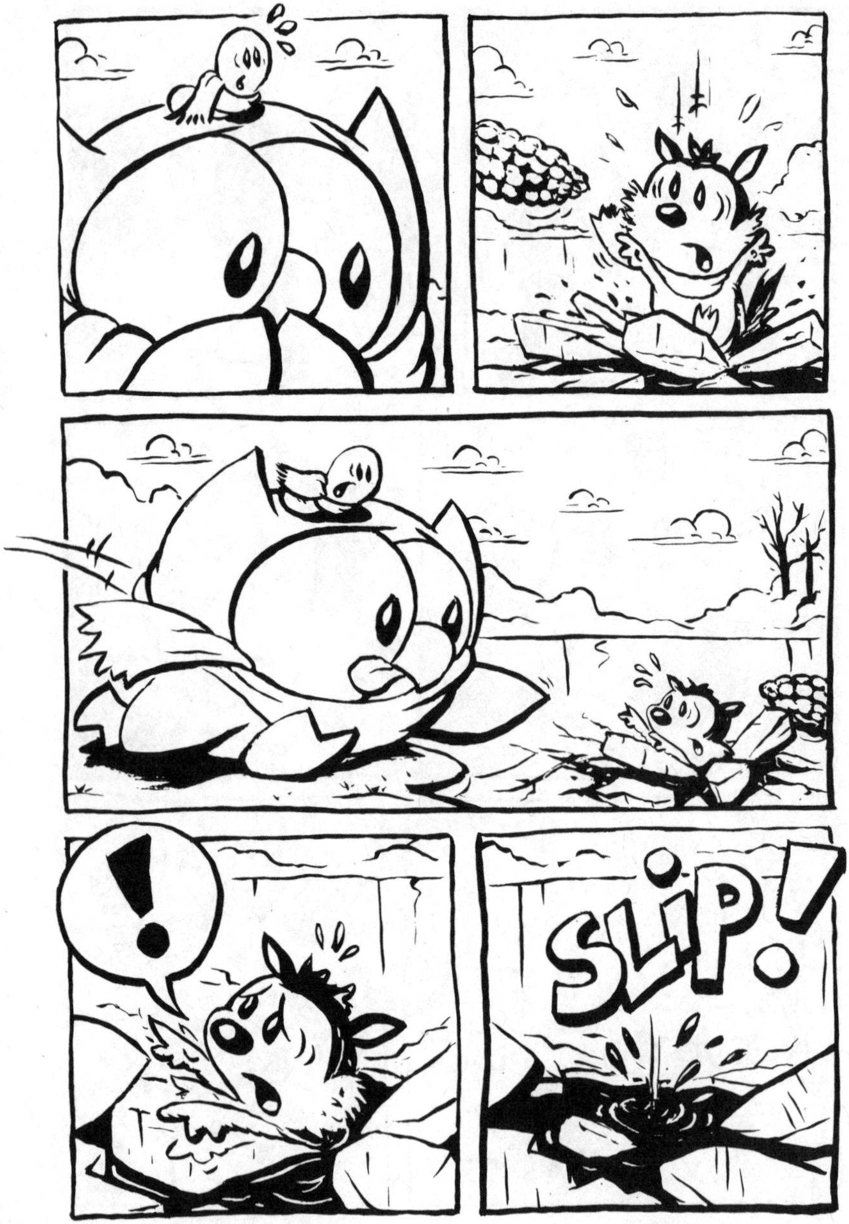
!
SLIP!

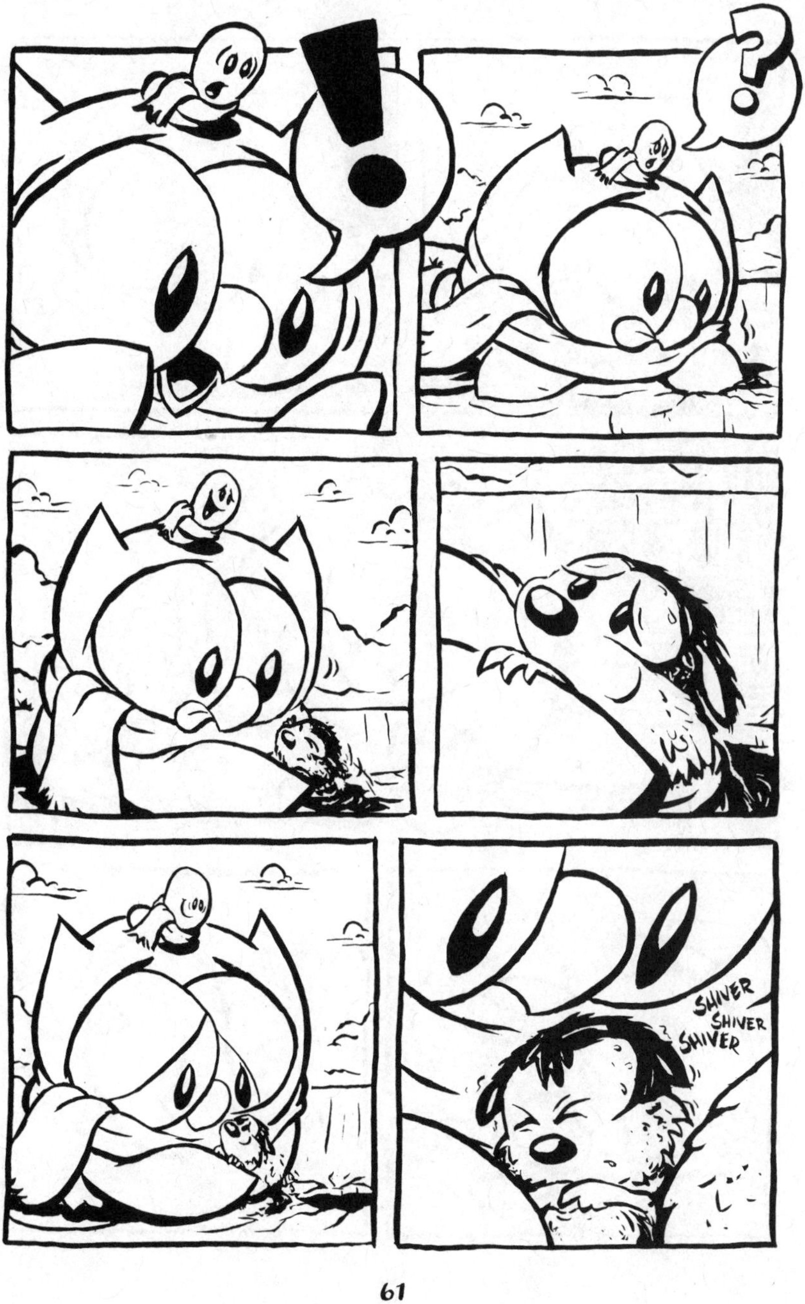
!
?
SHIVER
SHIVER
SHIVER

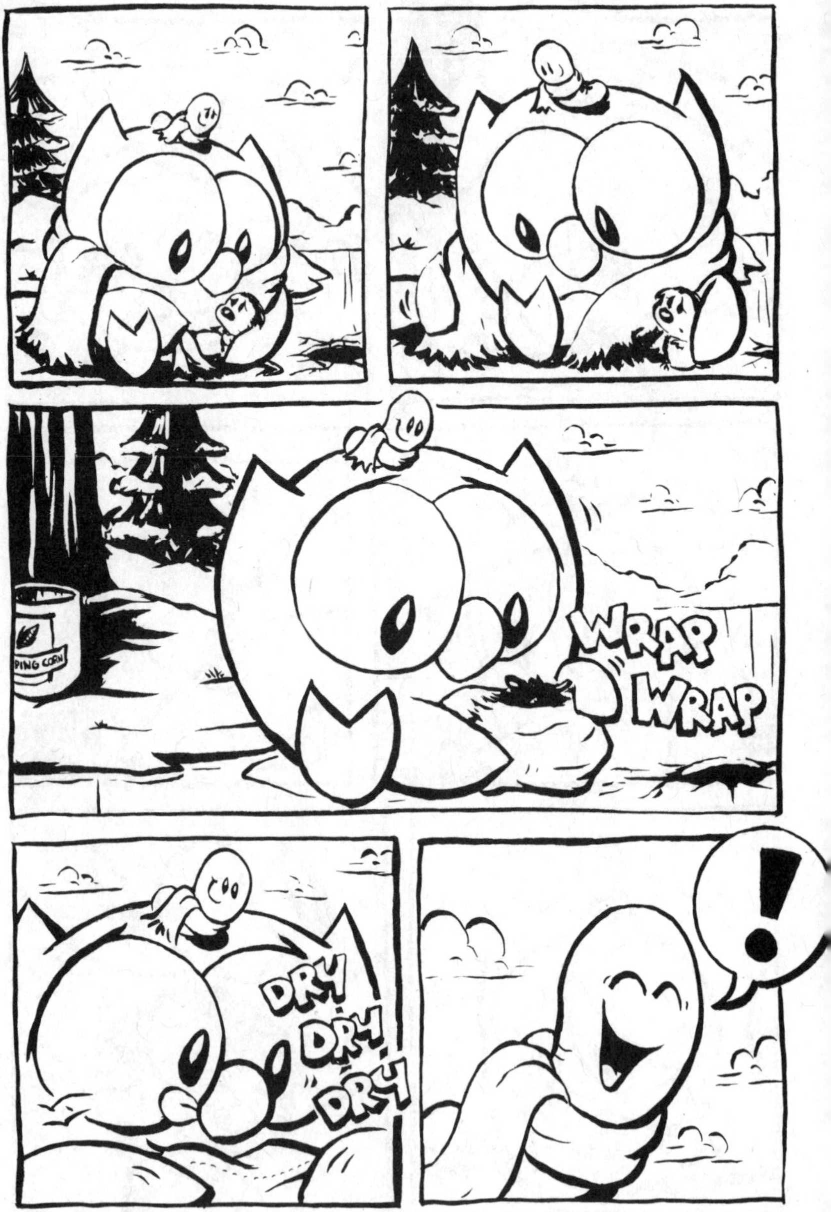
PING CORN
WRAP
WRAP
DRY
DRY
DRY
!

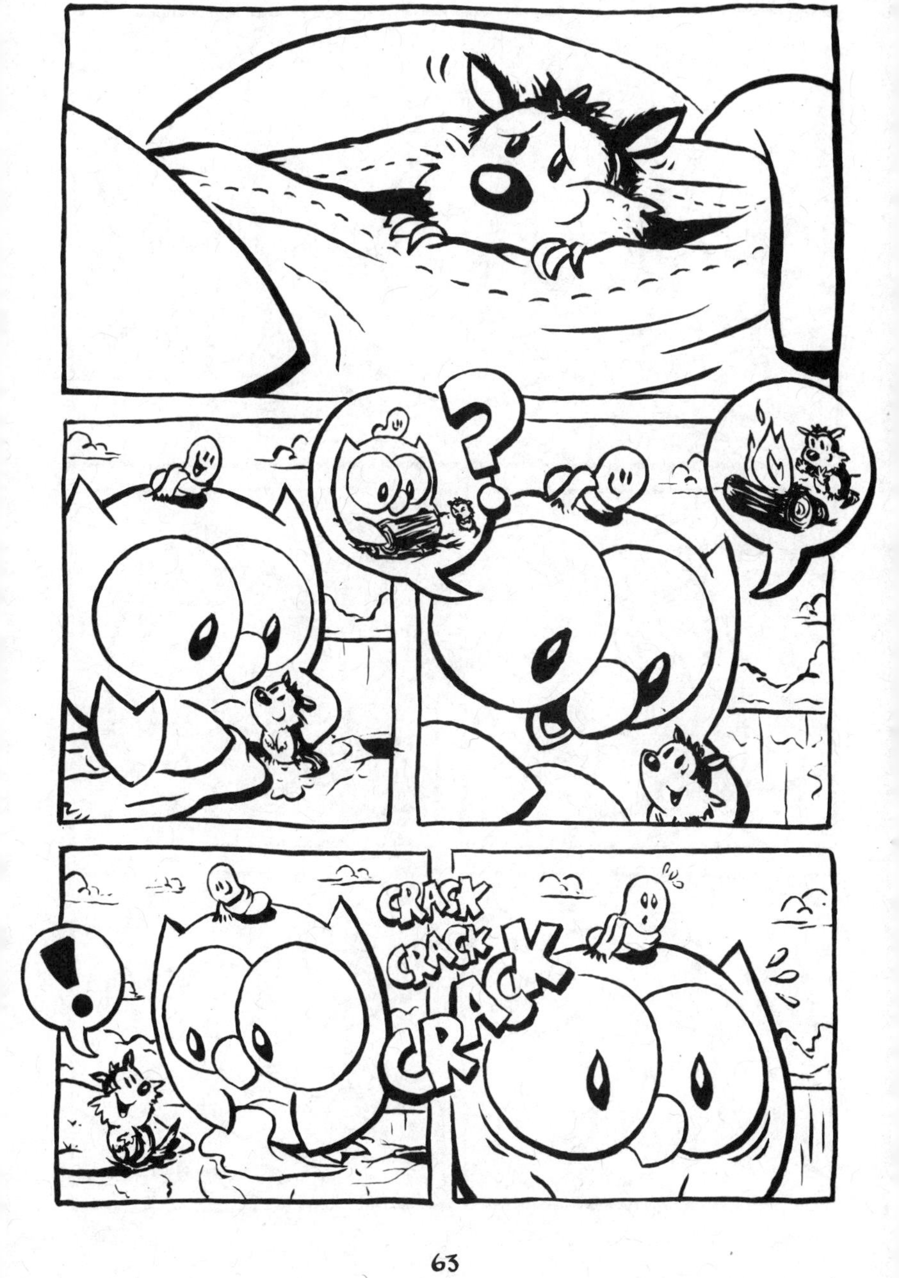
?
!
CRACK
CRACK
CRACK

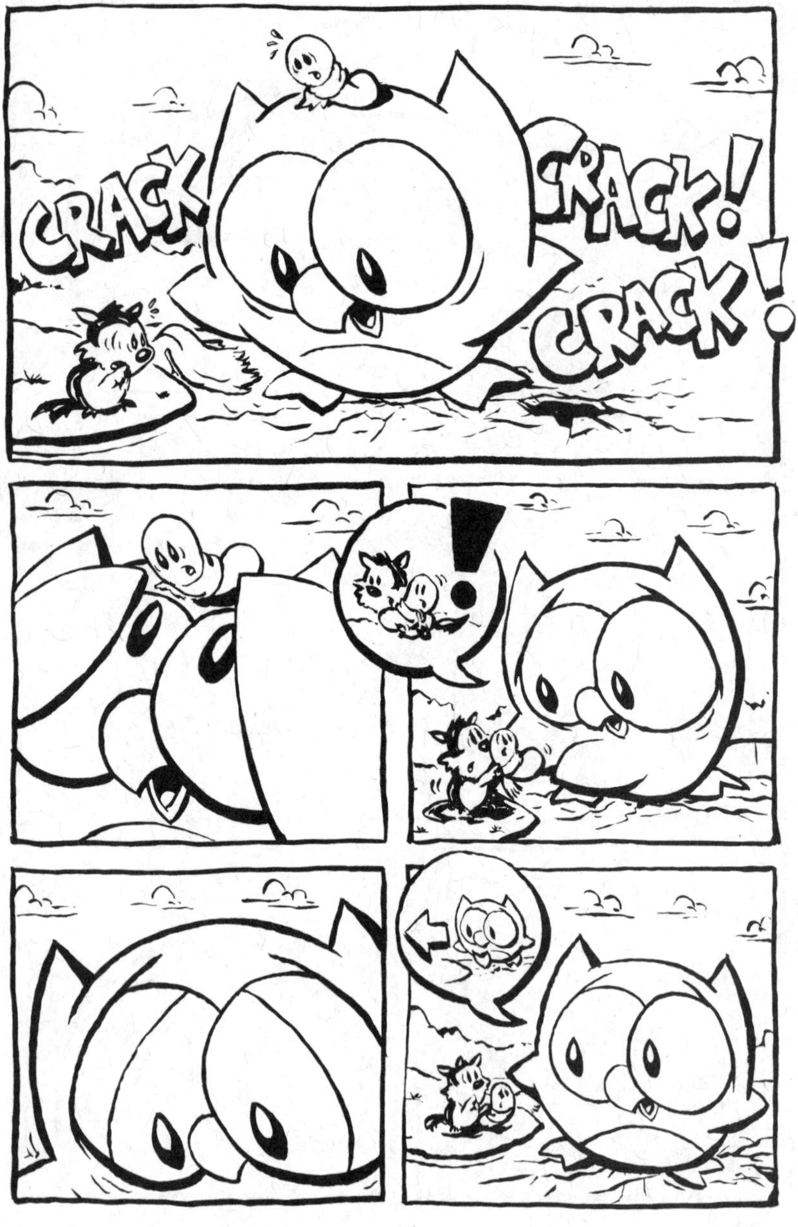
CRACK
CRACK!
CRACK!
!

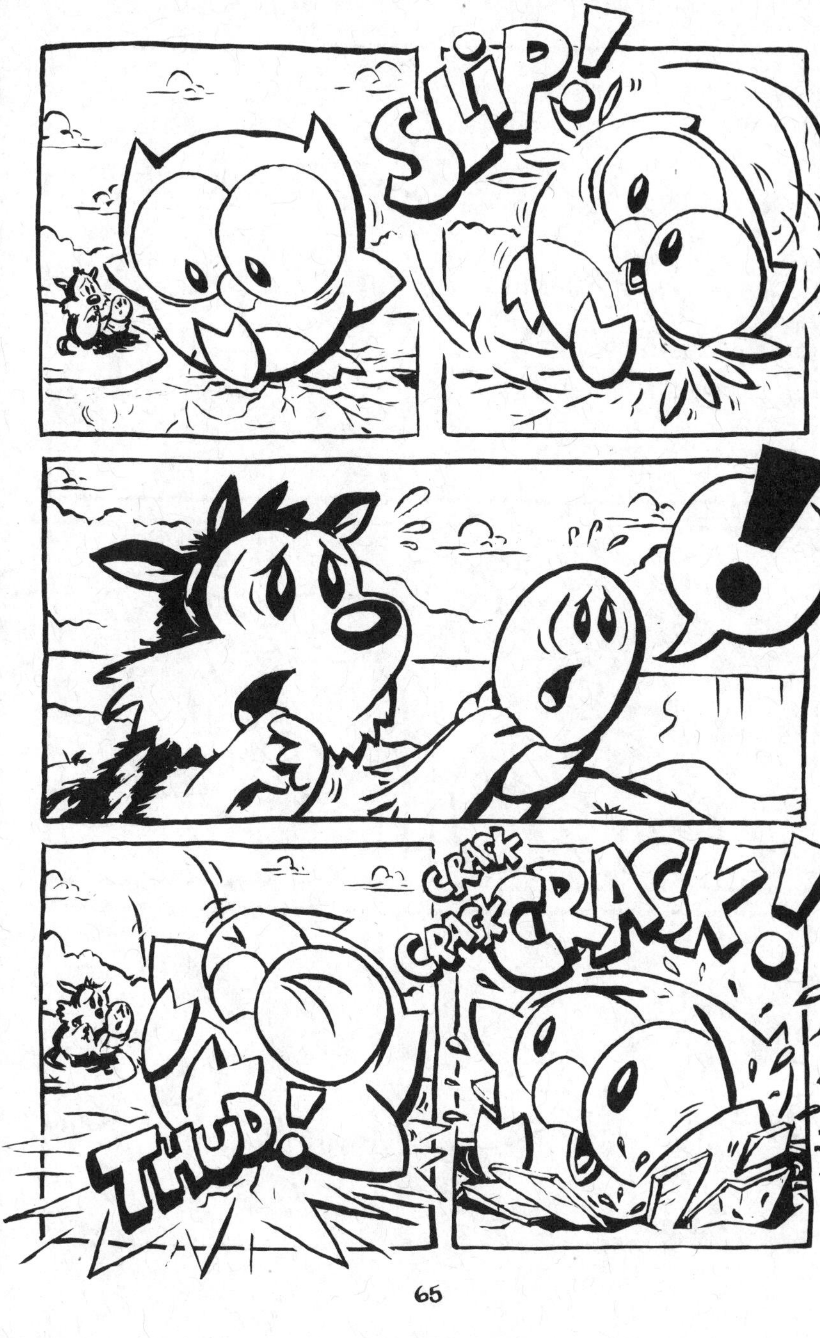
SLIP!
!
CRACK
CRACK
CRACK!
THUD!

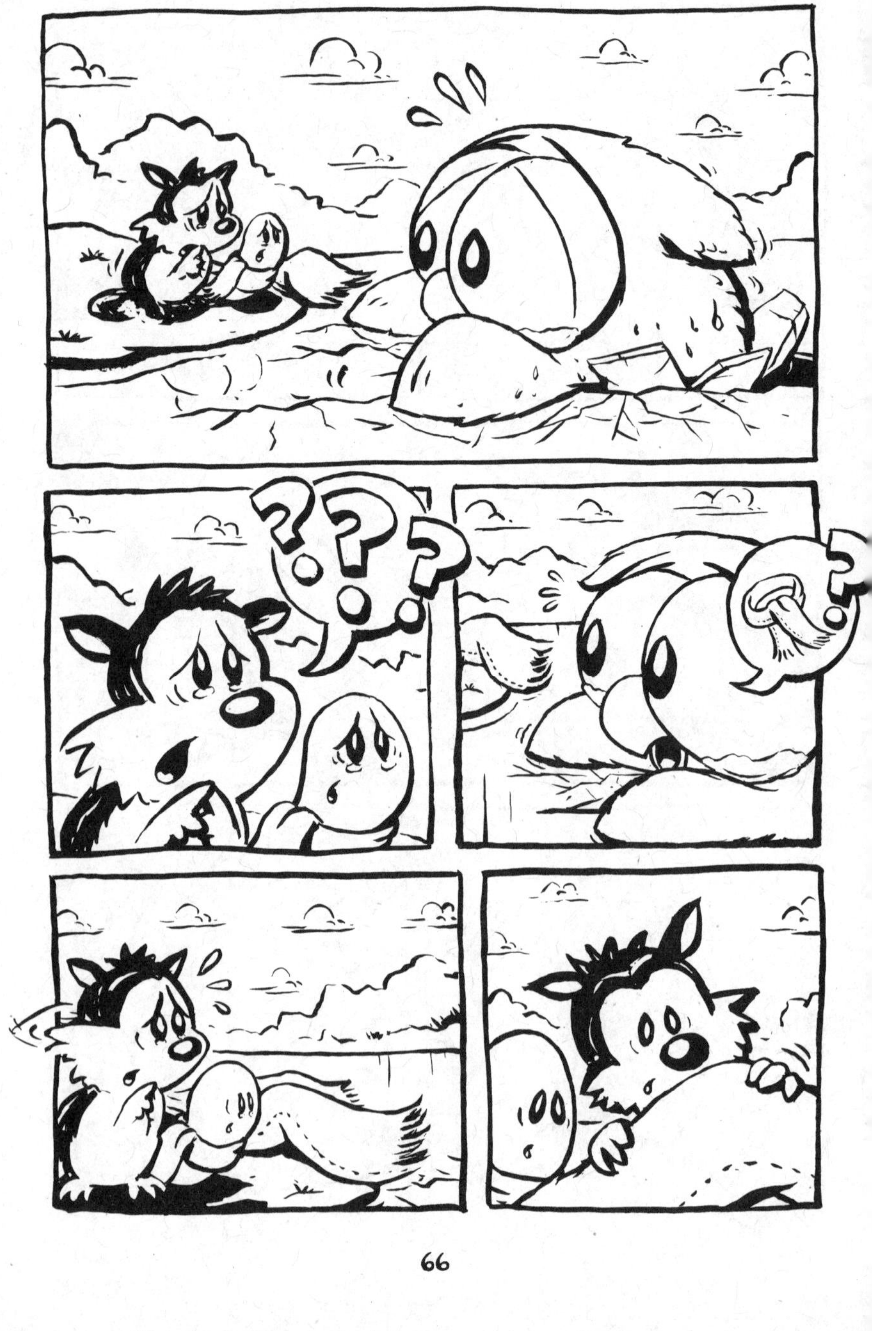
???
?

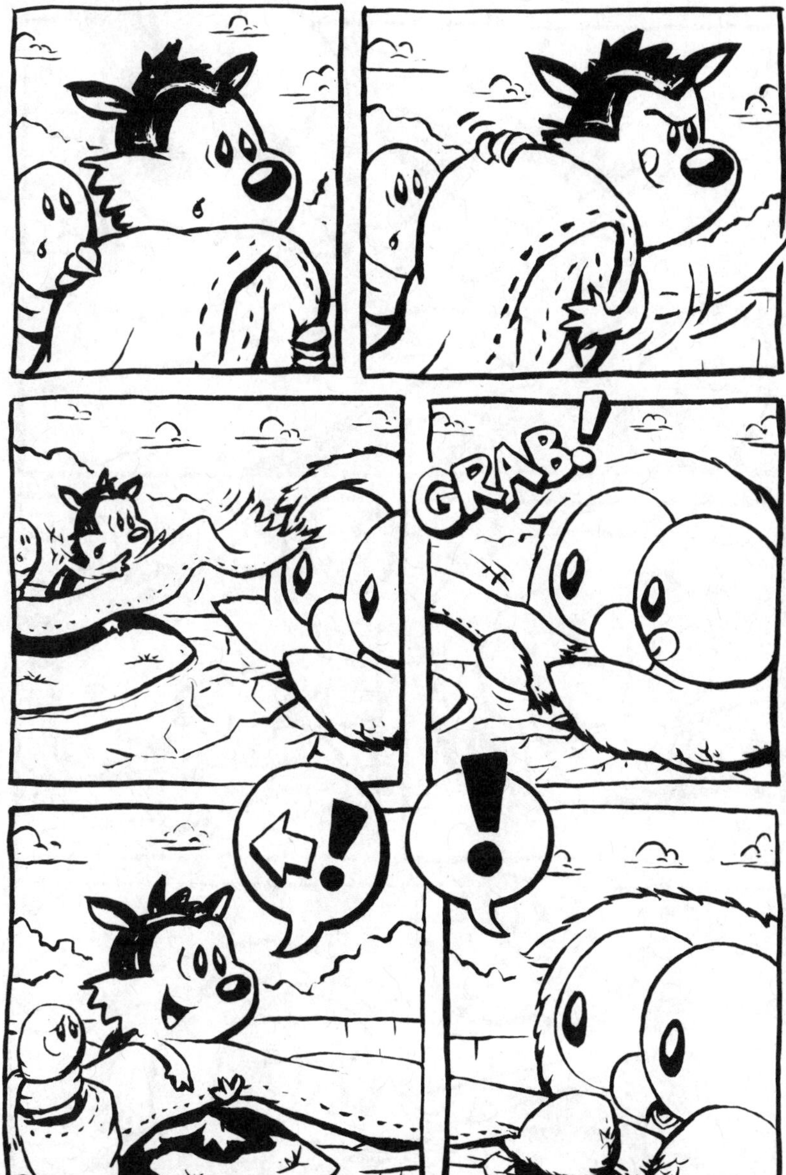
GRAB!
!
!

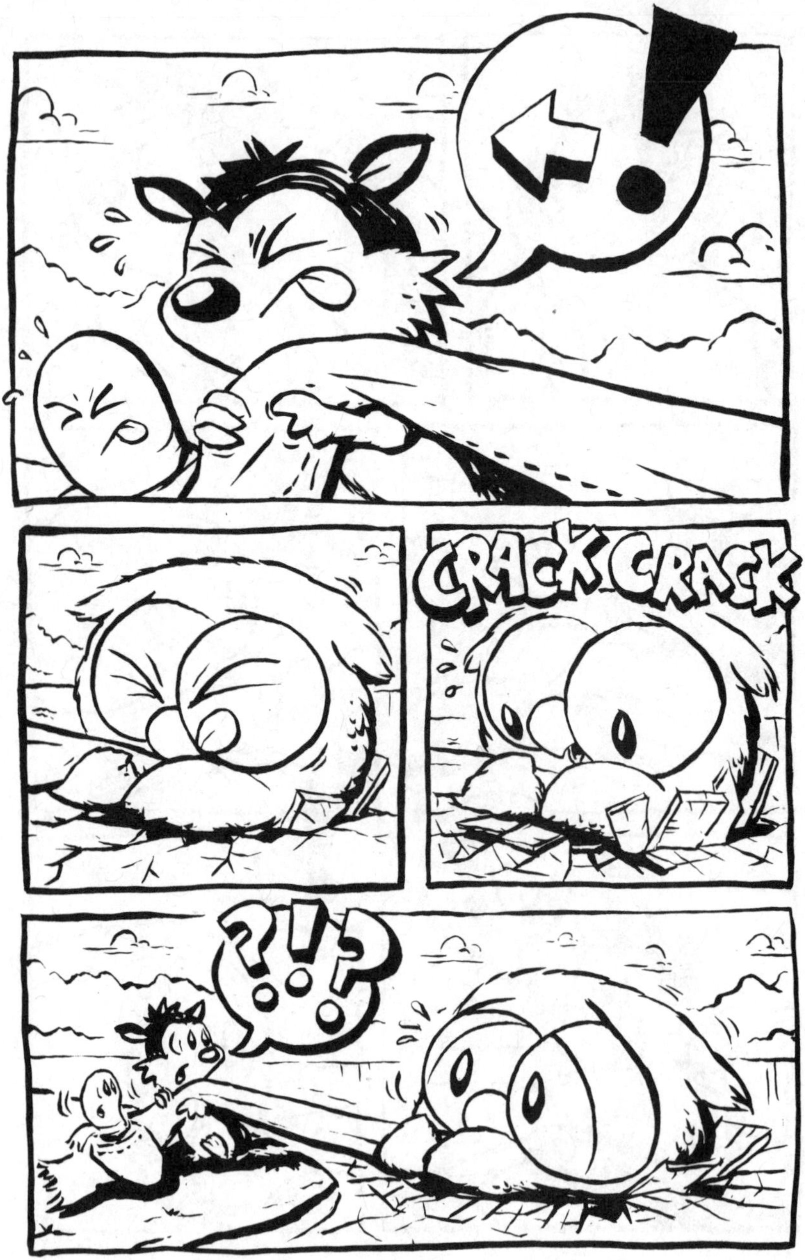
!
CRACK CRACK
?!?

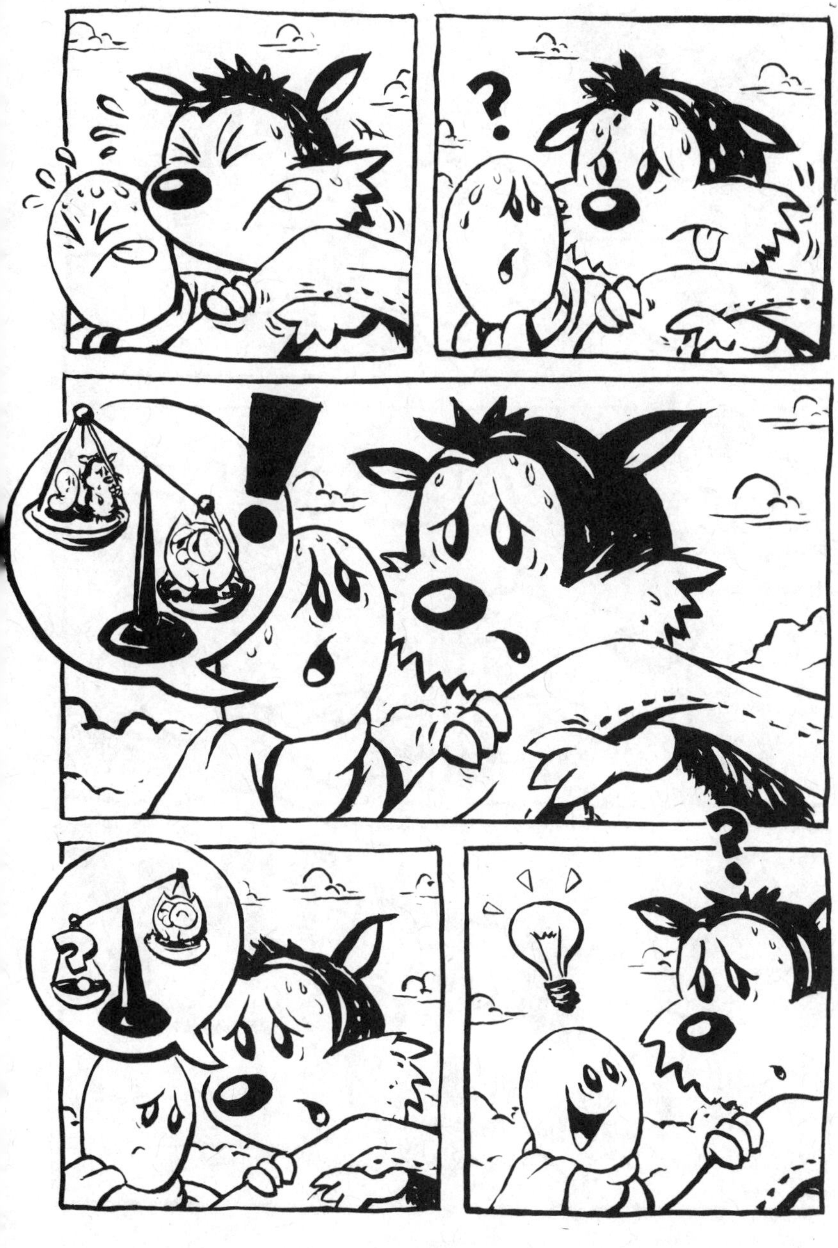

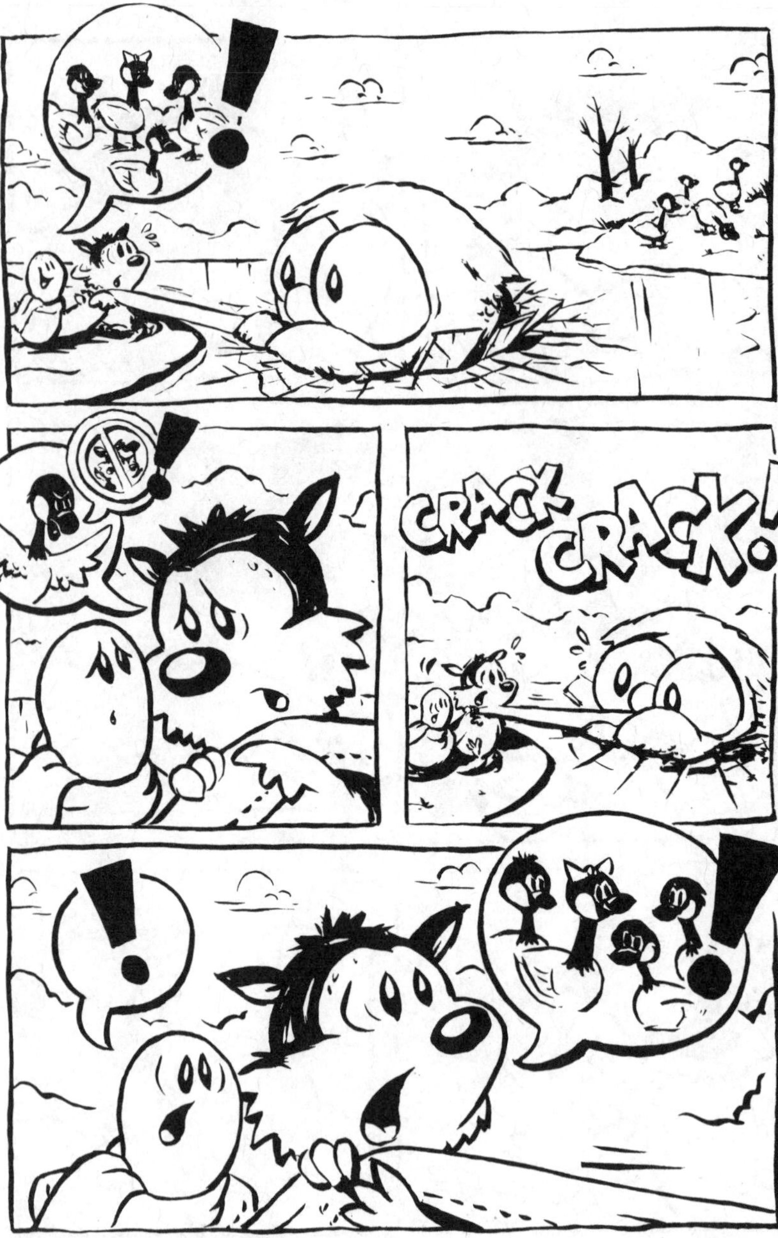
!
!
CRACK
CRACK!
!
!

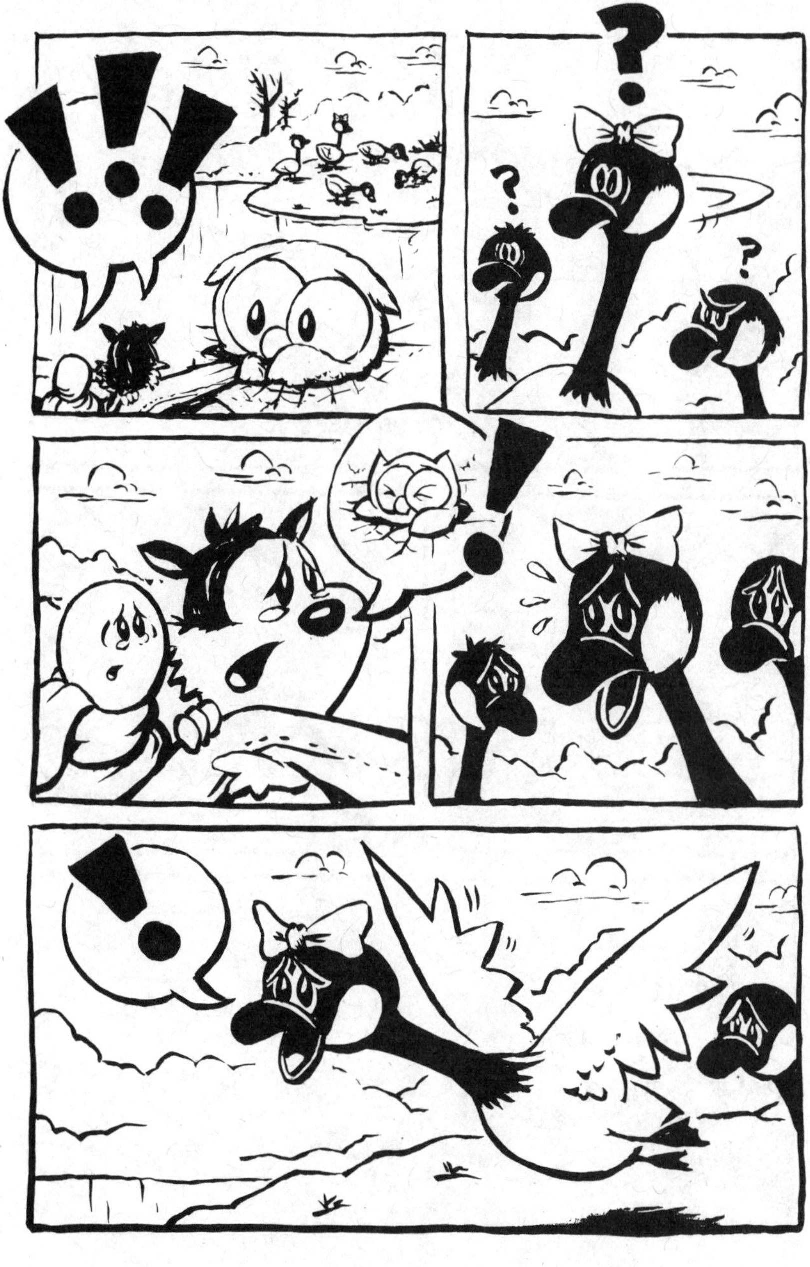
!!!
?
?
?
!
!

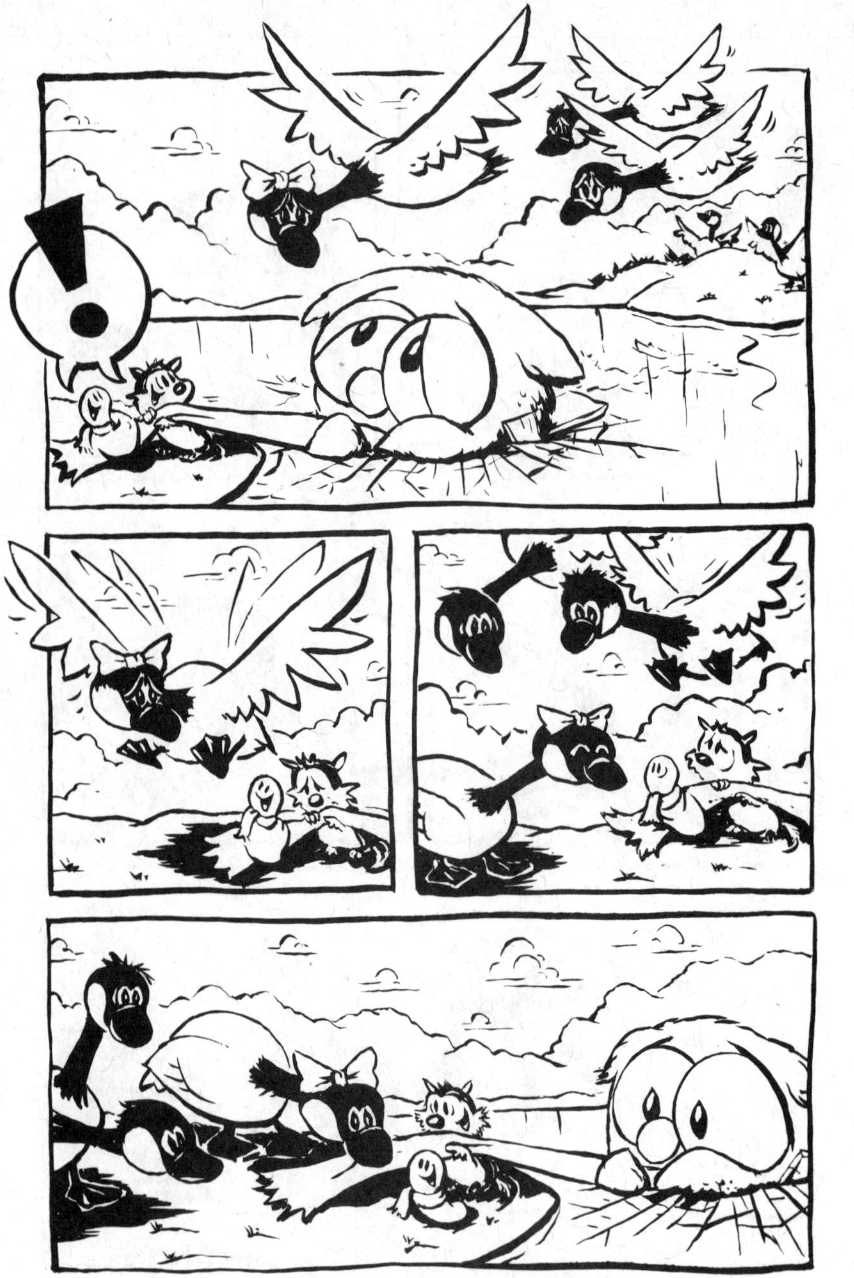
!

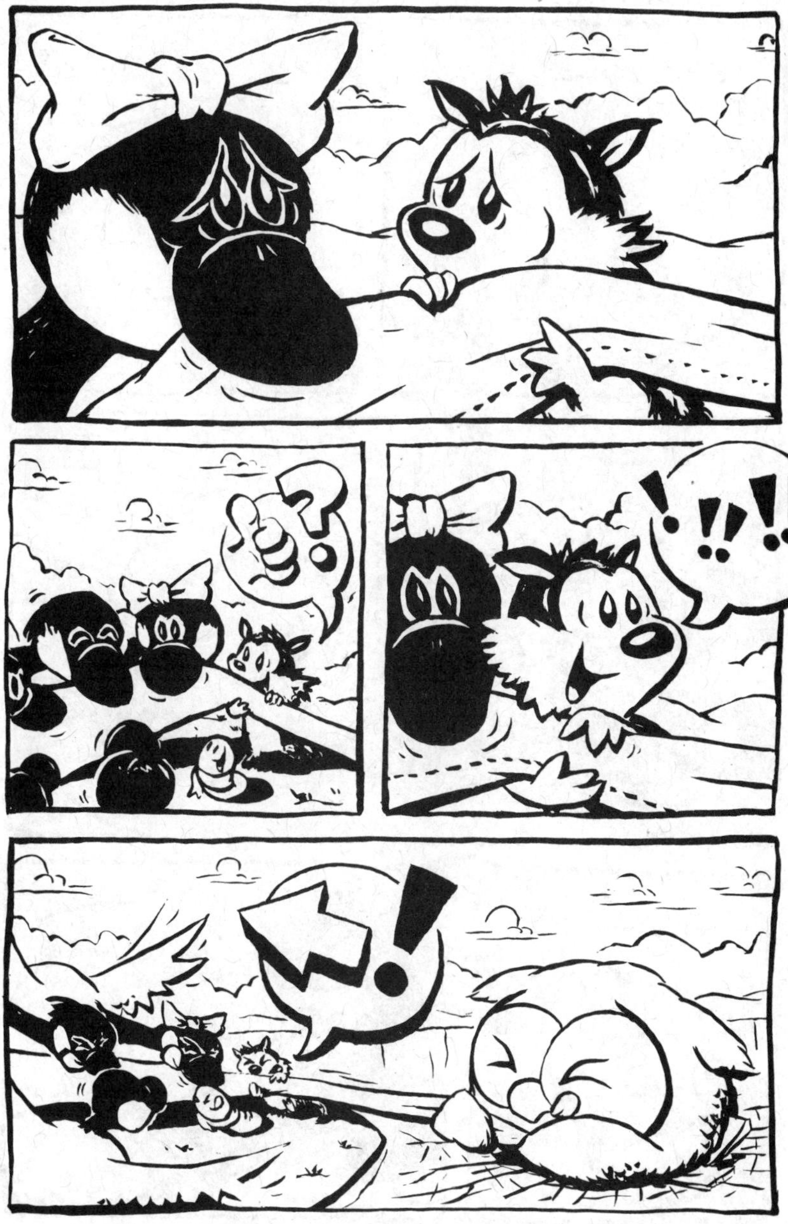
?
!!!!!
!

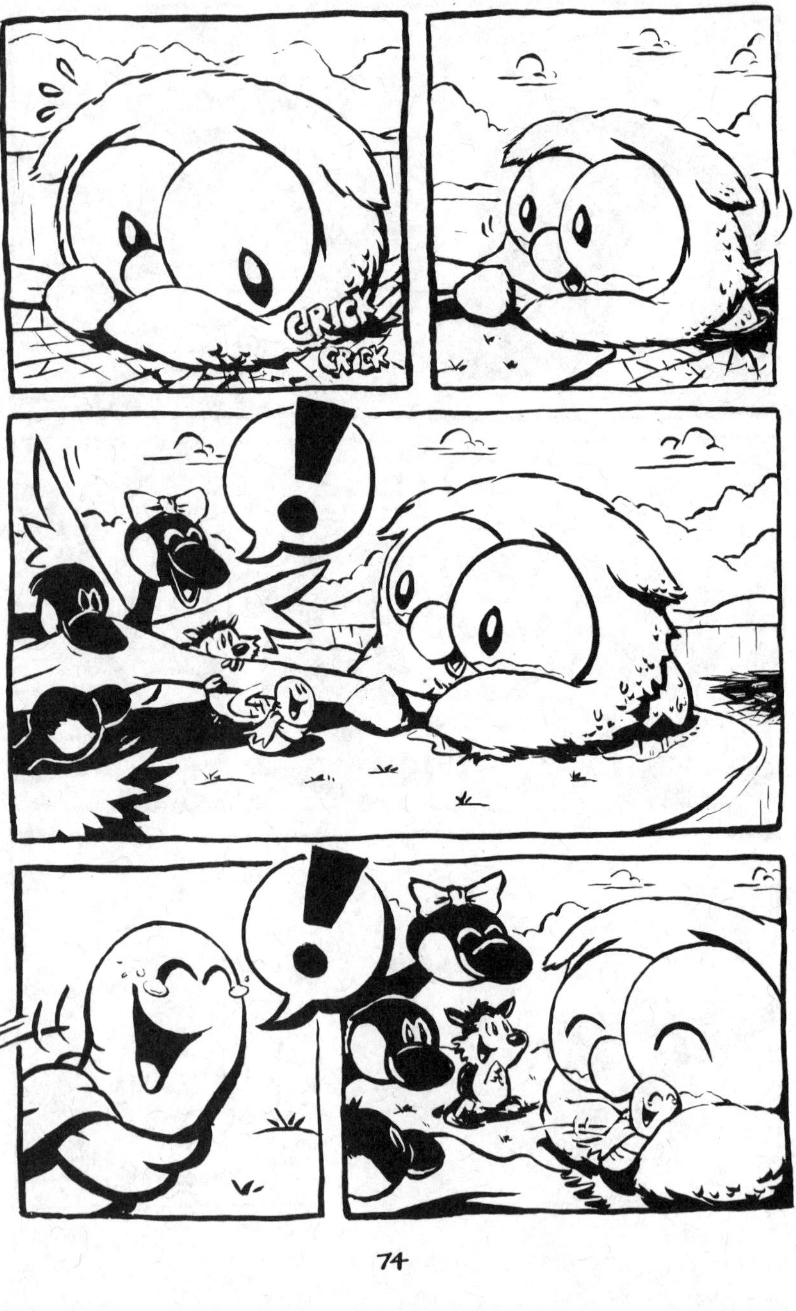
CRICK
CRICK
!
!

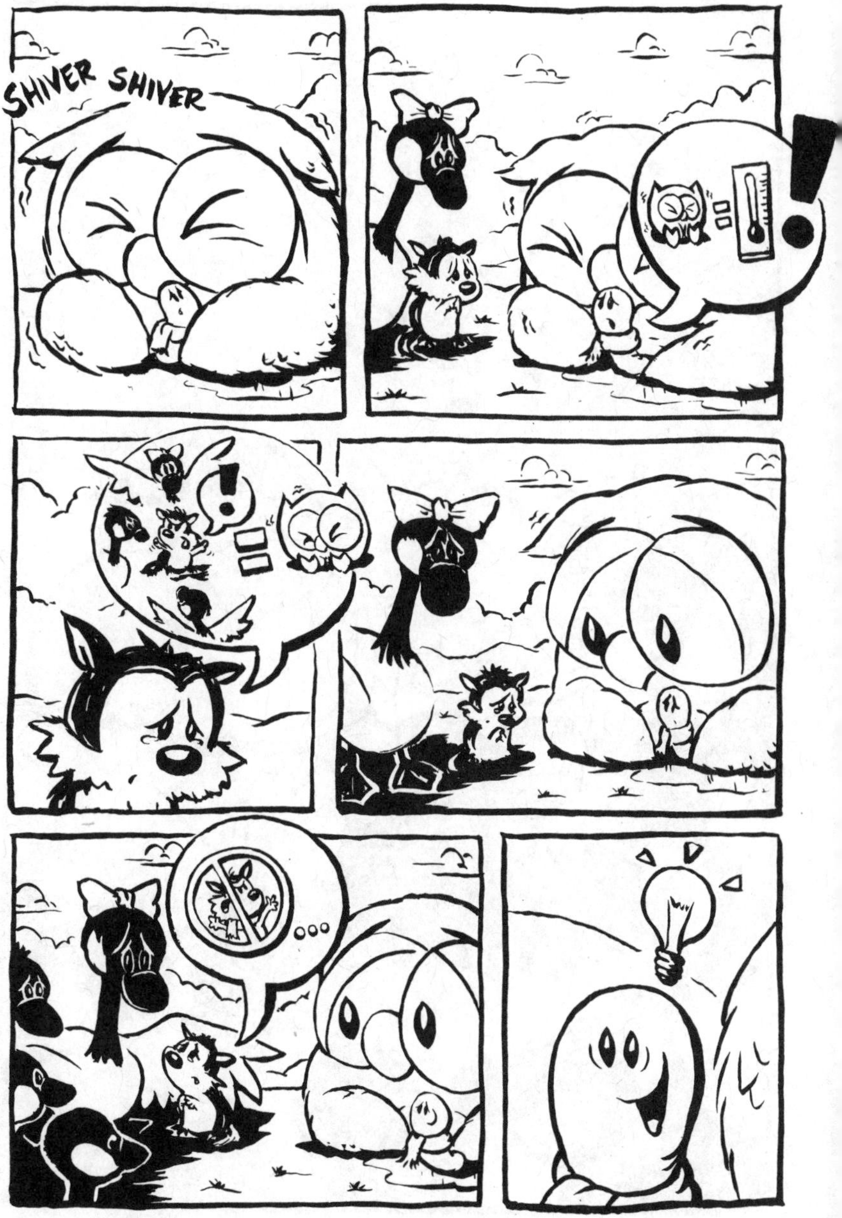
SHIVER SHIVER

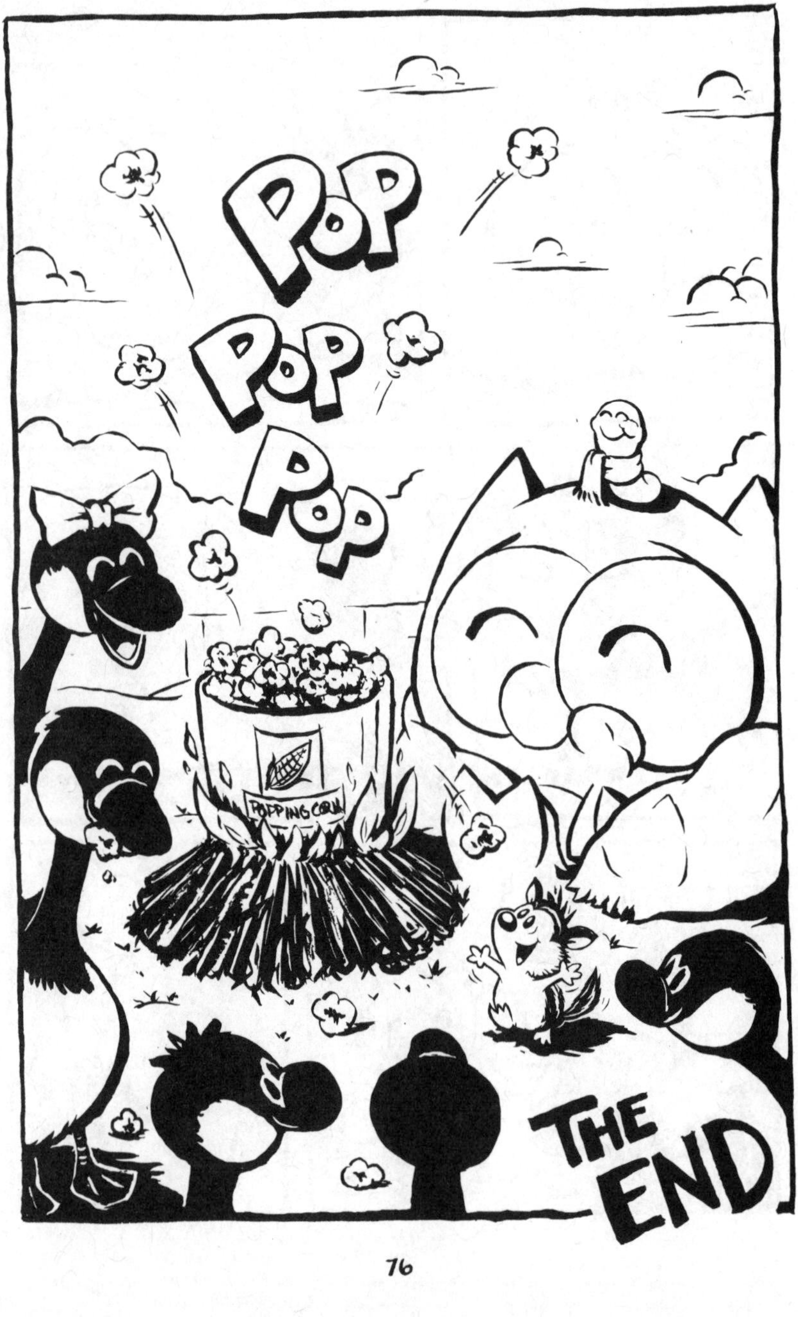
POP
POP
POP
POPPING CORN
THE END

HANGIN' UP TO DRY

JANUARY, 2006

THE END

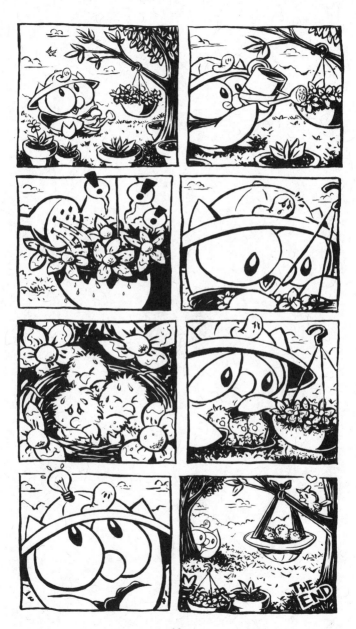

BEE NICE

JUNE, 2004

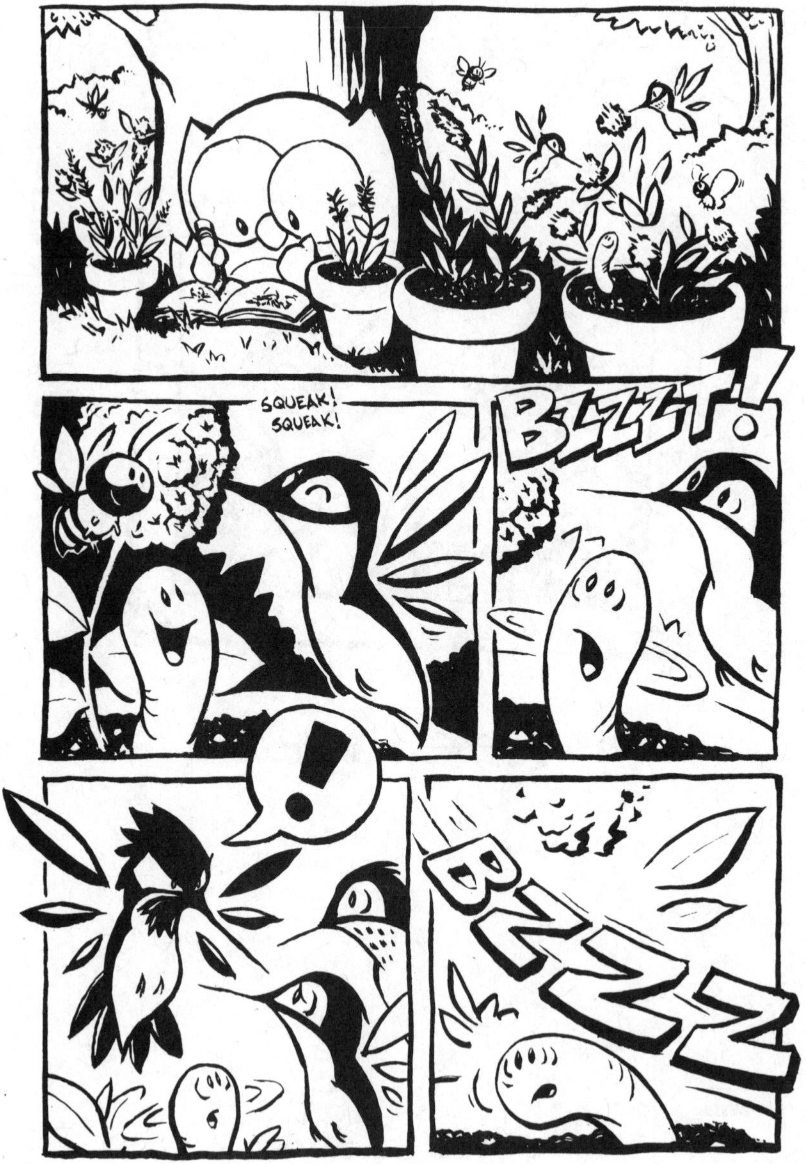
SQUEAK!
SQUEAK!
BZZZT!
!
BZZZZ

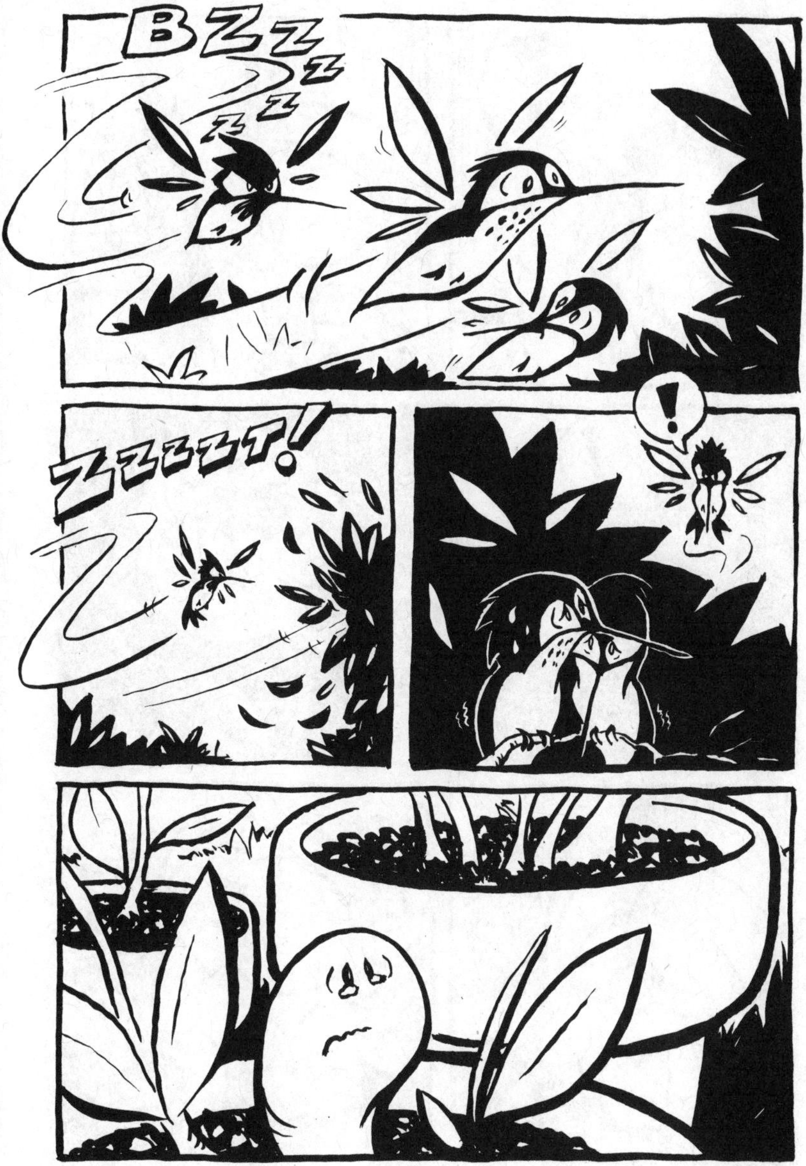
BZZZZZ
ZZZZZT!
!

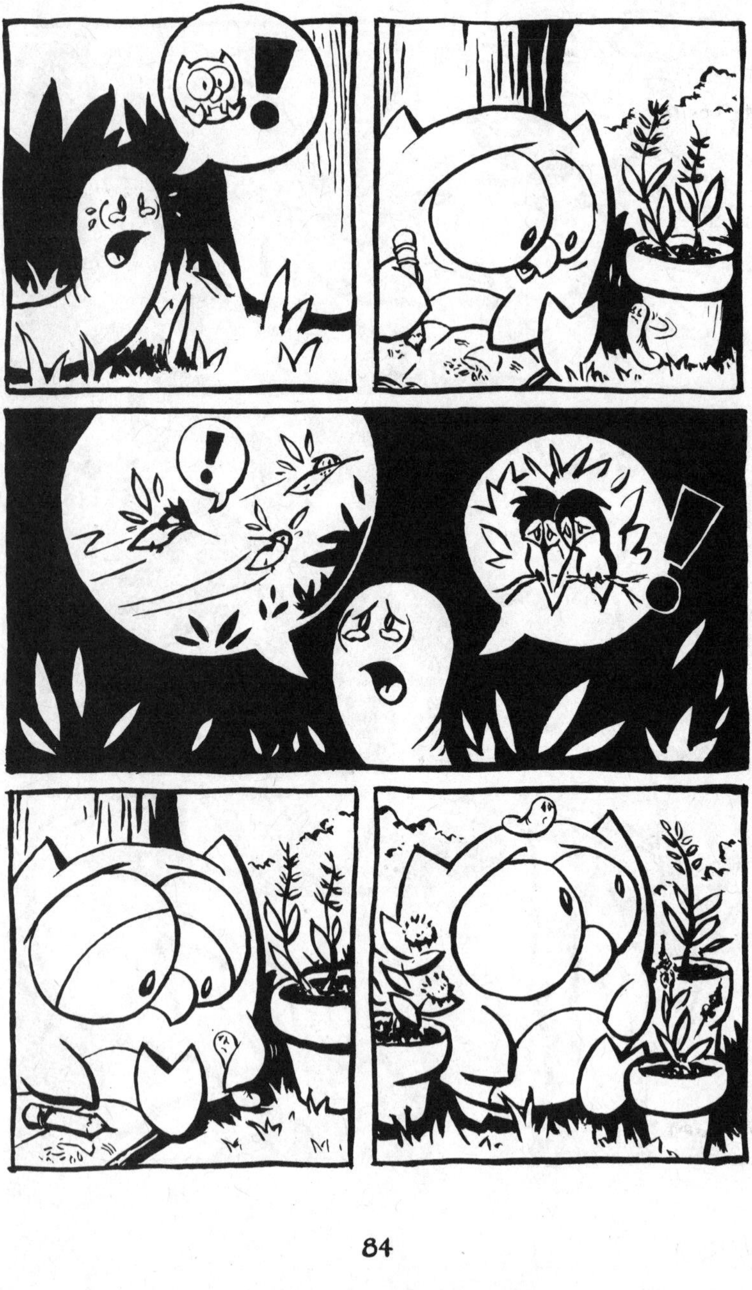
!
!
!

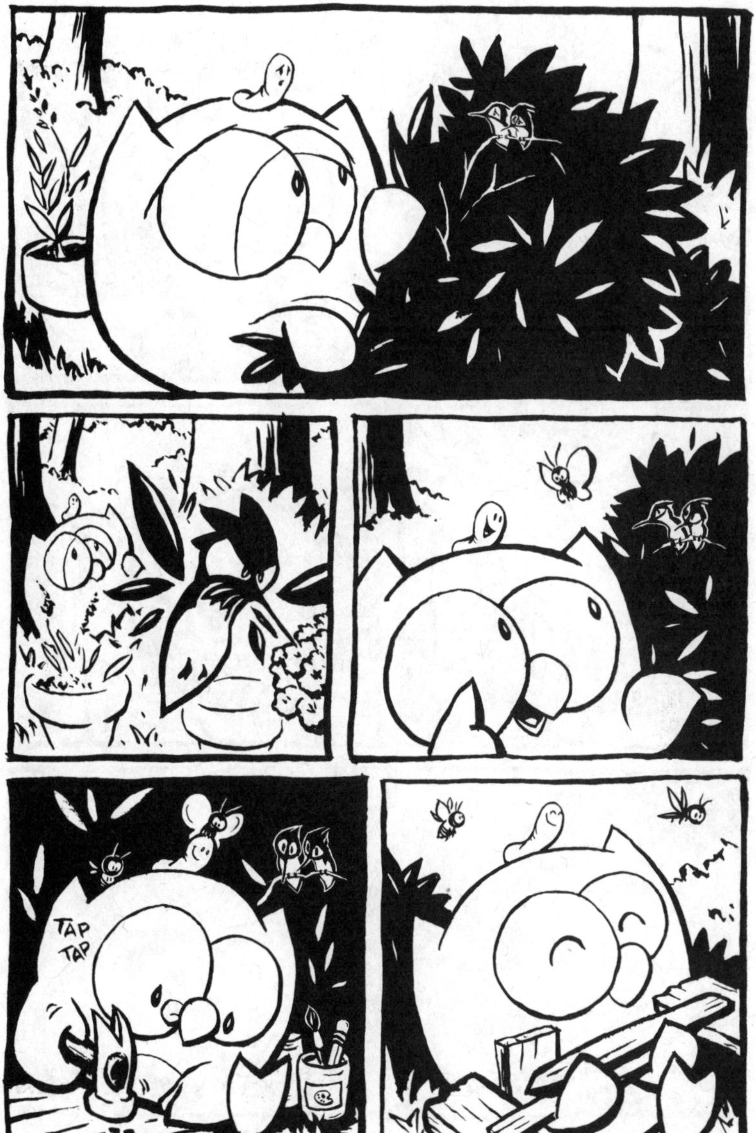
TAP
TAP

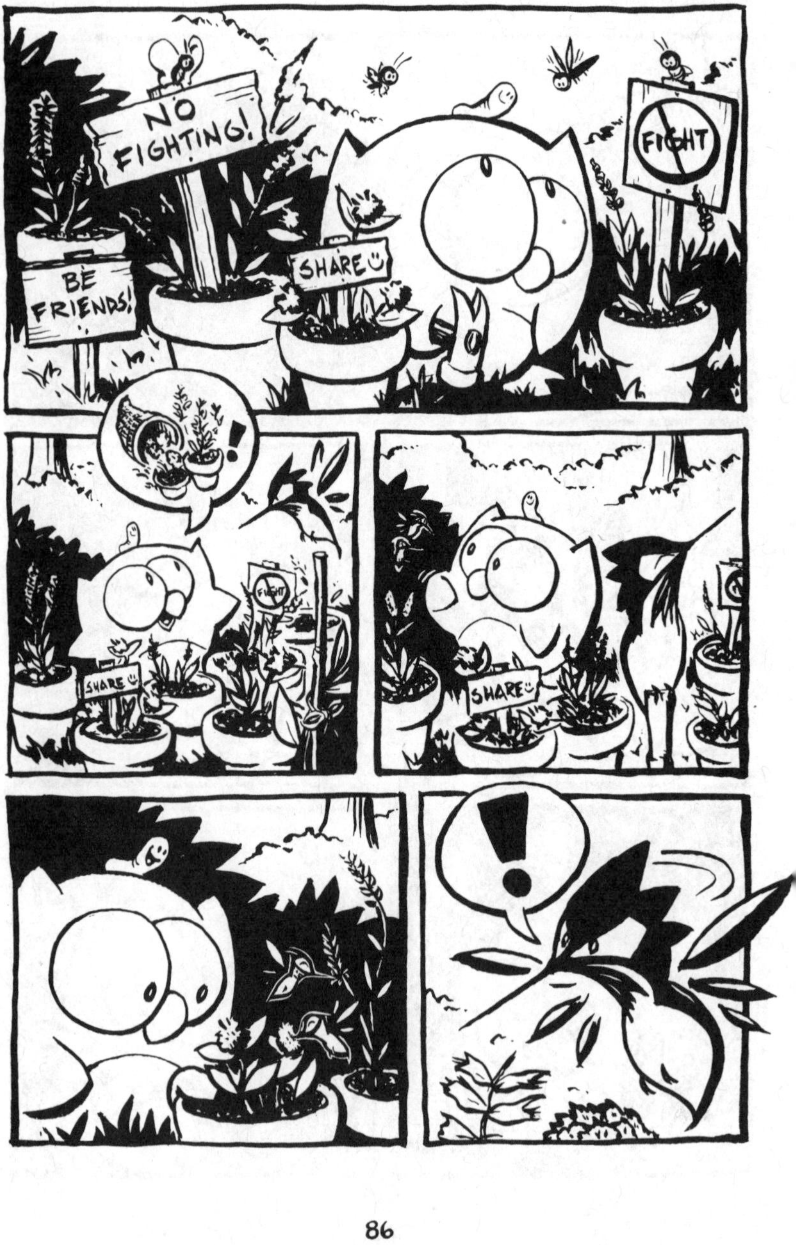
NO FIGHTING!
BE FRIENDS!
SHARE
FIGHT
!
SHARE
FIGHT
SHARE
!

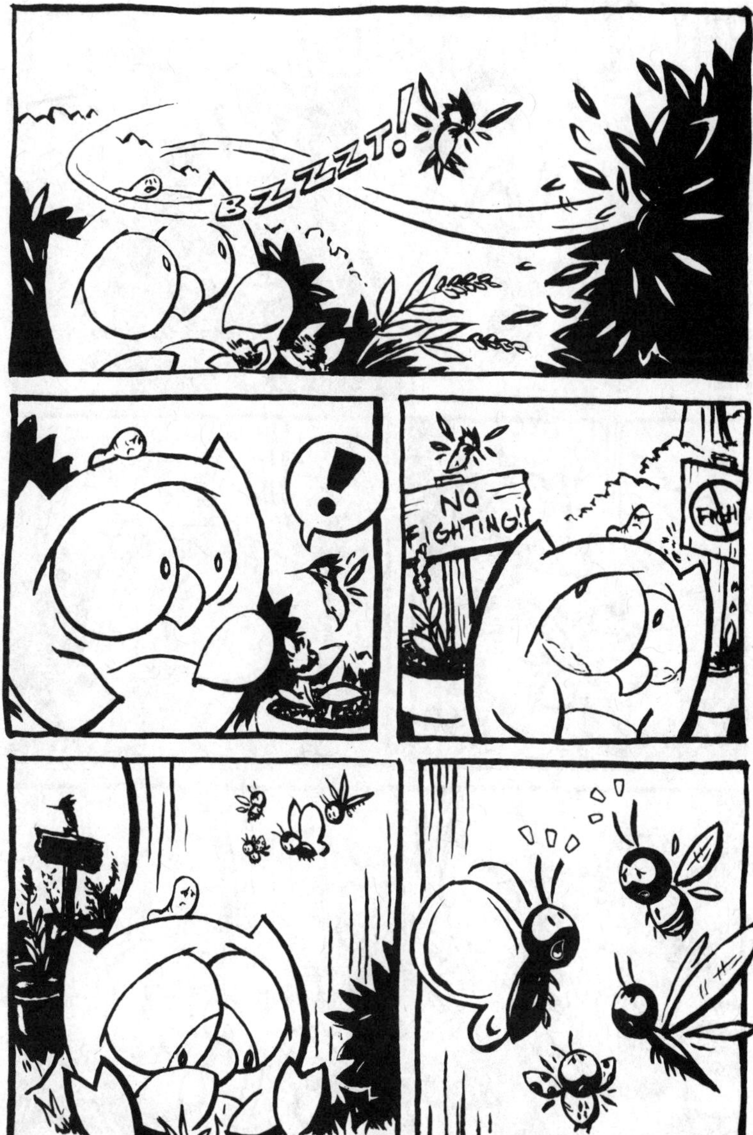
BZZZZT!
!
NO FIGHTING!

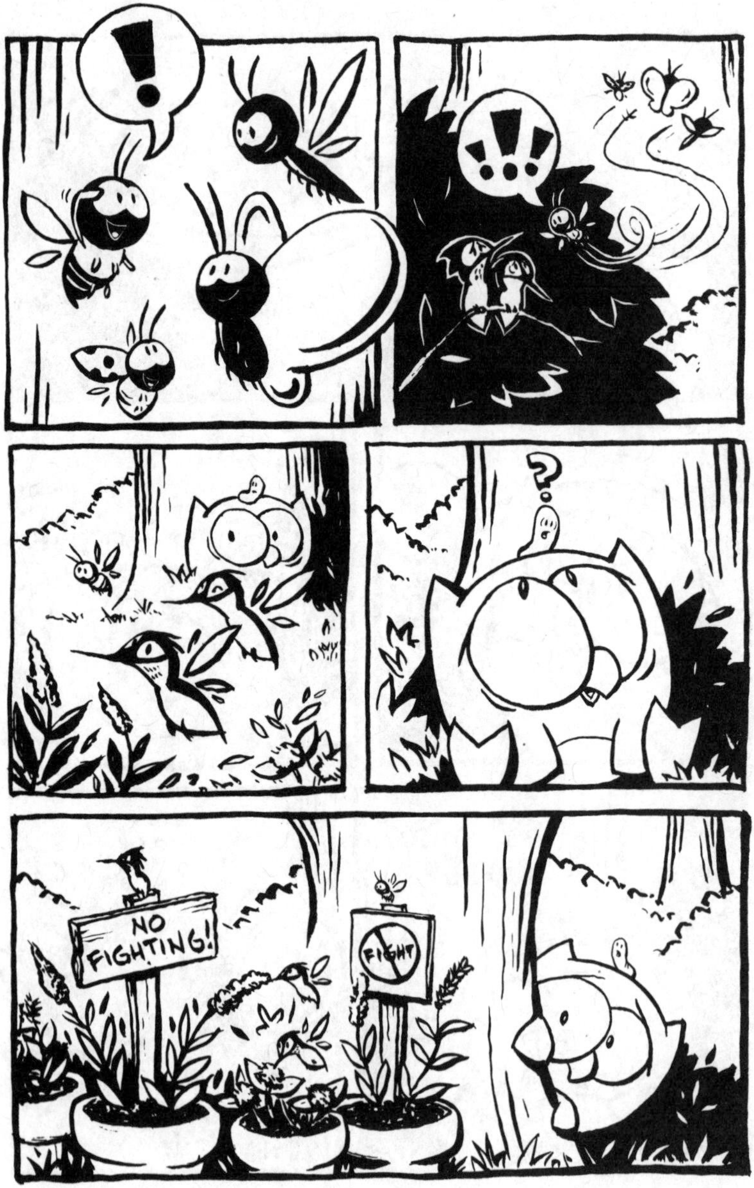
!
!...
?
NO FIGHTING!
FIGHT

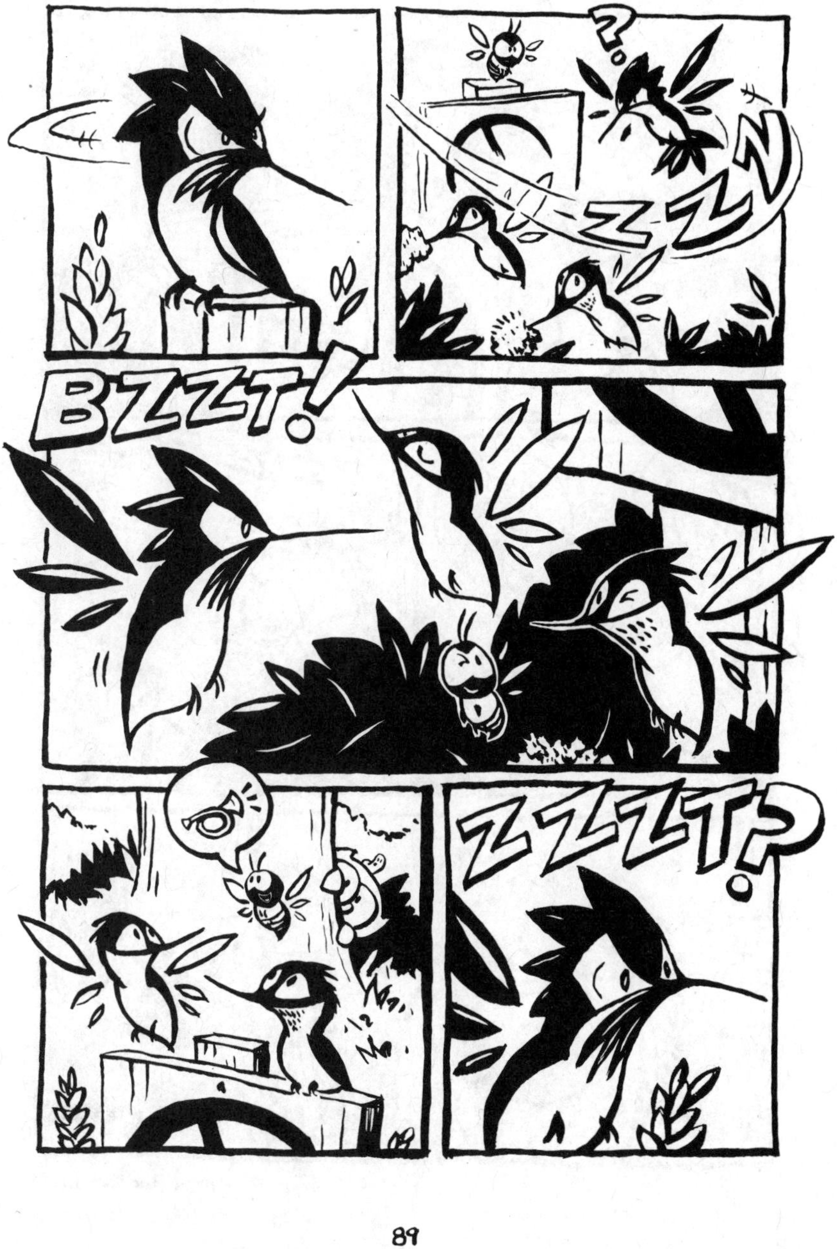
?
ZZZN
BZZZT!
ZZZZT?

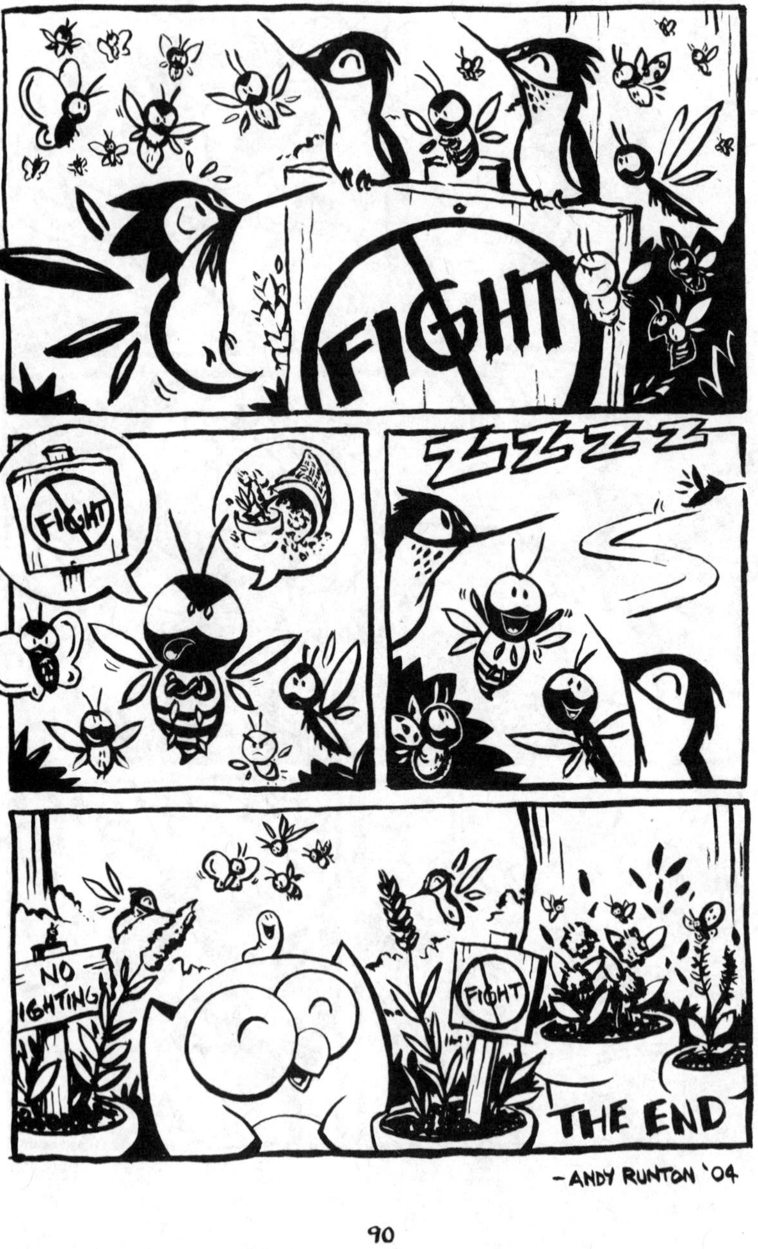
FIGHT
ZZZZZZ
NO
IGHTING
FIGHT
THE END
- ANDY RUNTON '04

GONE SWIMMIN'

OCTOBER, 2003

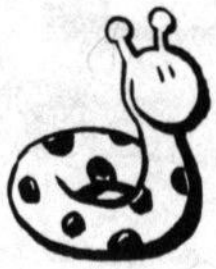

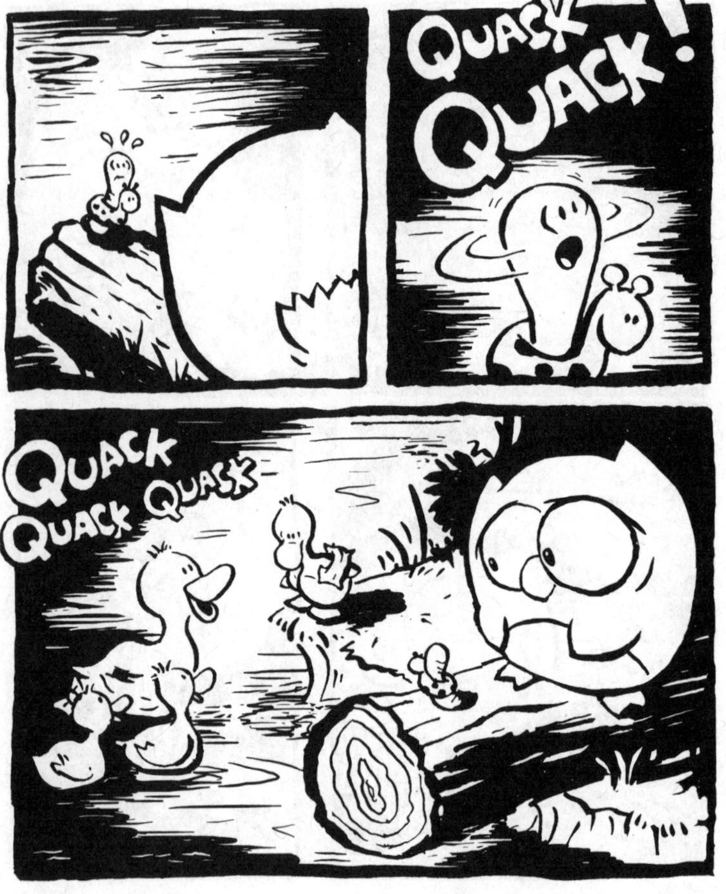
QUACK QUACK!
QUACK
QUACK QUACK

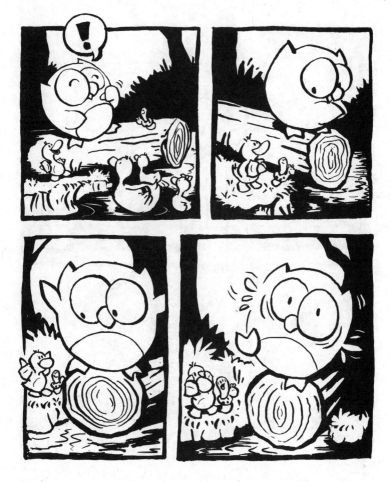

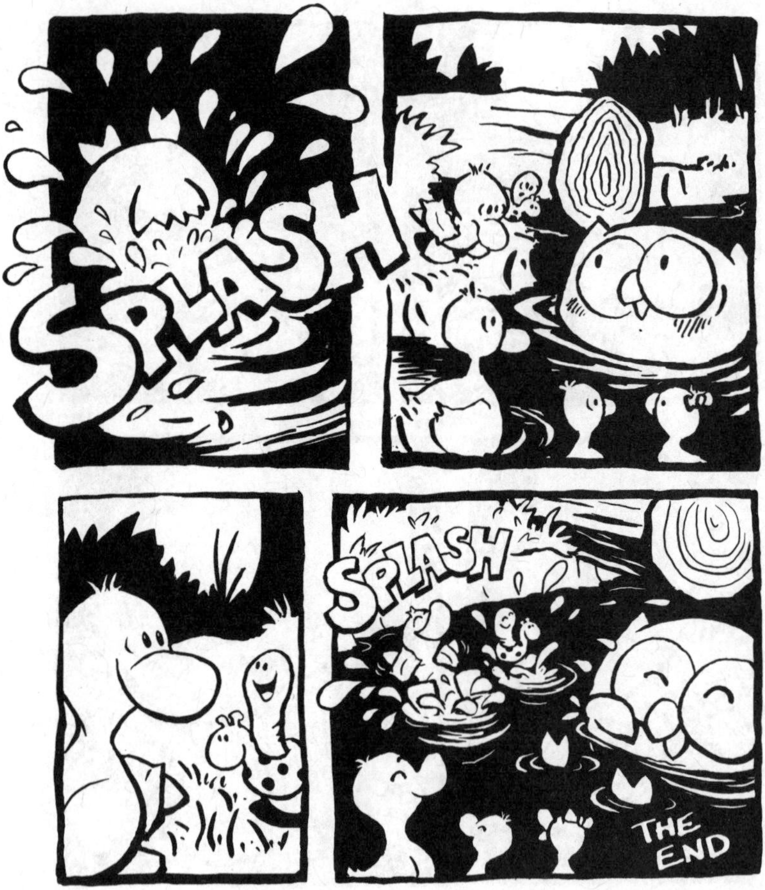
SPLASH
SPLASH
THE END

LET'S GO FLY A KITE

DECEMBER, 2003

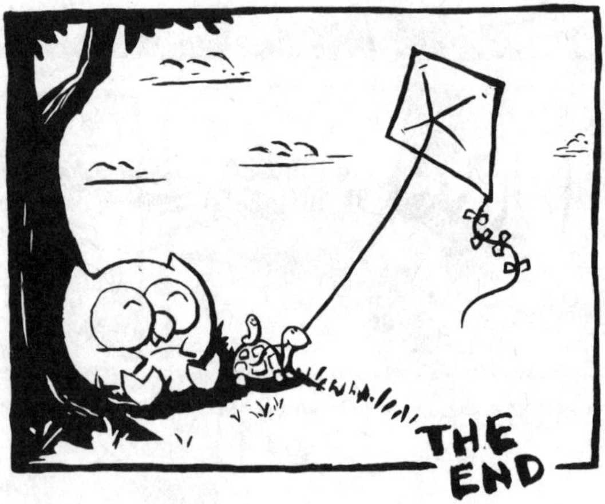
THE END

HELPING HANDS

APRIL, 2007

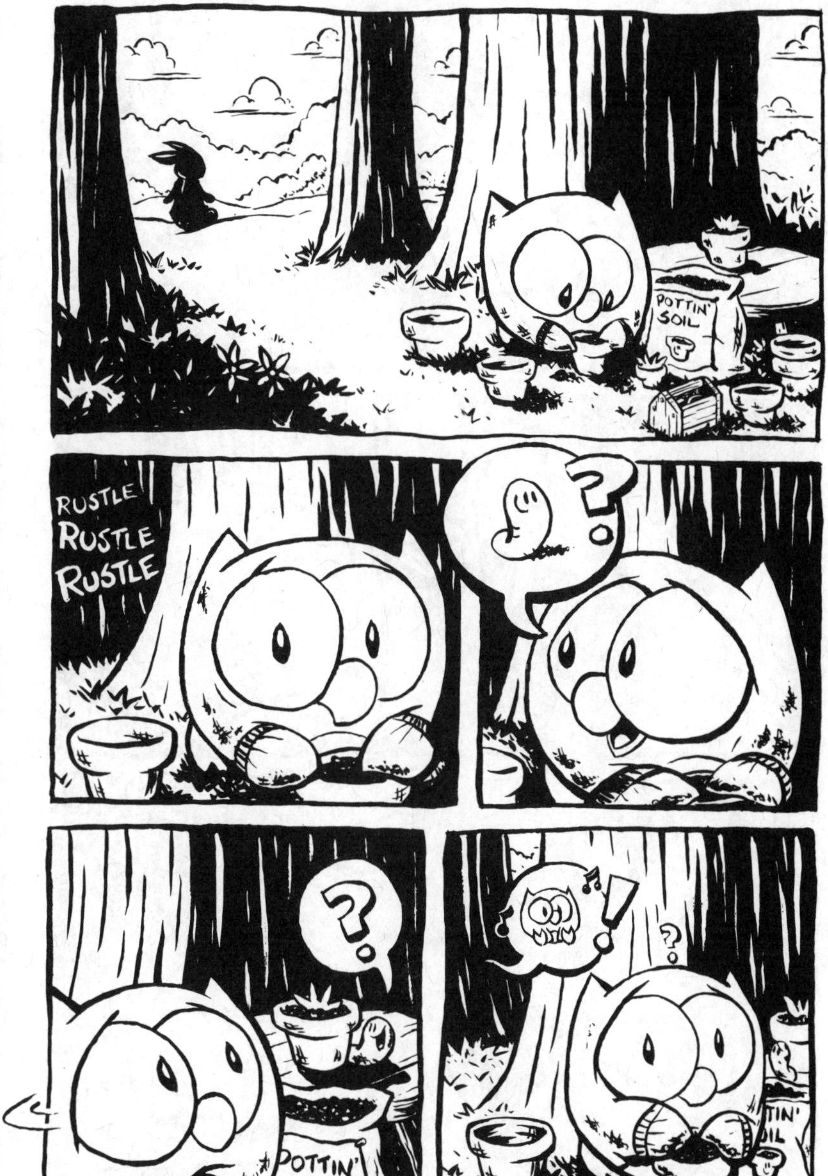
POTTIN' SOIL
RUSTLE
RUSTLE
RUSTLE
?
?
POTTIN' SOIL
!
?
TIN' OIL

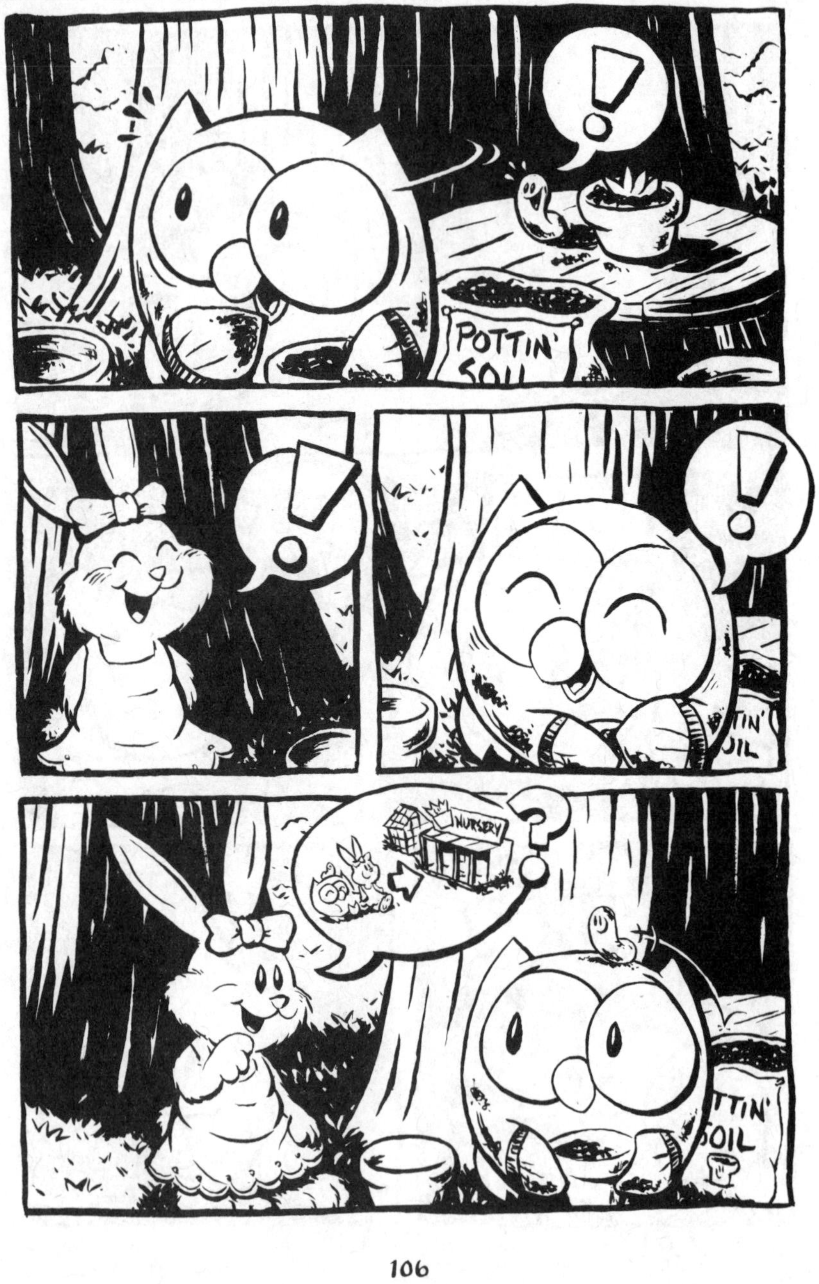
!
POTTIN' SOIL
!
!
NURSERY
?

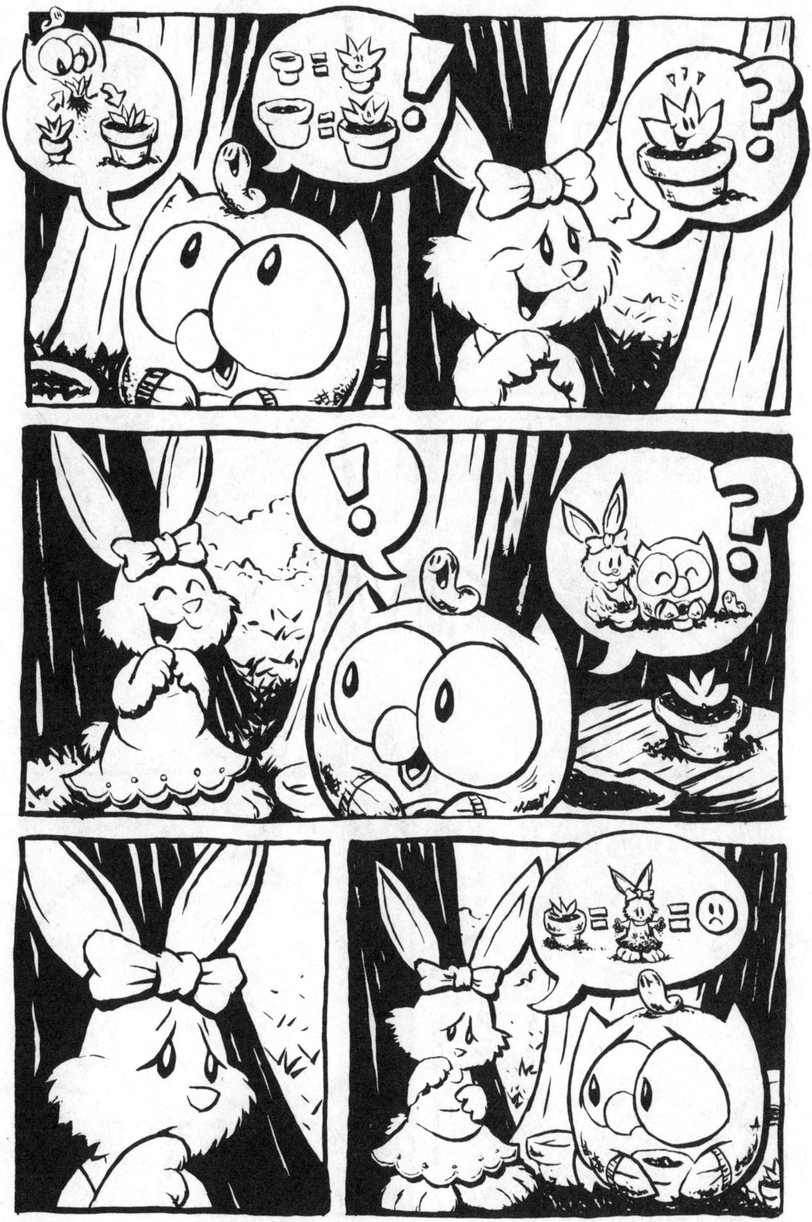
!
?
!
?

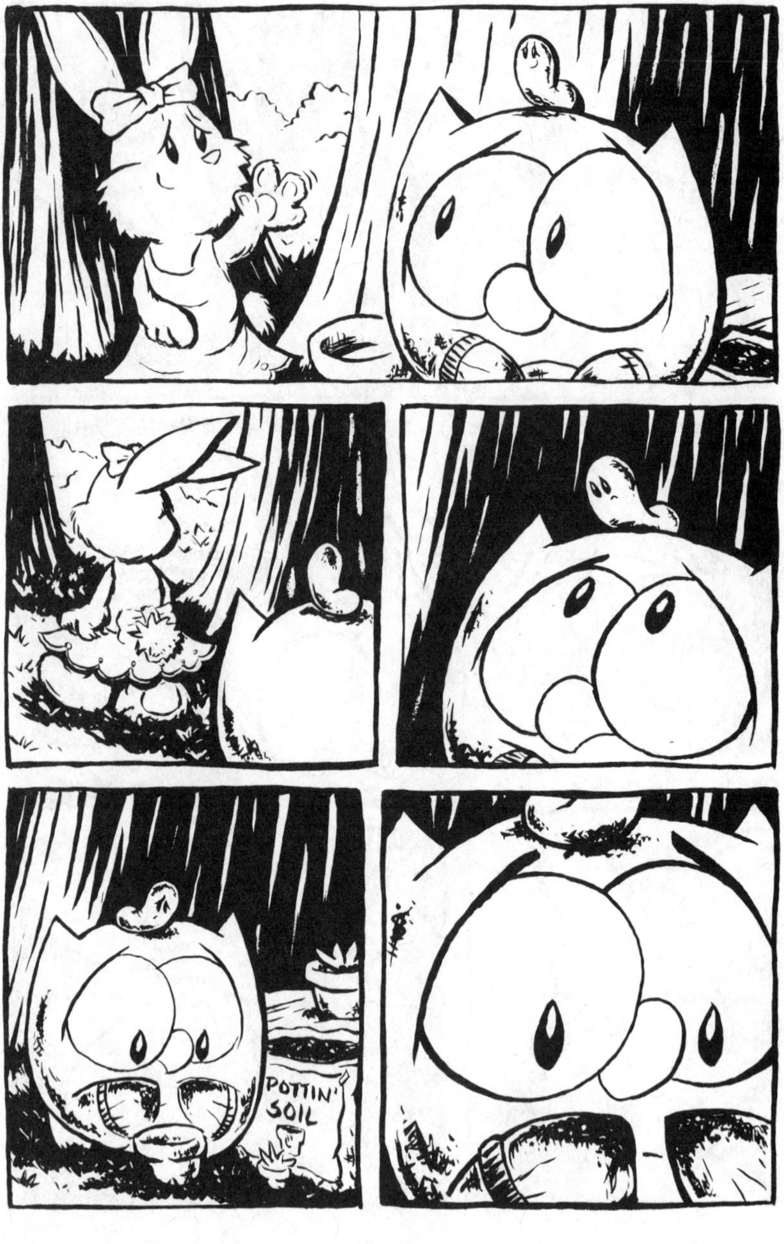
POTTIN' SOIL

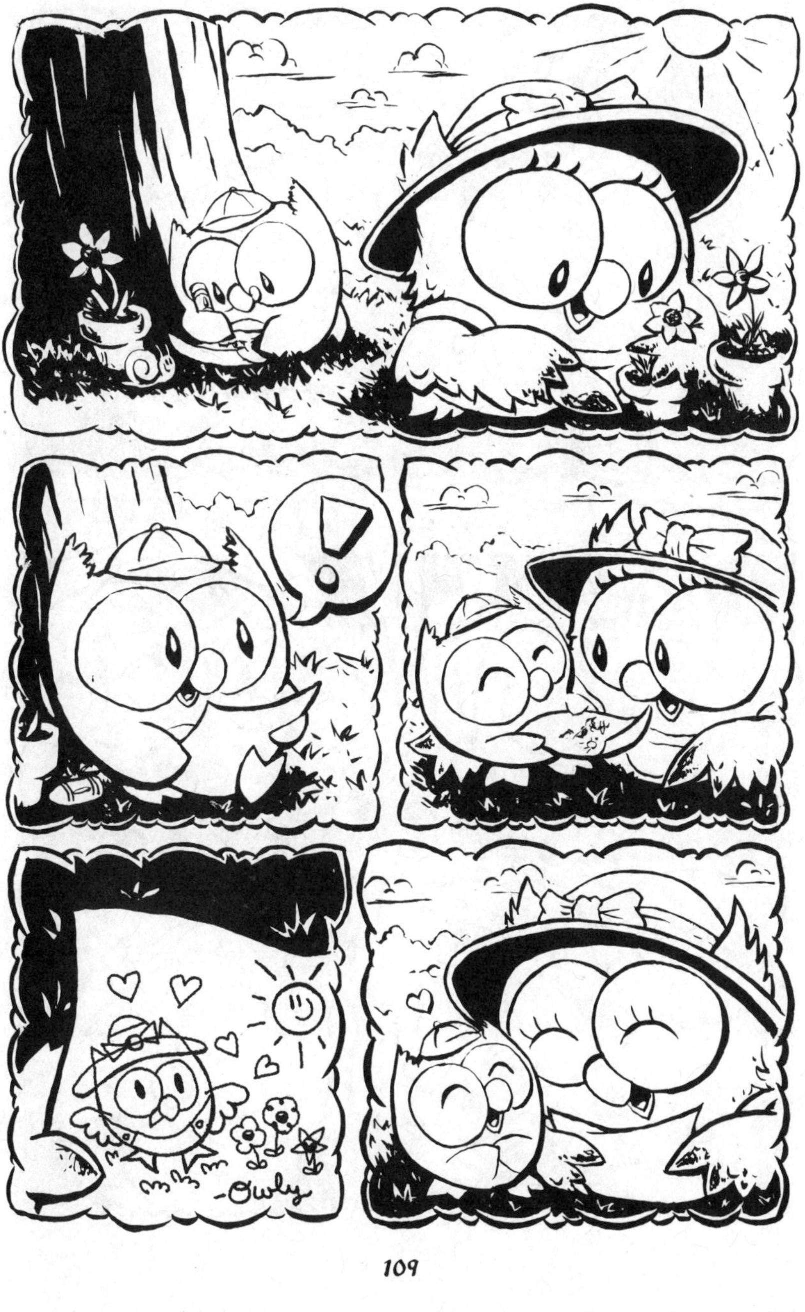
!
-Owly

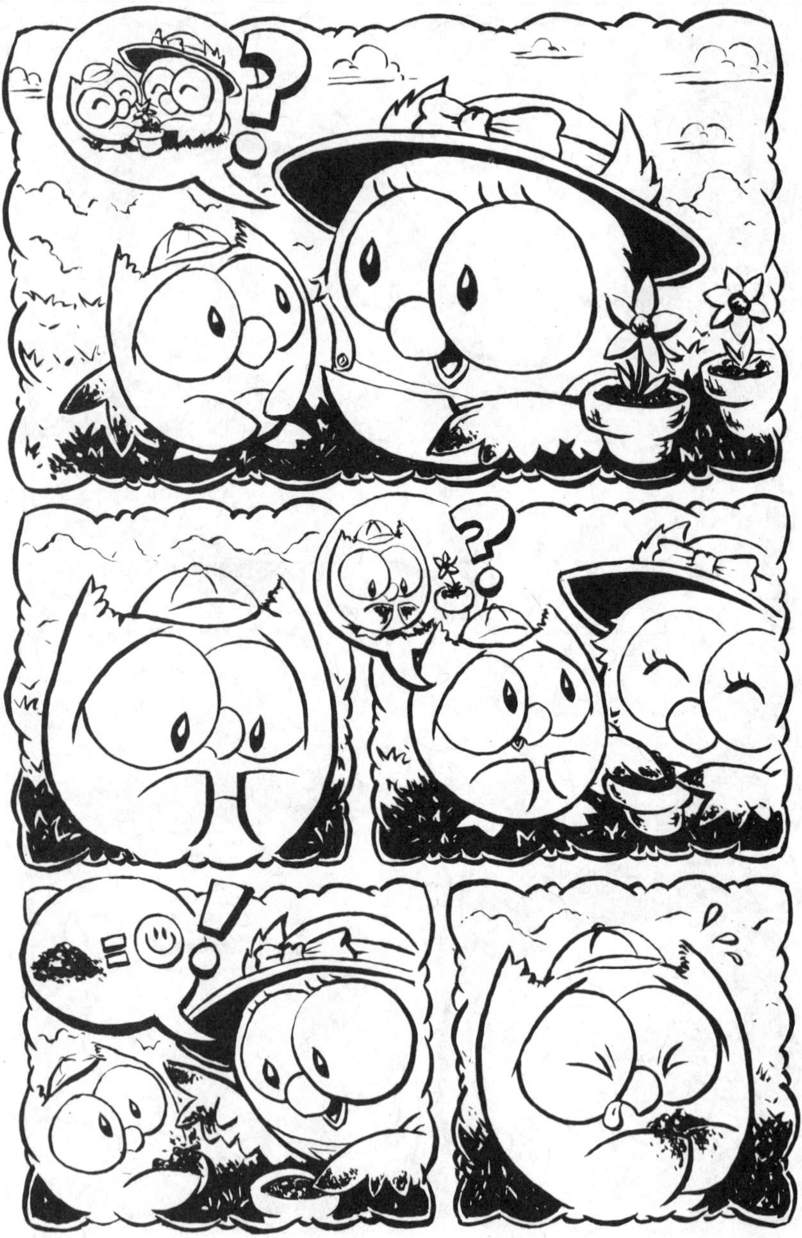

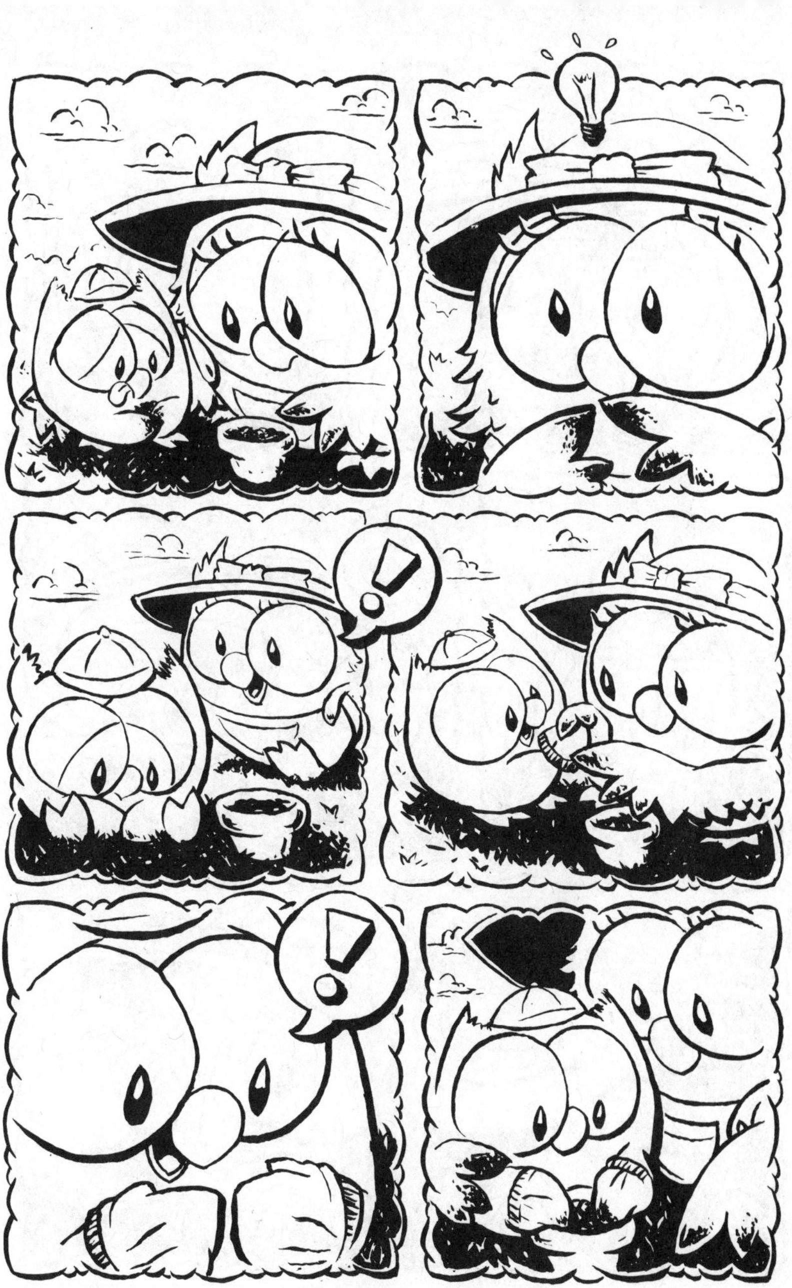
!
!

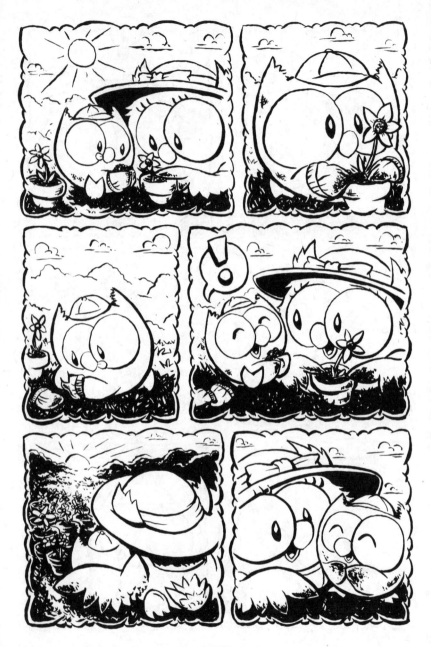

112

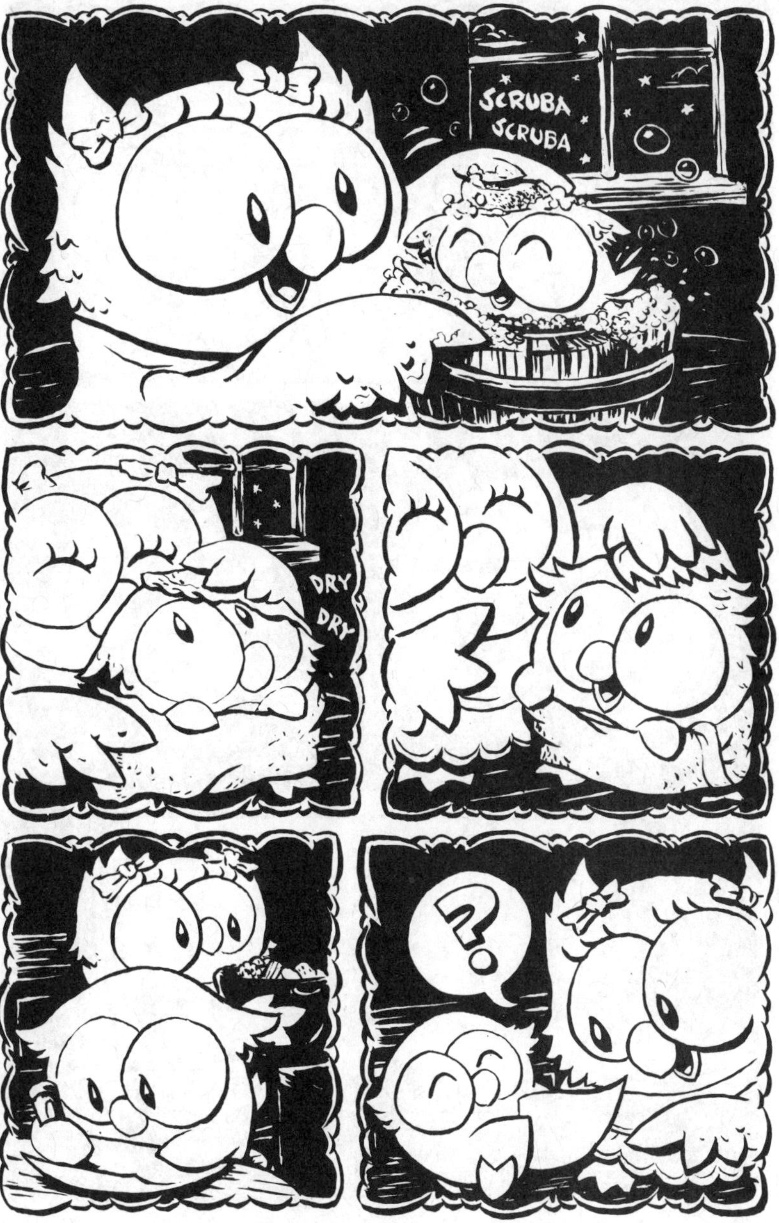
SCRUBA
SCRUBA
DRY
DRY
?

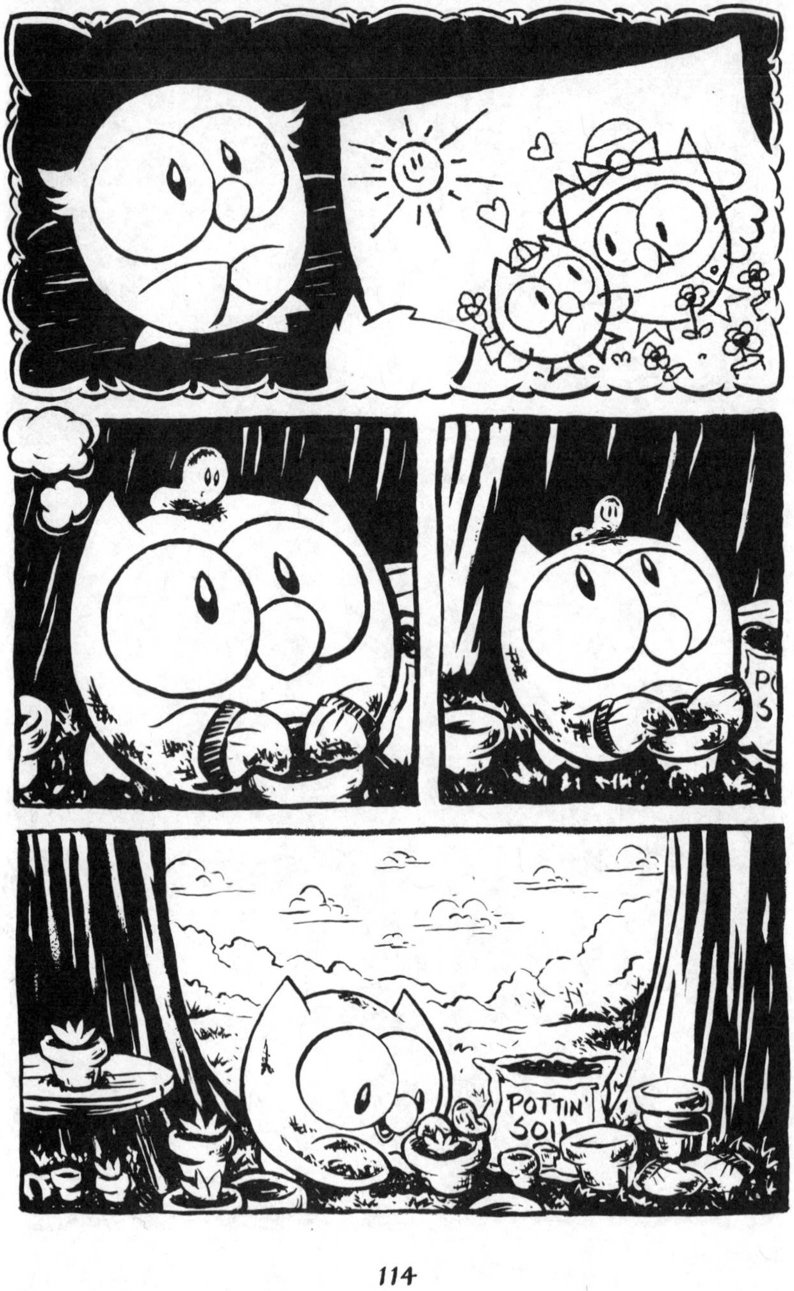
POTTIN' SOIL

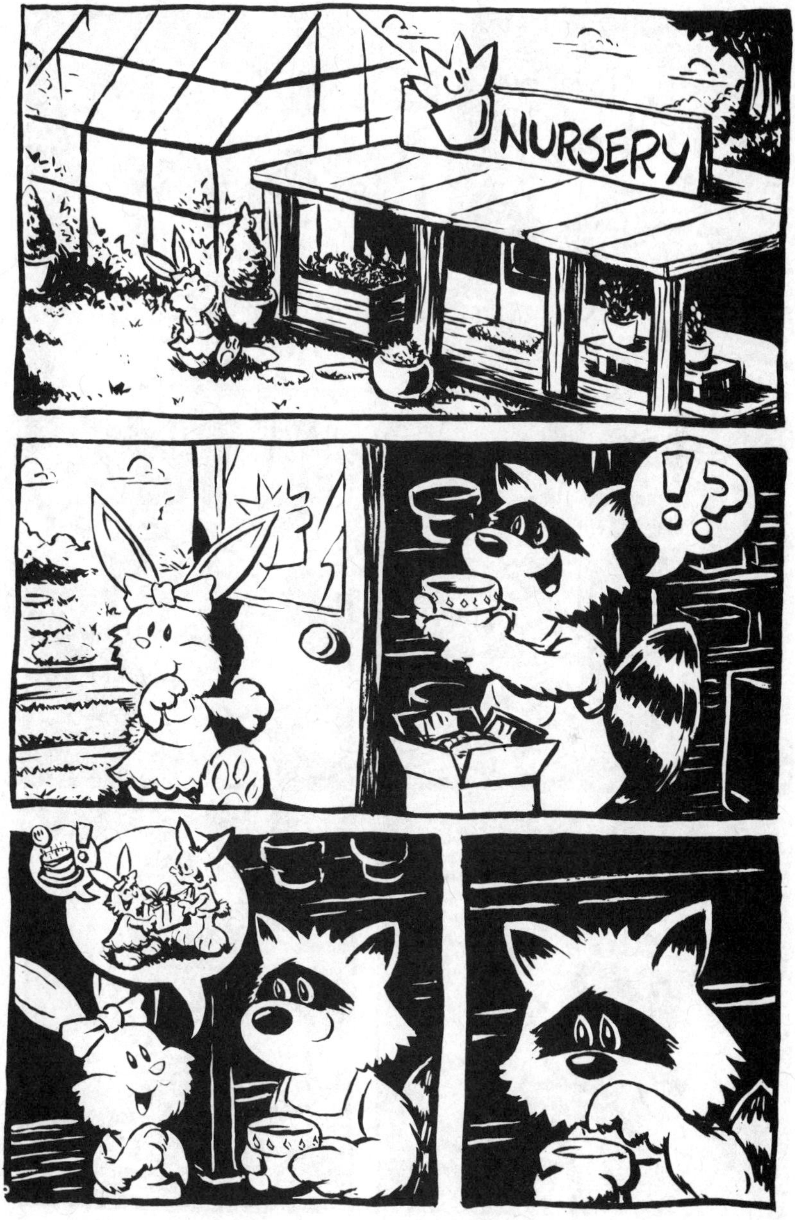
NURSERY
!?

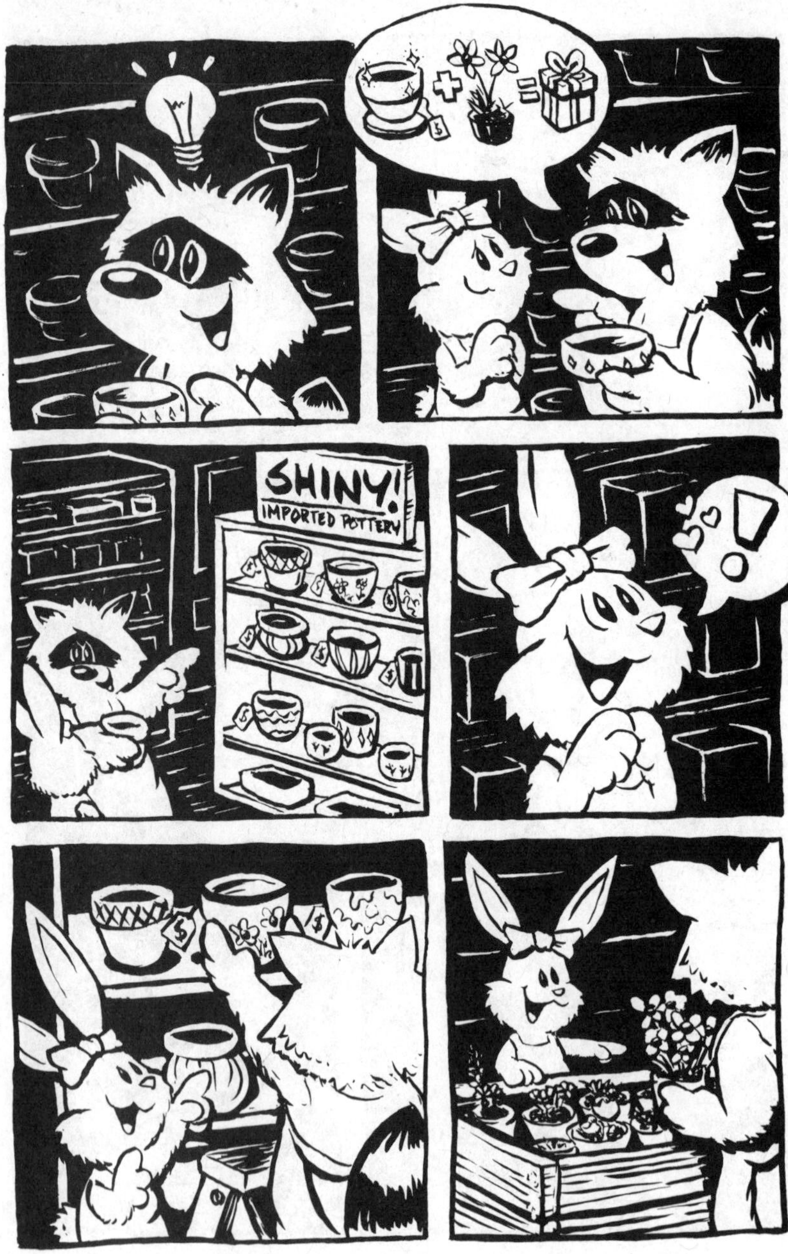
SHINY!
IMPORTED POTTERY

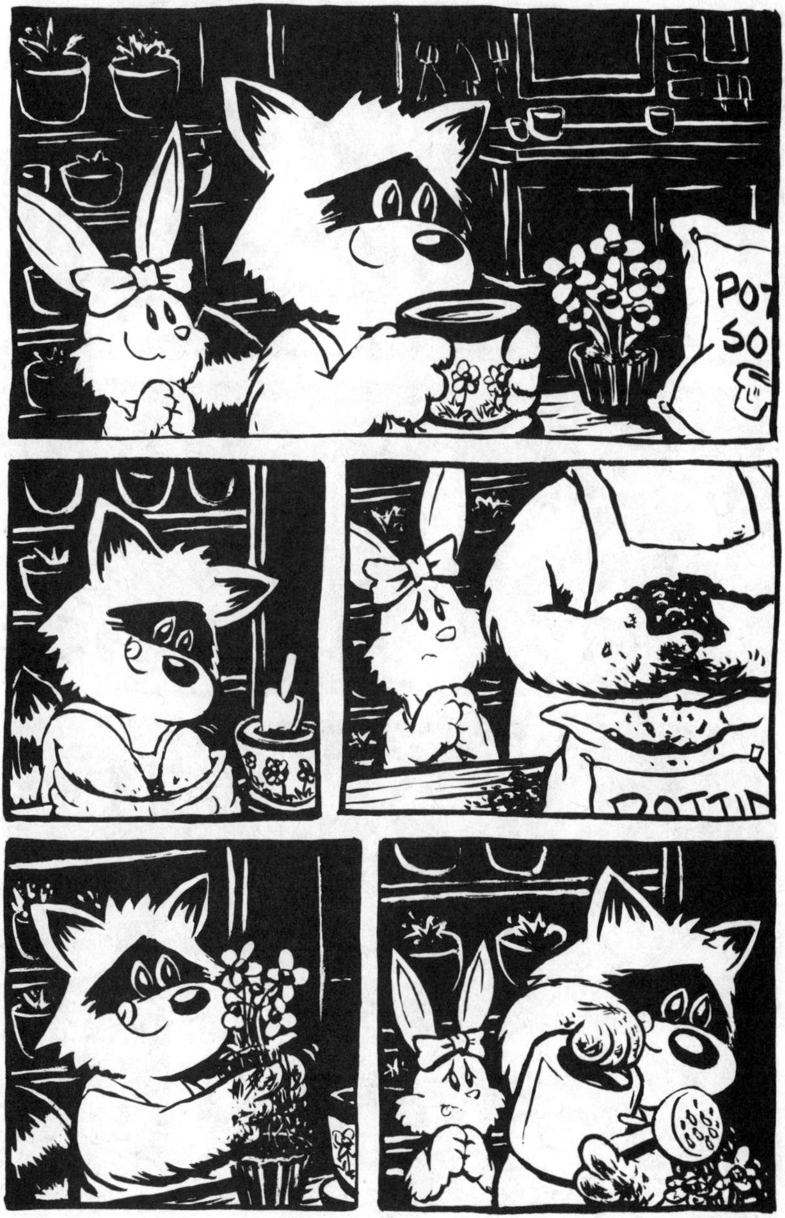
POT
SO

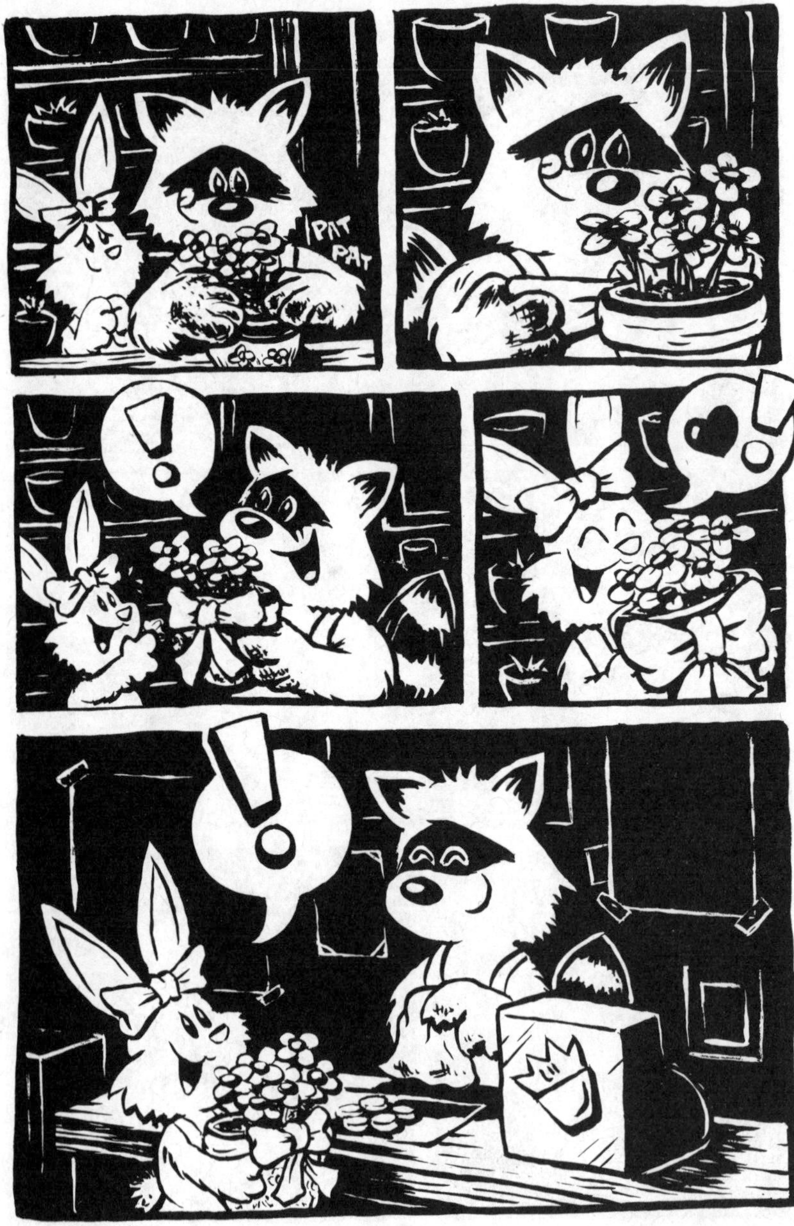
PAT
PAT
!
!
!

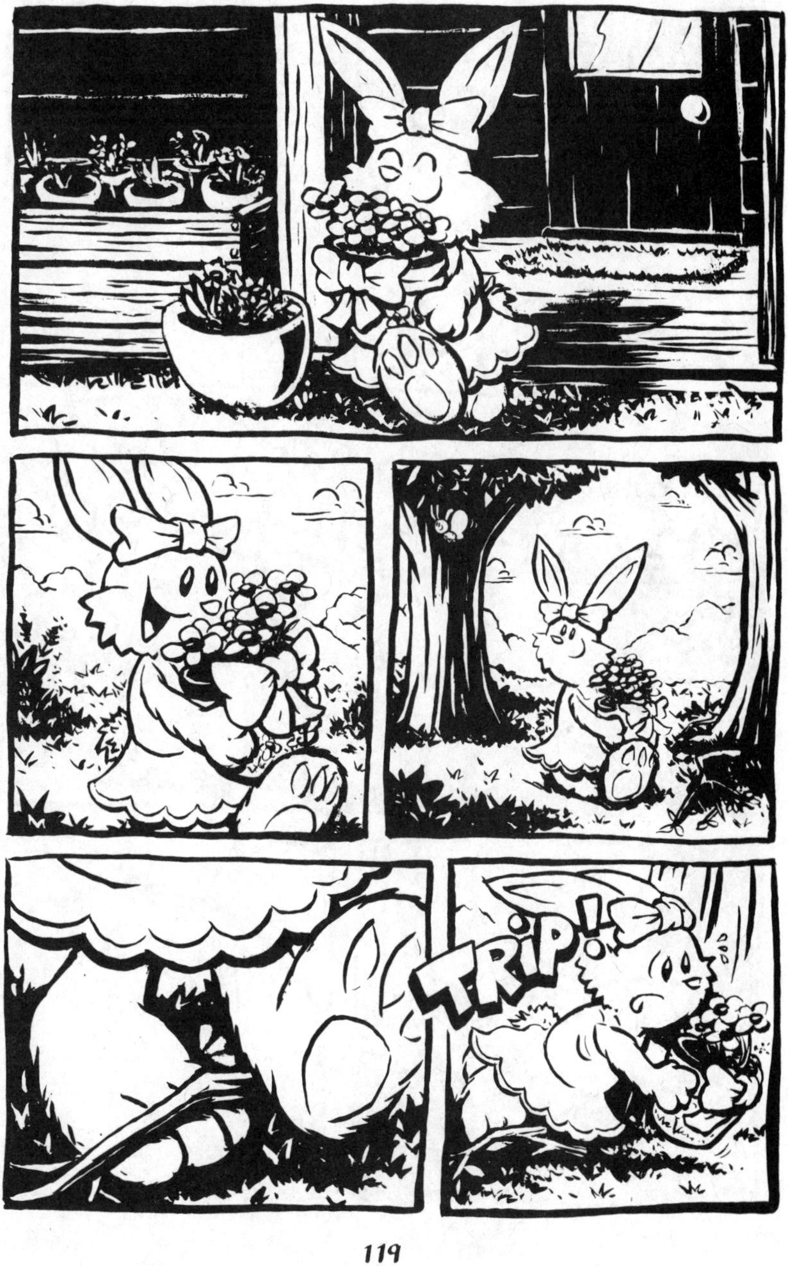
TRIP!

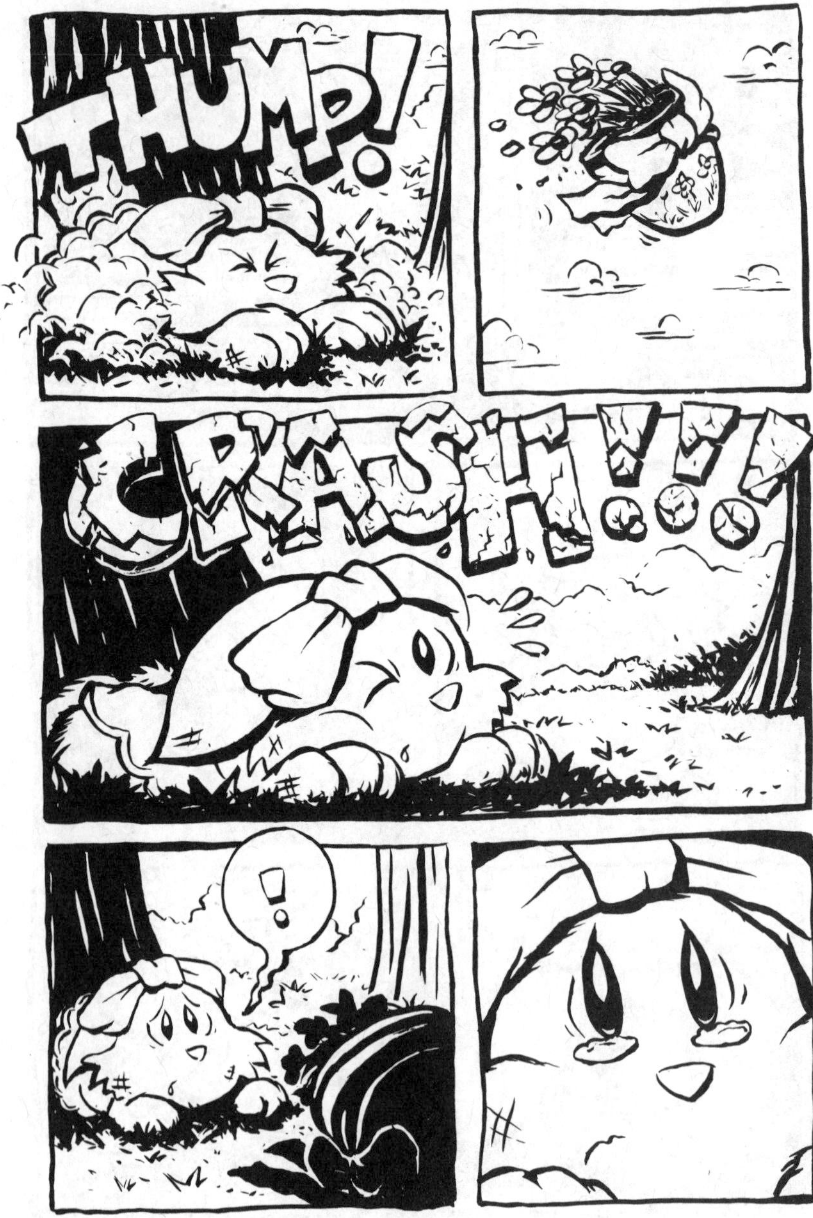
THUMP!
CRASH!!!
!

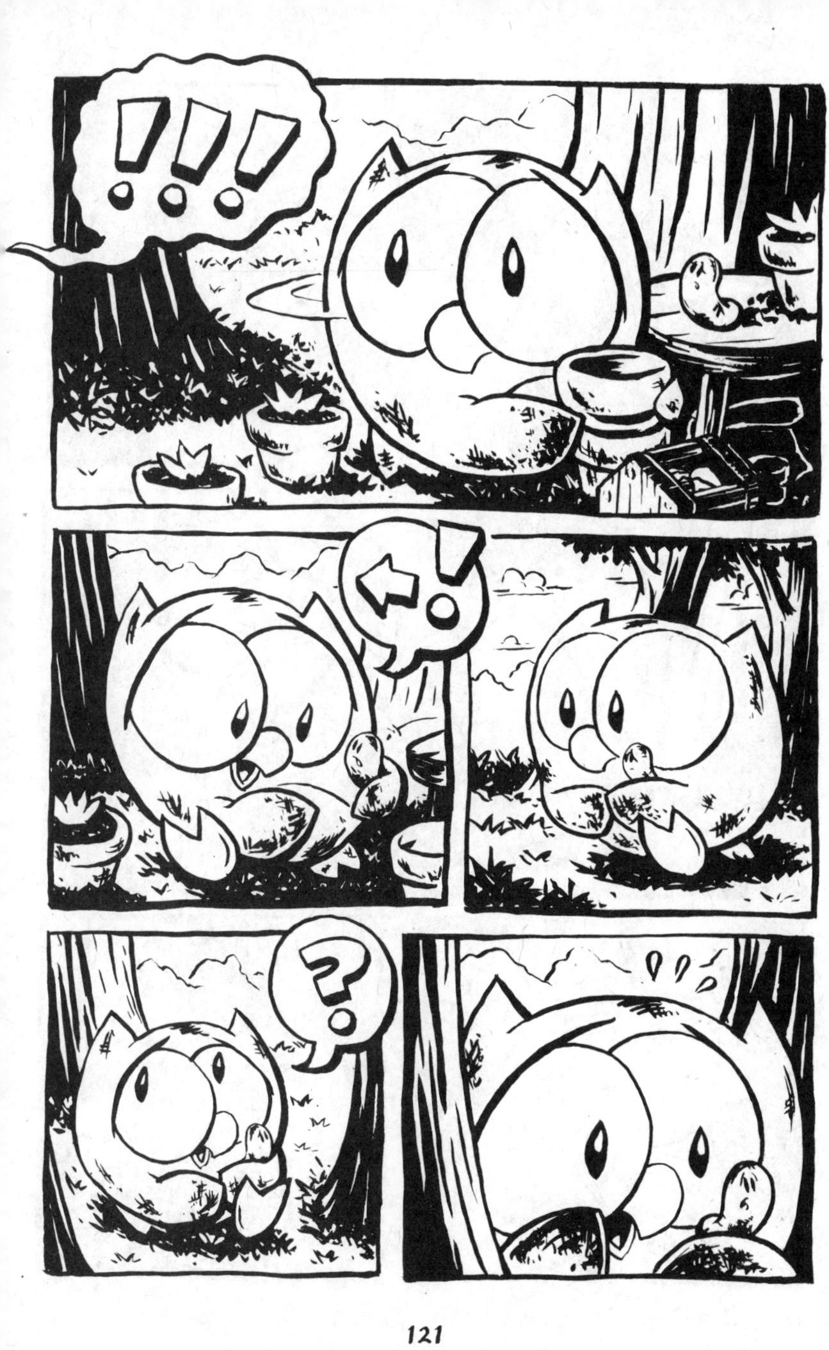
!!!
!
?
!!

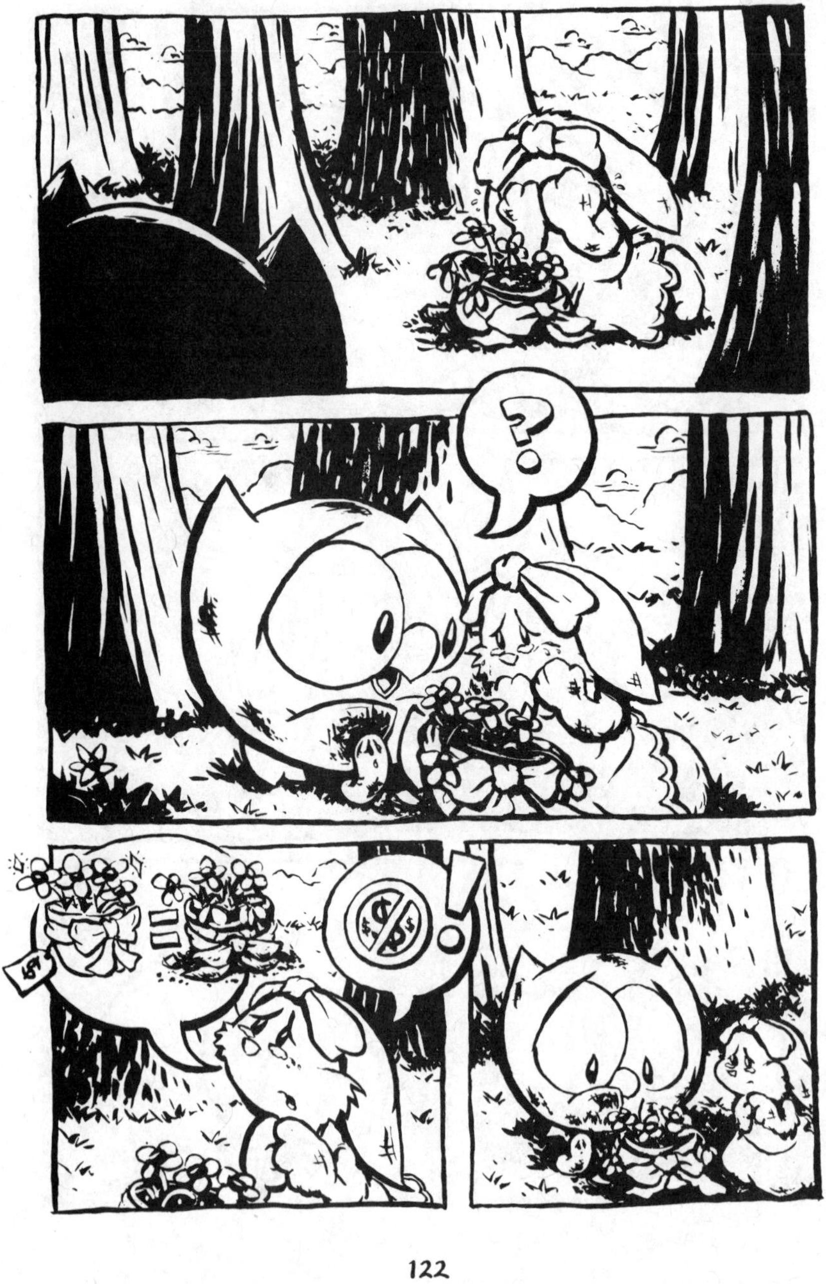
?
!

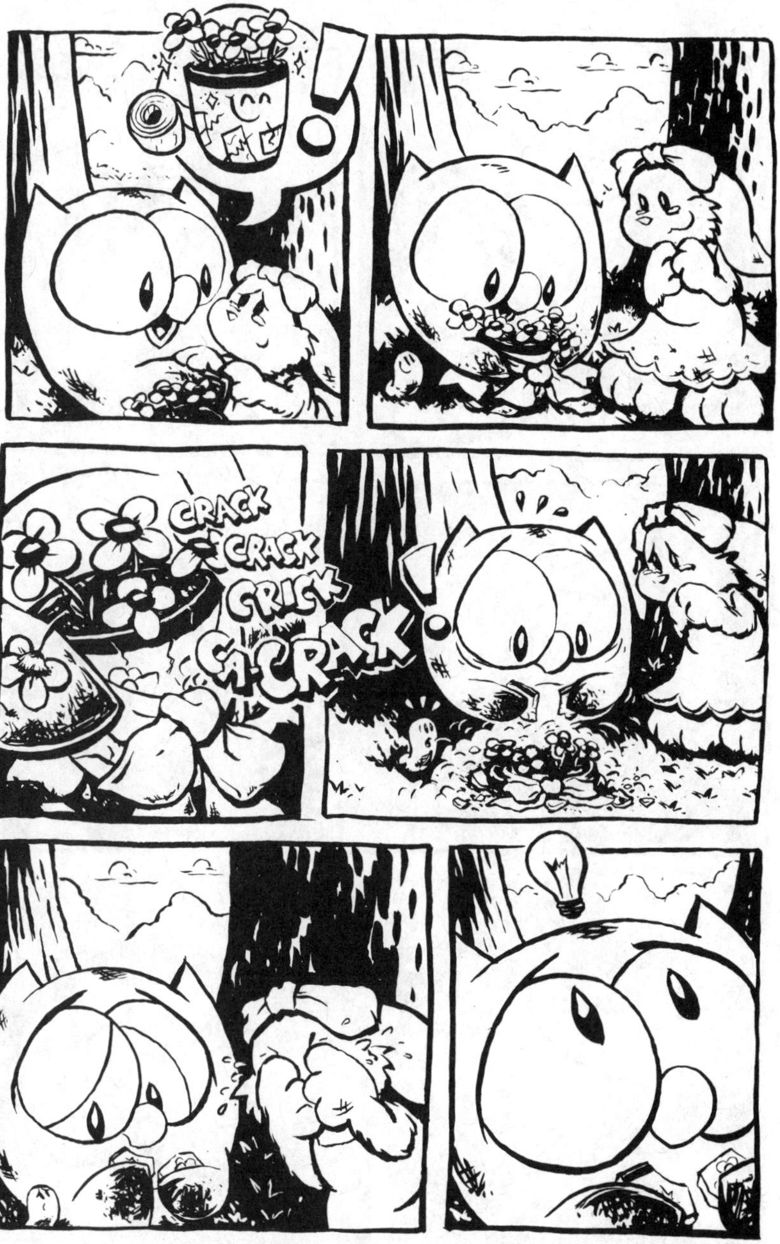
CRACK
CRACK
CRICK
CA-CRACK

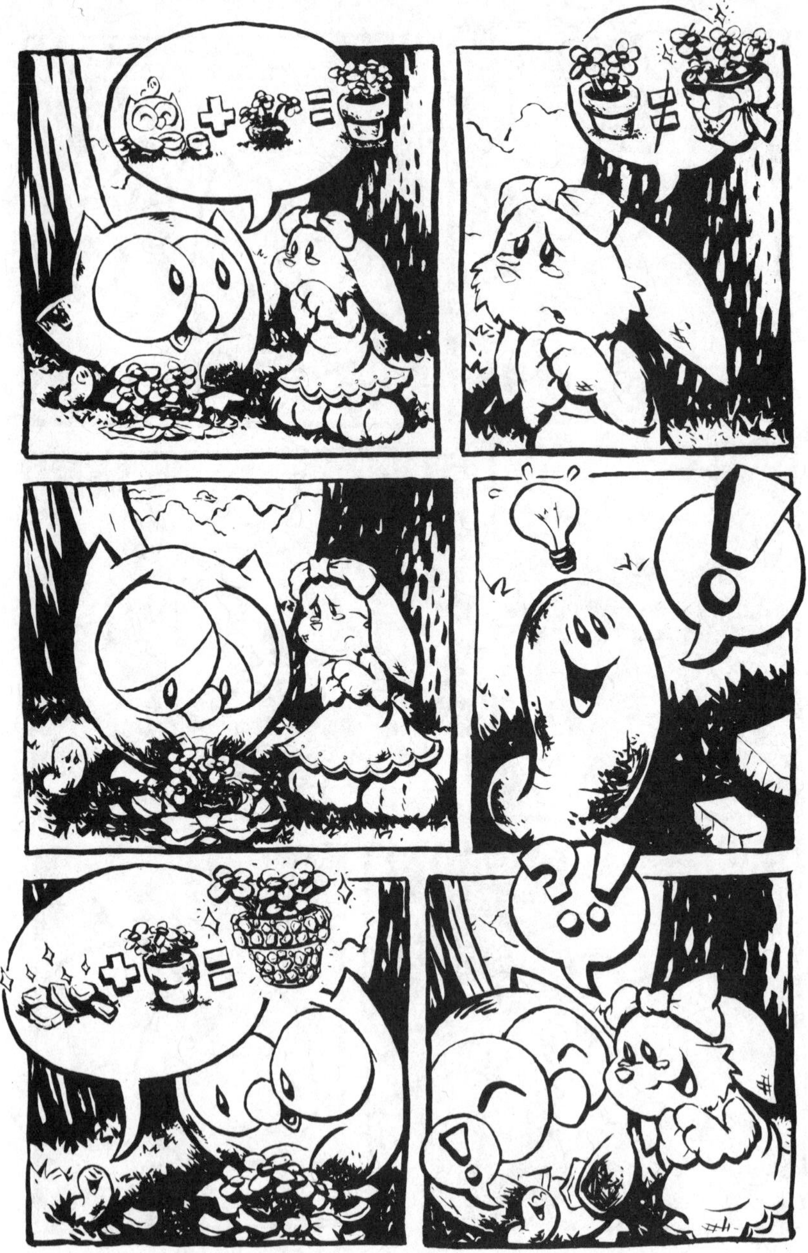

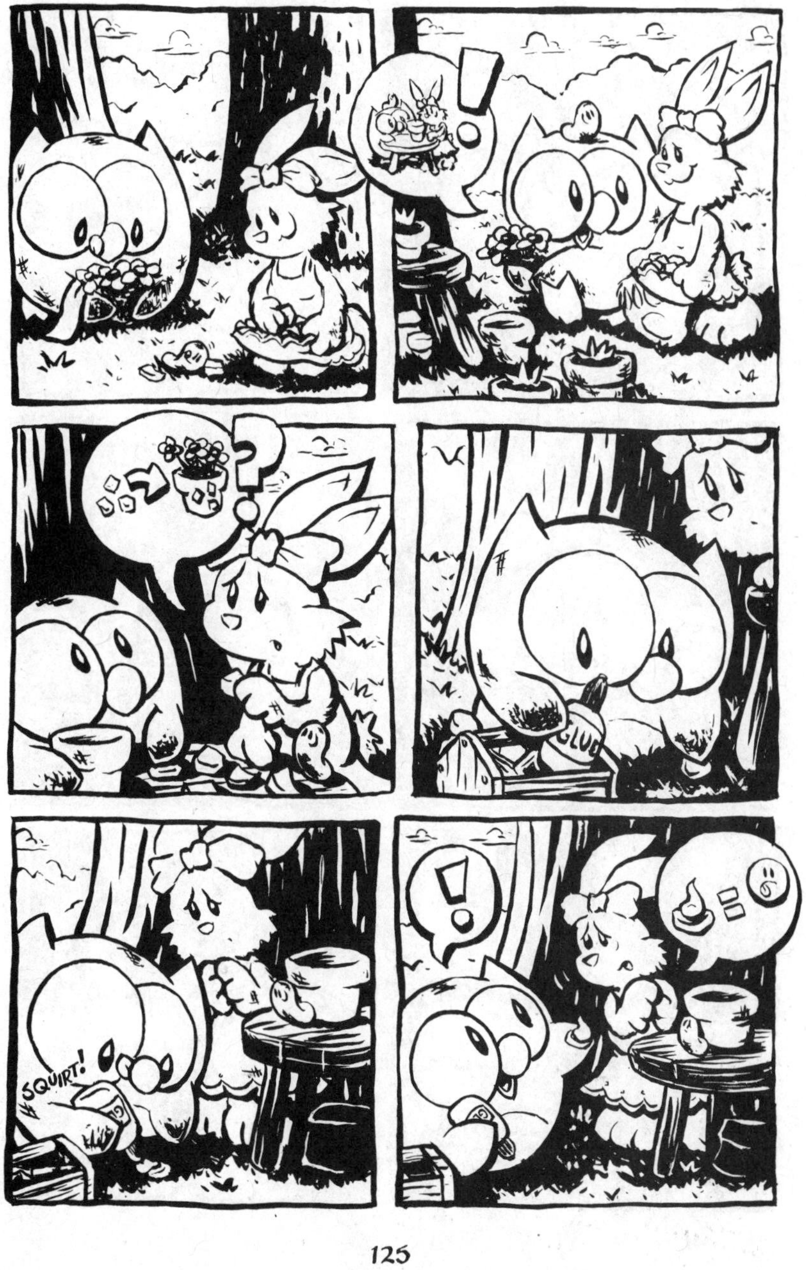
GLUE
SQUIRT!

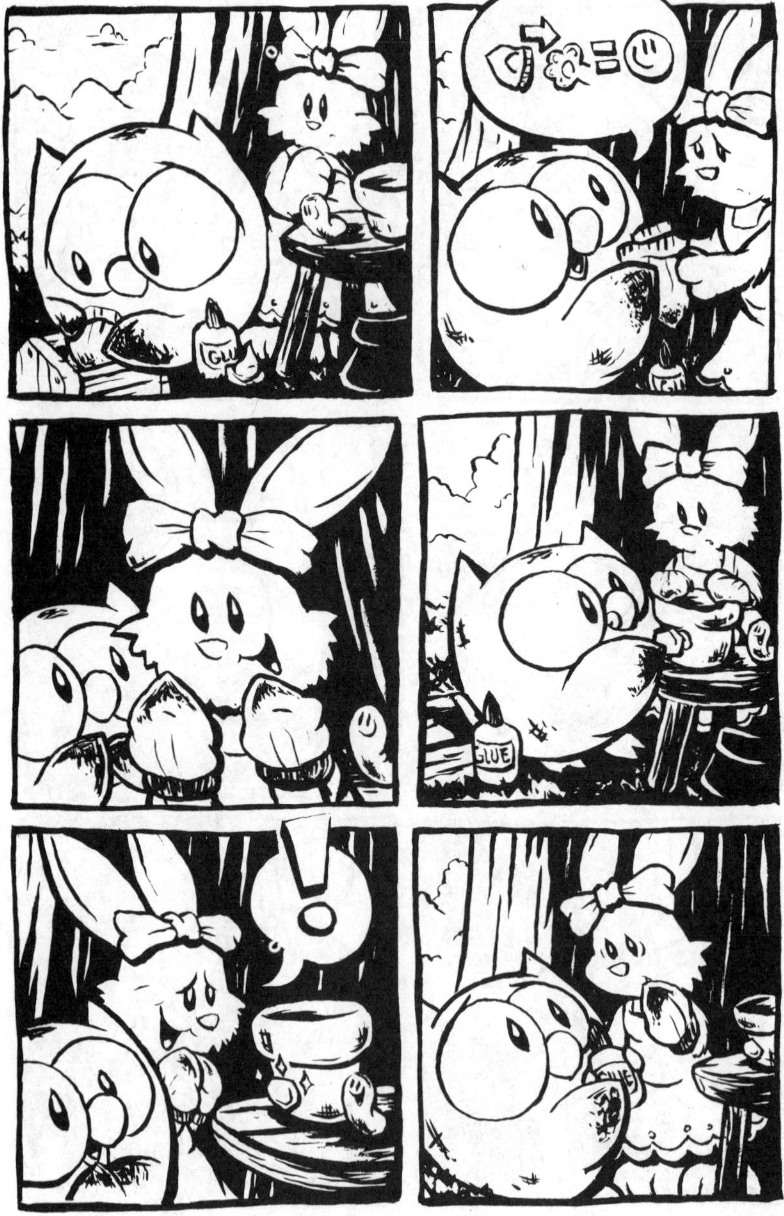
GLUE
GLUE
!
GLUE

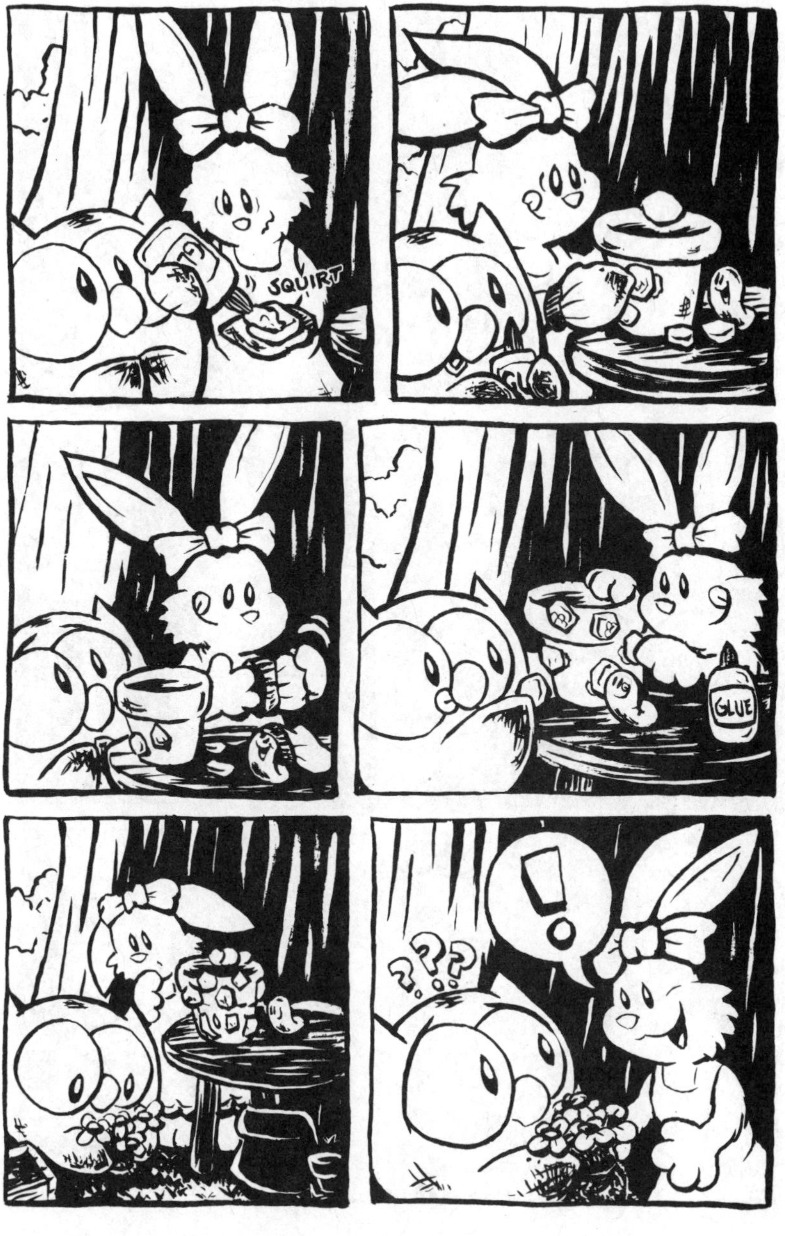
SQUIRT
GLUE
!
???

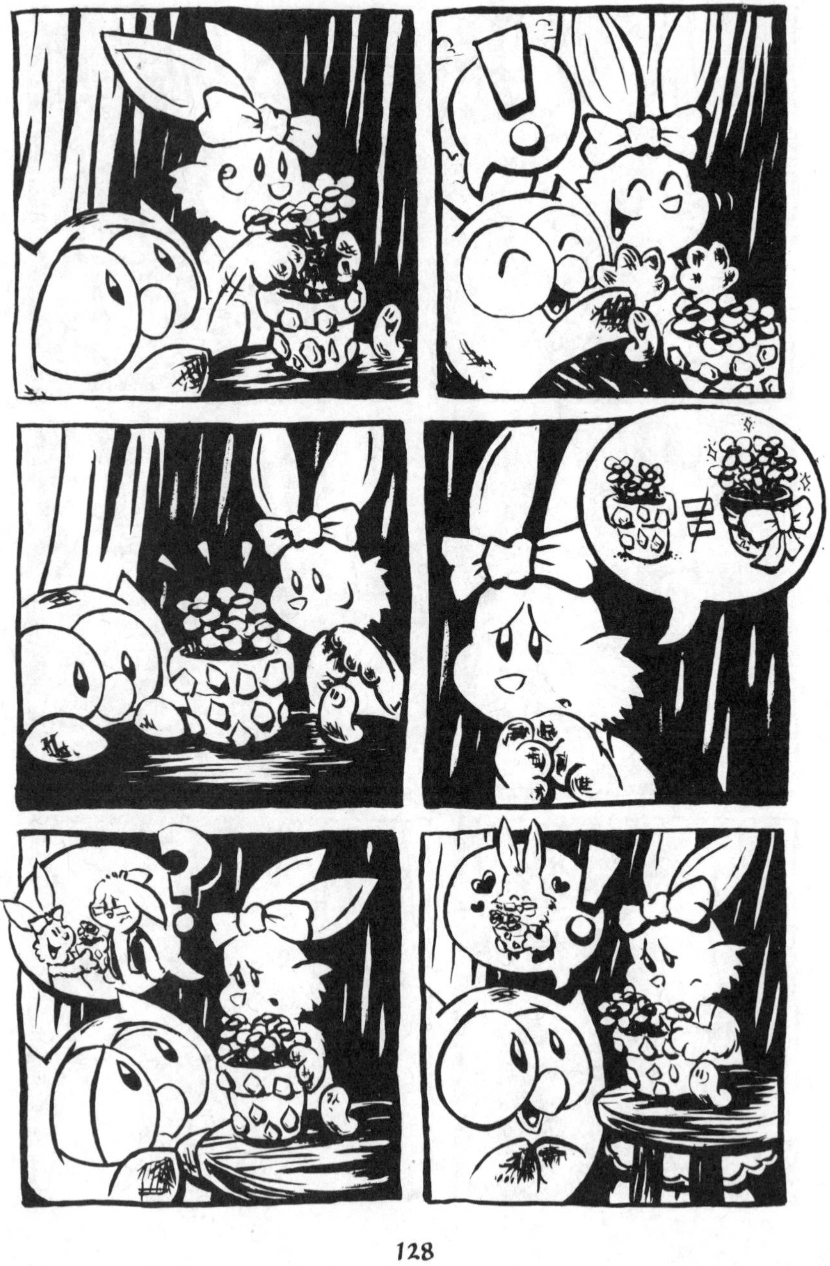

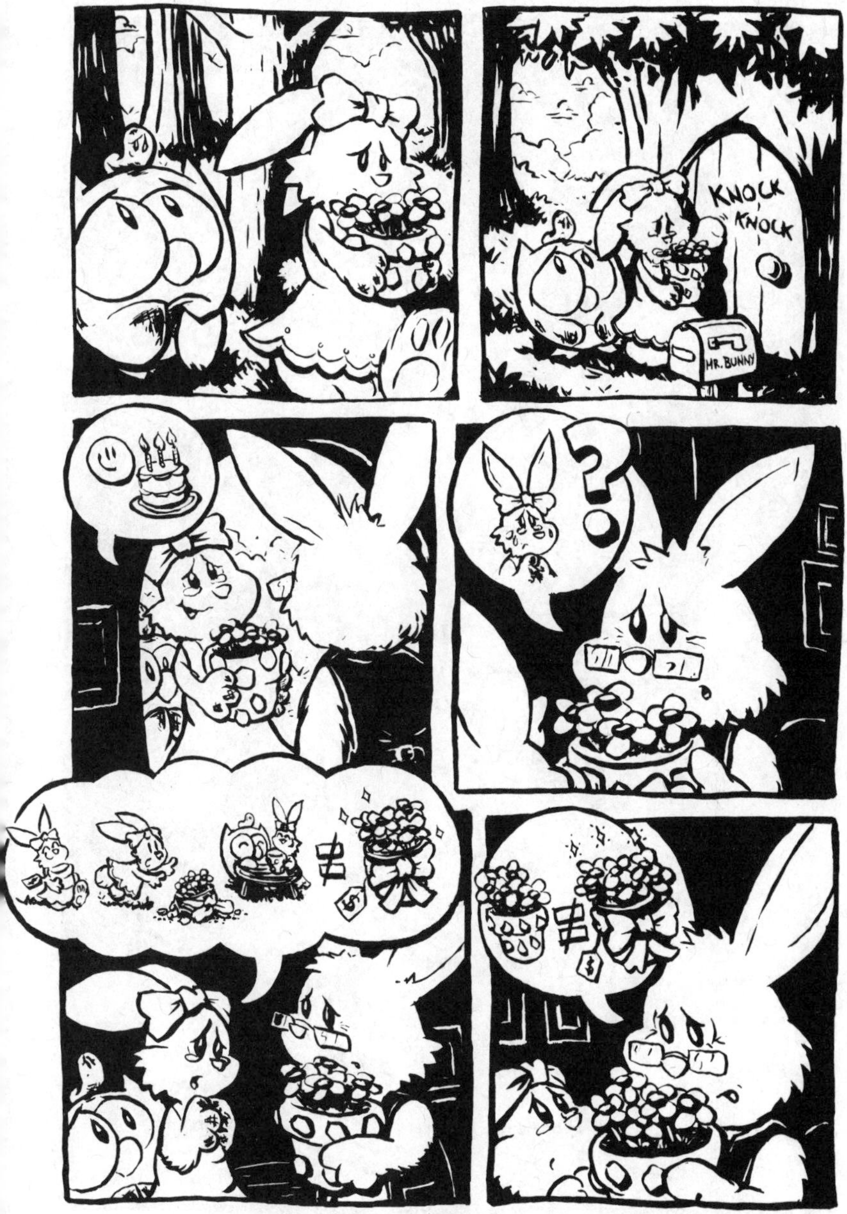
KNOCK
KNOCK
MR. BUNNY

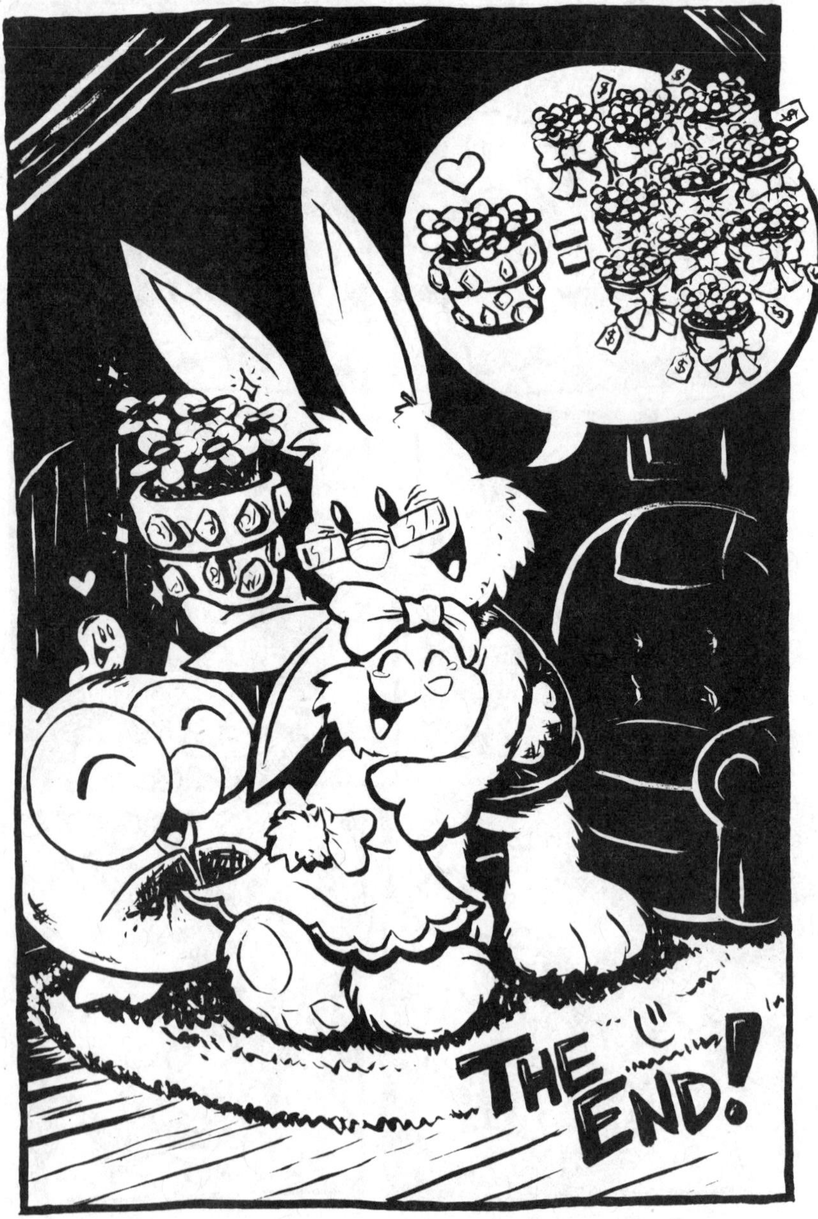
THE END!

MISSIN' YOU

AUGUST, 2006

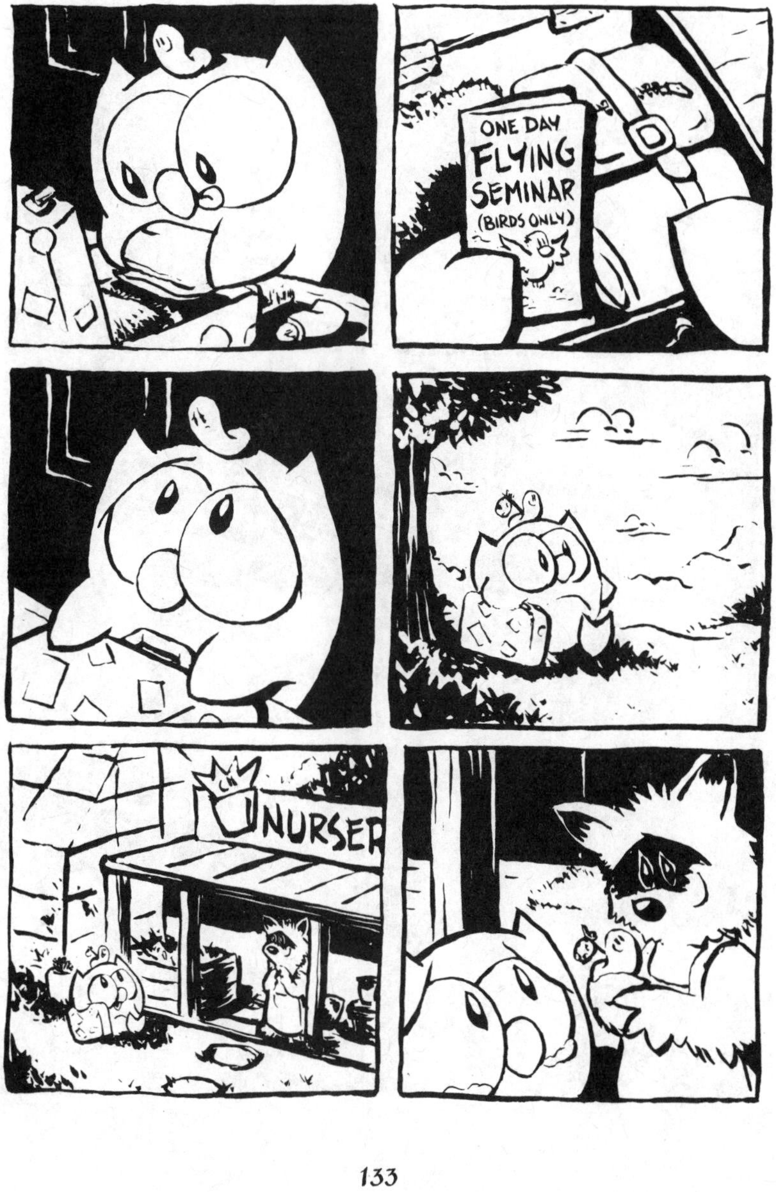
ONE DAY
FLYING
SEMINAR
(BIRDS ONLY)
NURSER

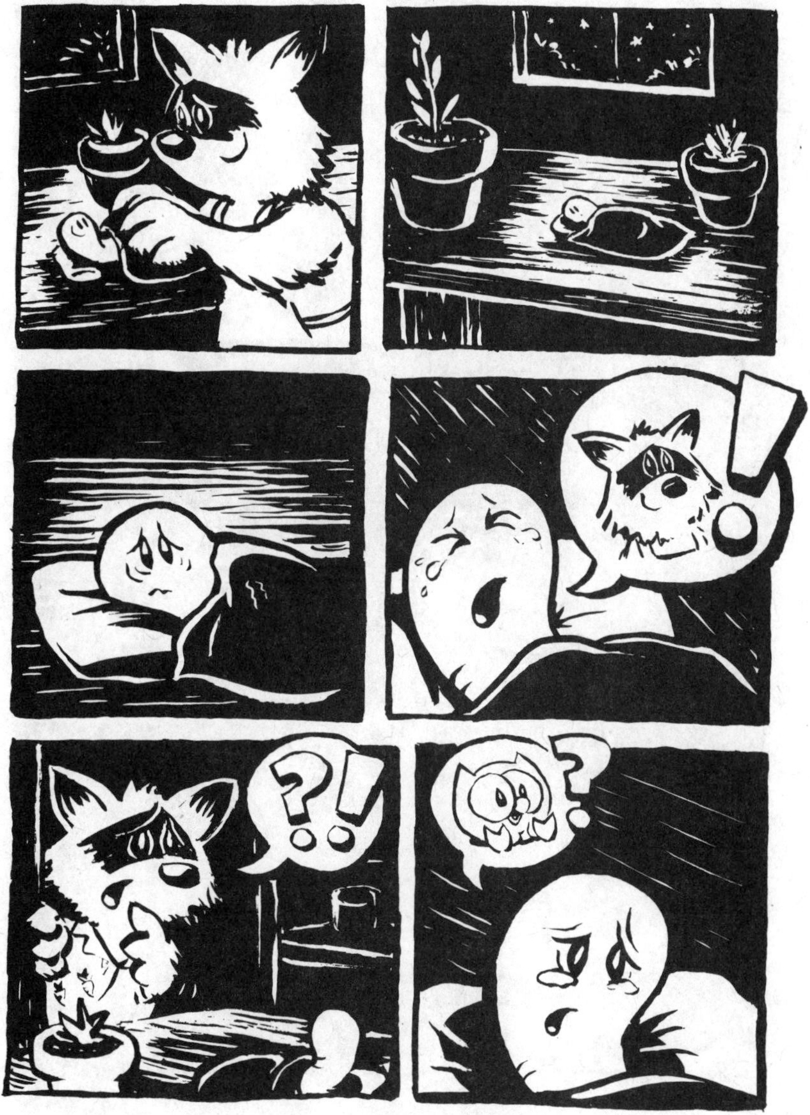
!
?!
?

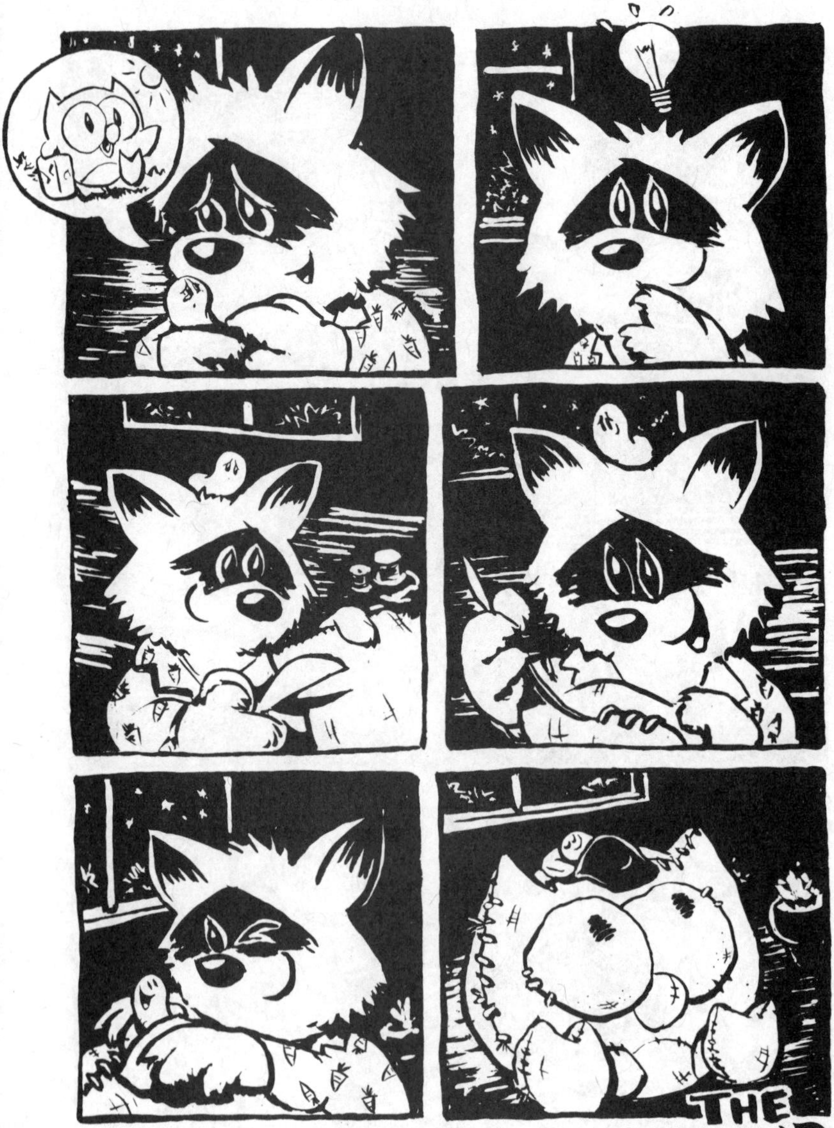
THE END

HATCHIN' FRIENDS

APRIL, 2008

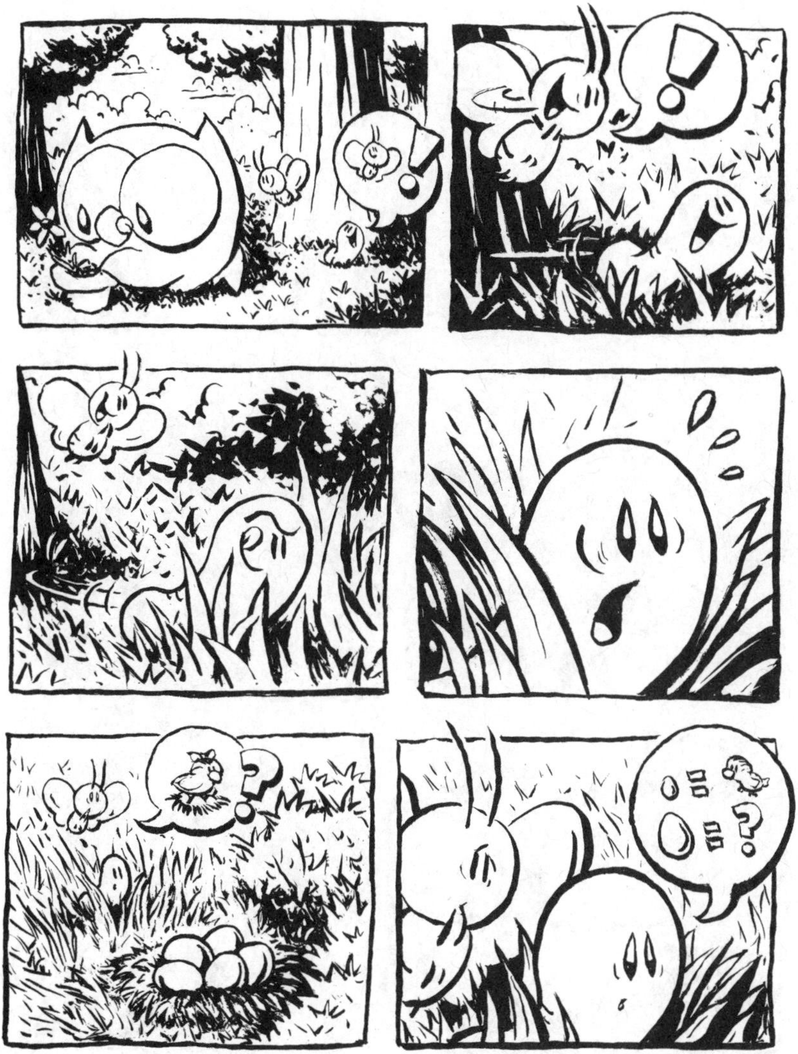

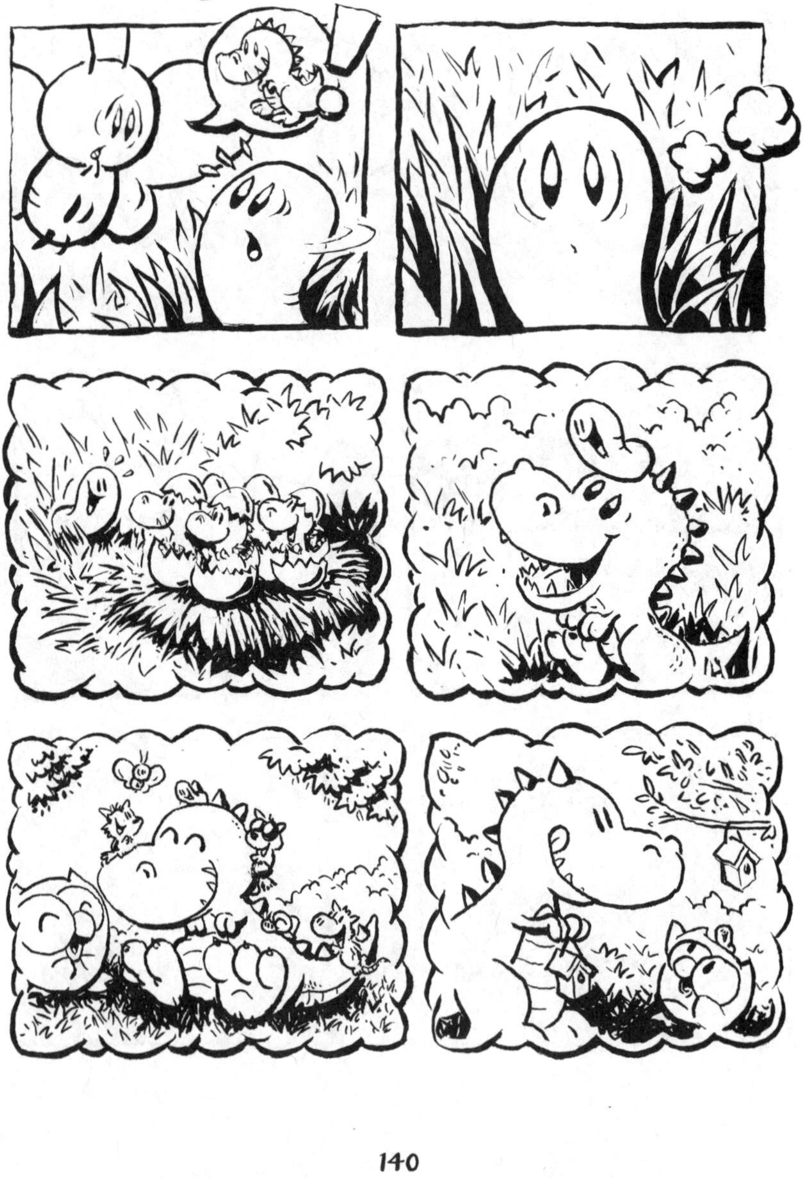

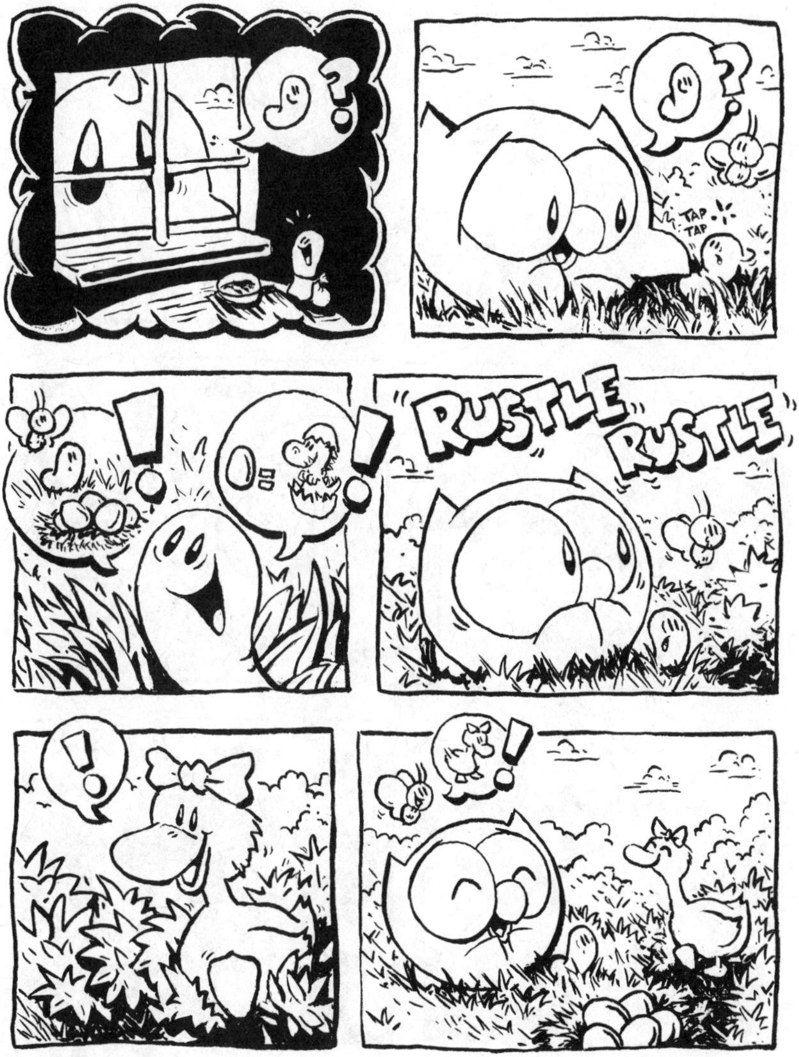
TAP
TAP
RUSTLE
RUSTLE

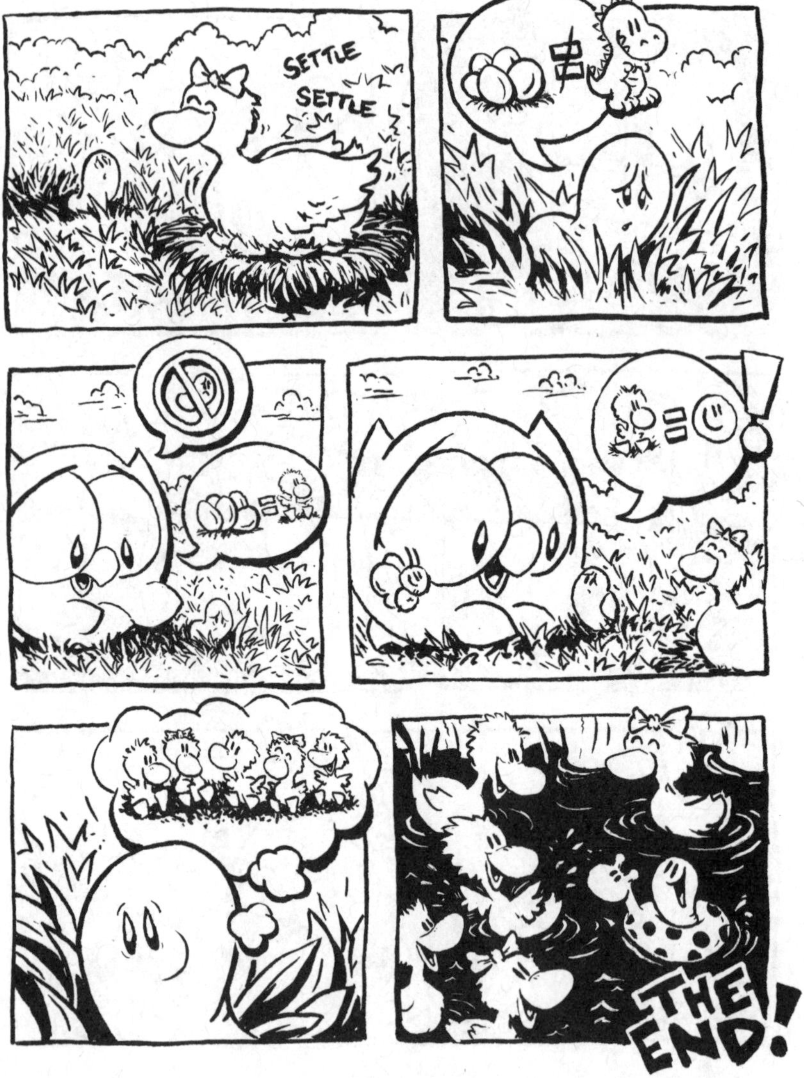
SETTLE
SETTLE
THE END!

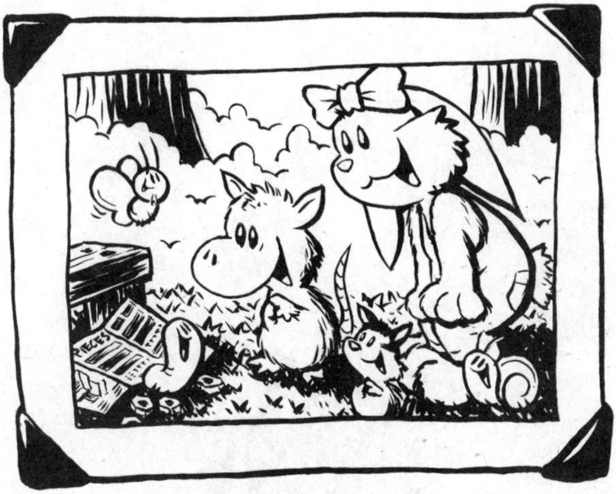
PIECES

IN A FIX!

MARCH, 2008

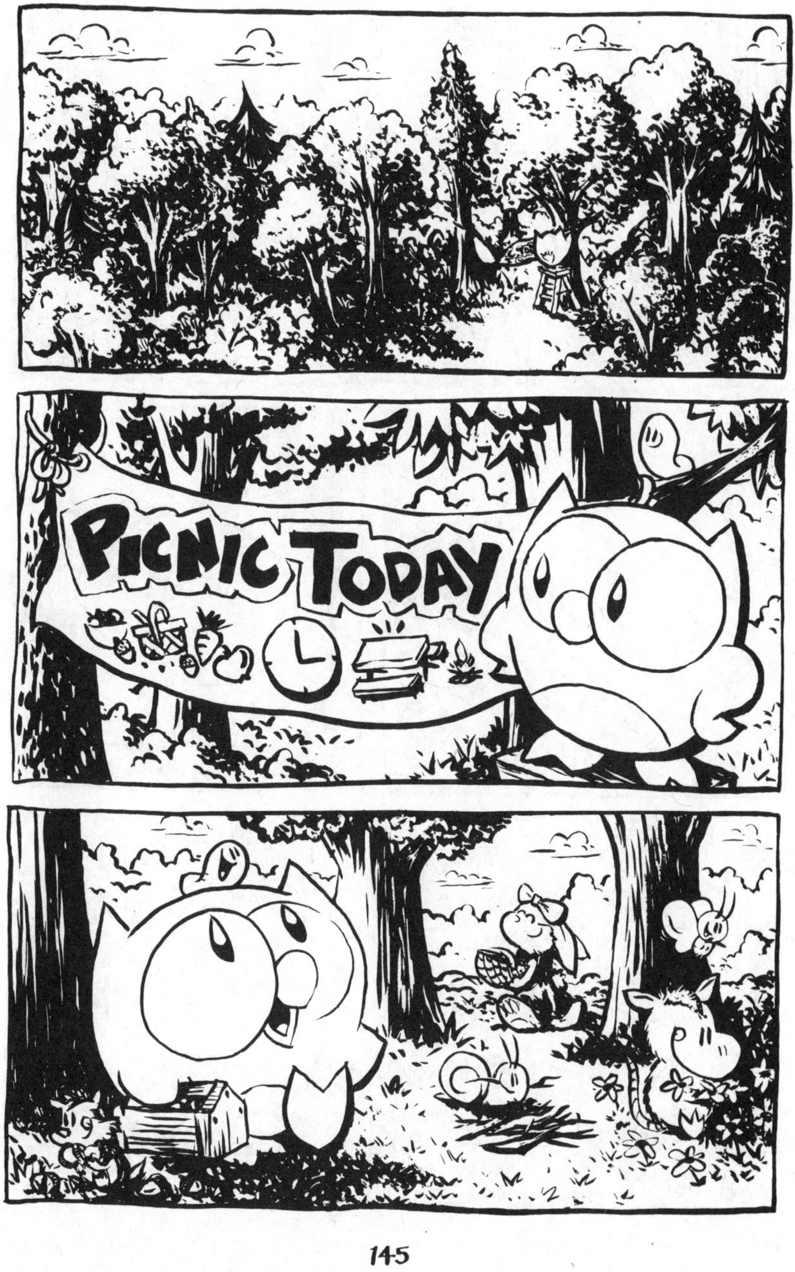
PICNIC TODAY

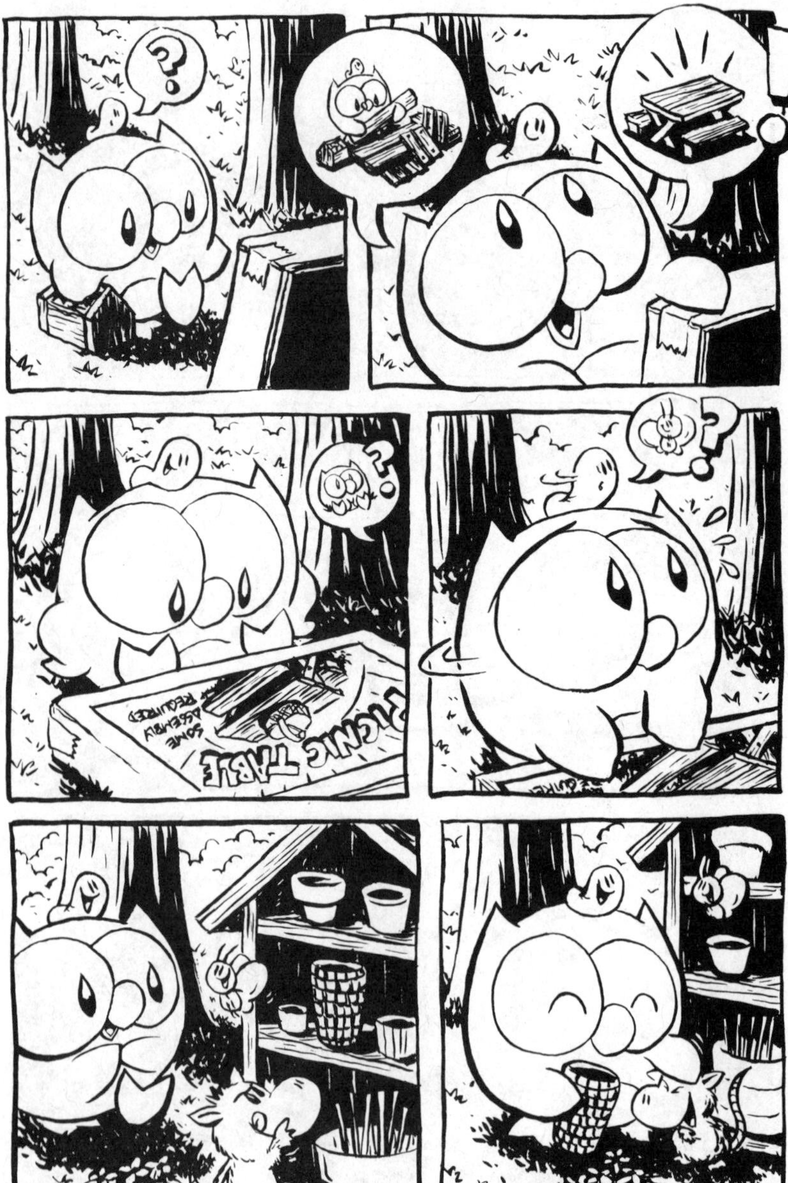
TABLE
SOME ASSEMBLY REQUIRED

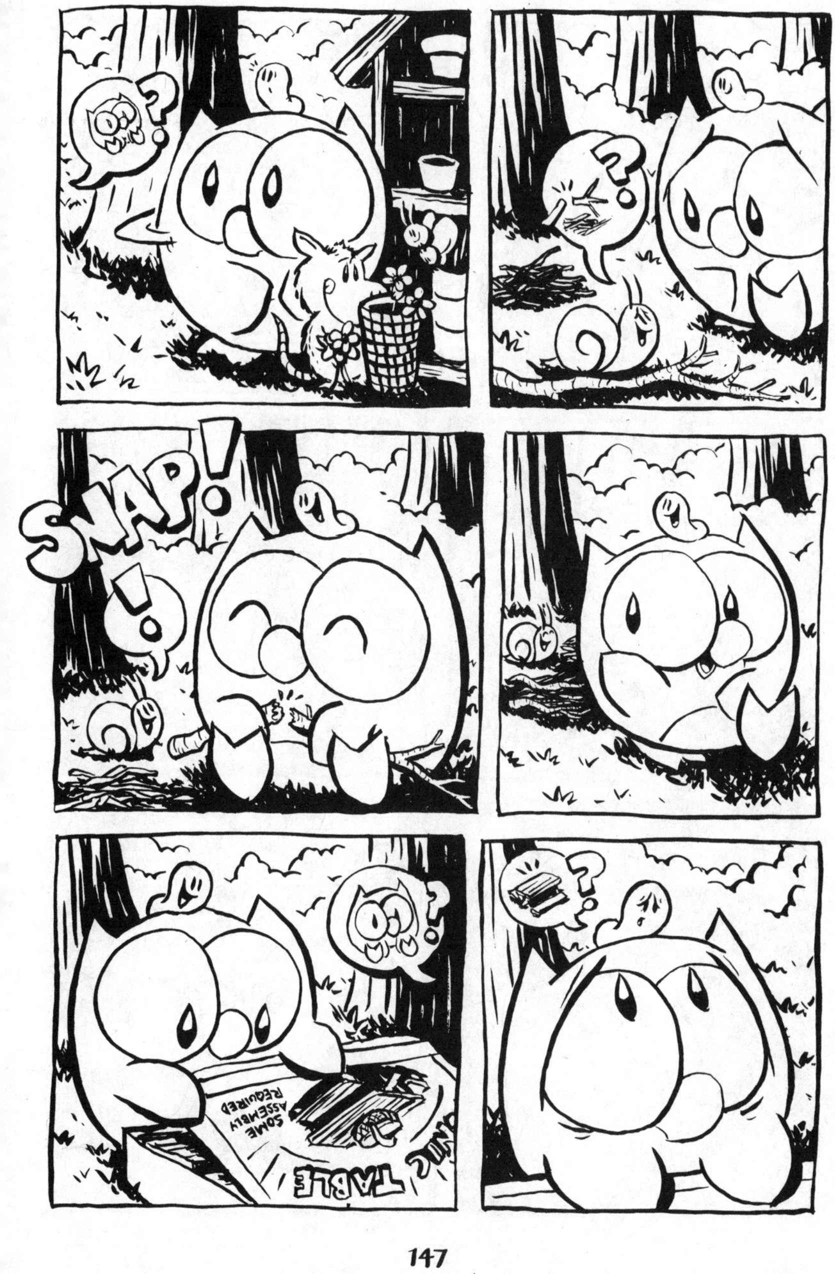
?
?
SNAP!
!
?
SOME ASSEMBLY REQUIRED
TABLE
?

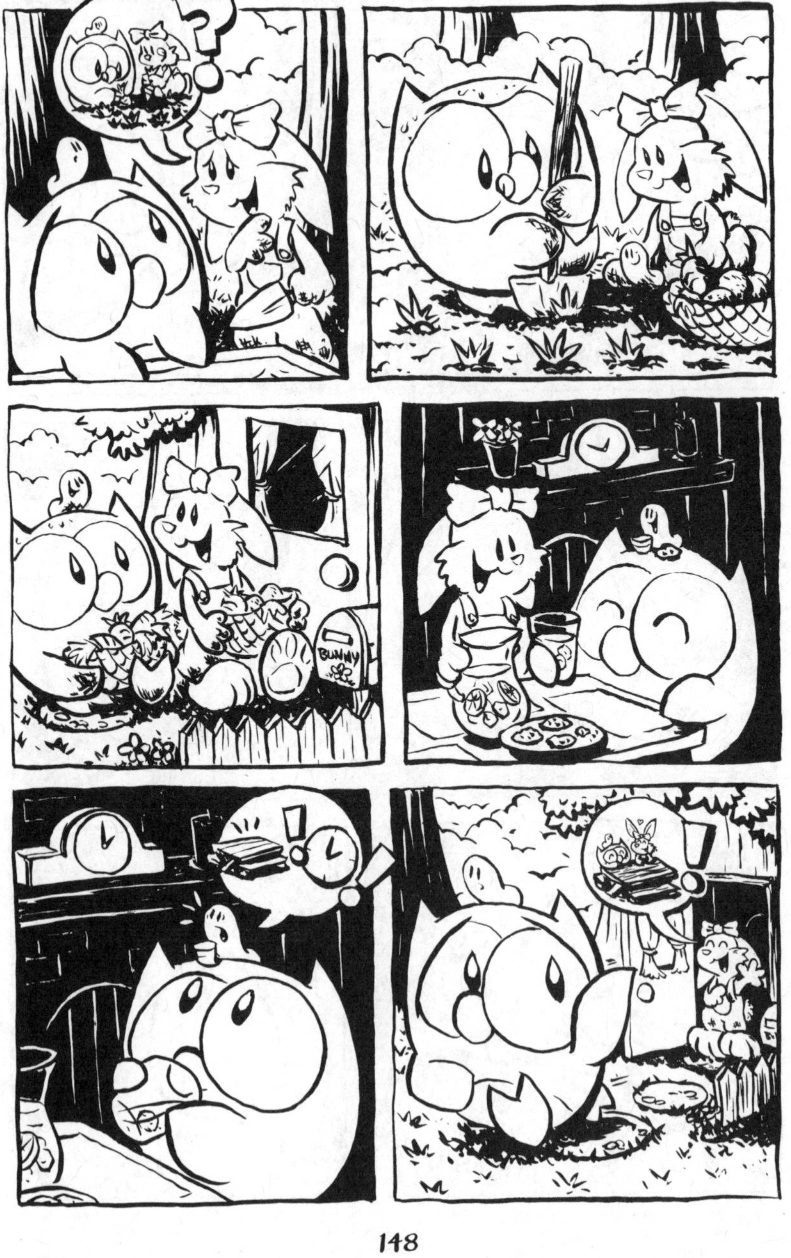
BUNNY

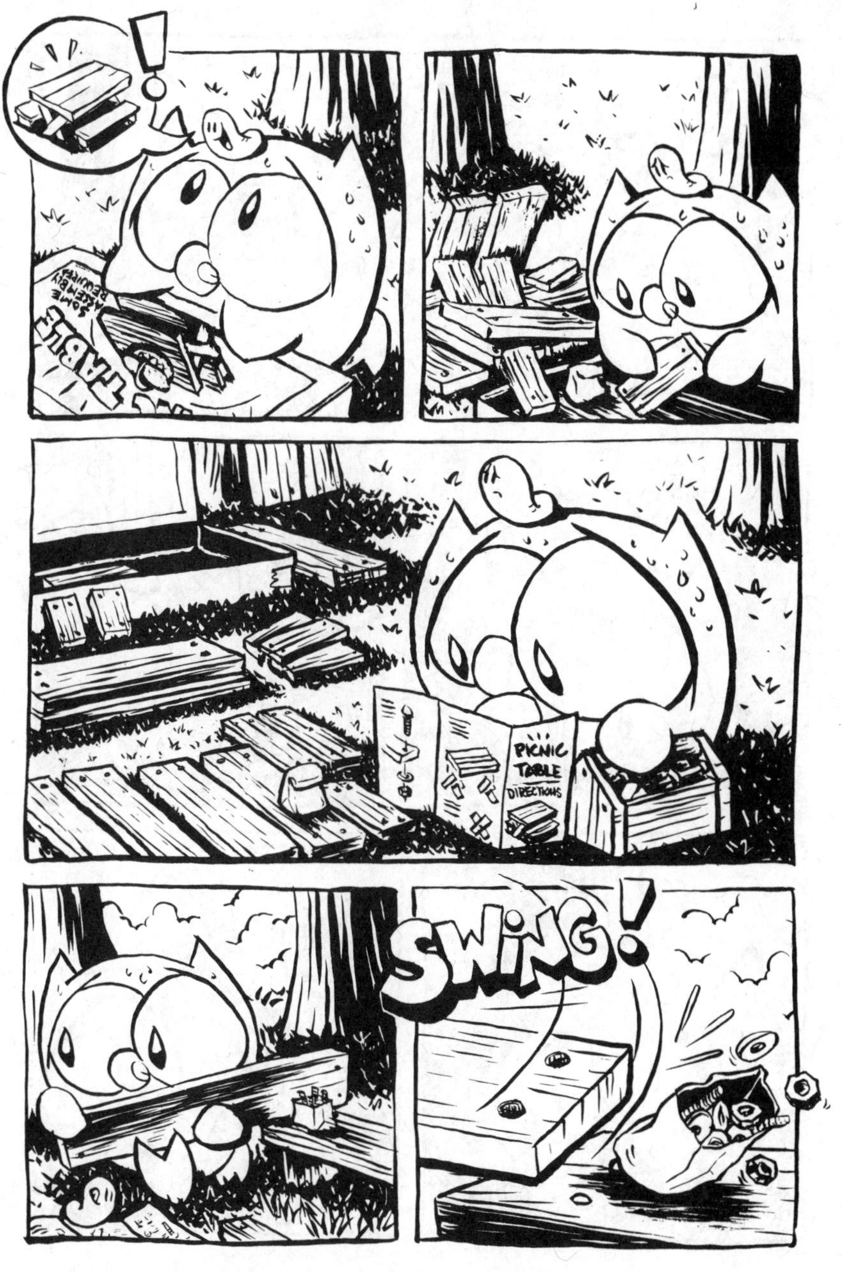
!
TABLE
SOME ASSEMBLY REQUIRED
PICNIC TABLE DIRECTIONS
SWING!

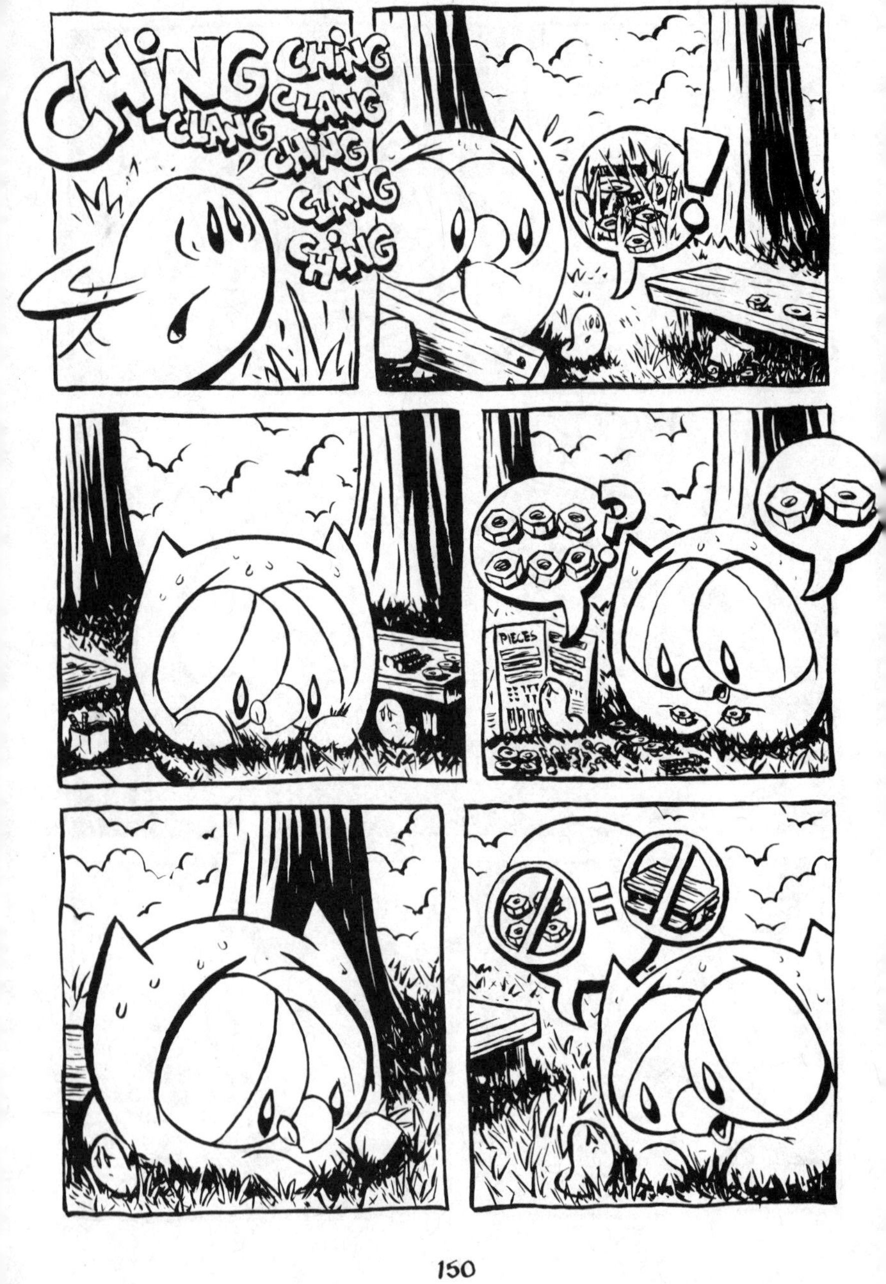
CHING CLANG
CHING CLANG CHING CLANG CHING
!
PIECES
?

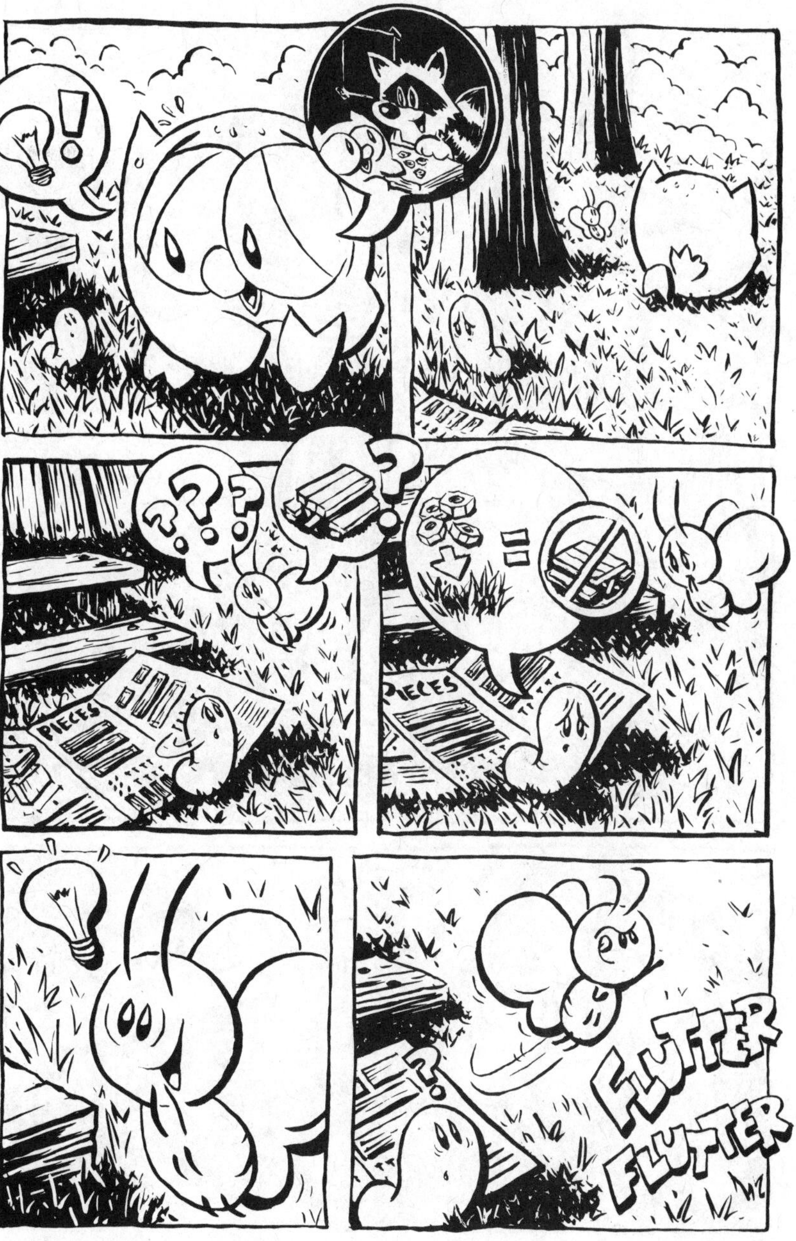
!
???
?
=
PIECES
PIECES
?
FLUTTER
FLUTTER

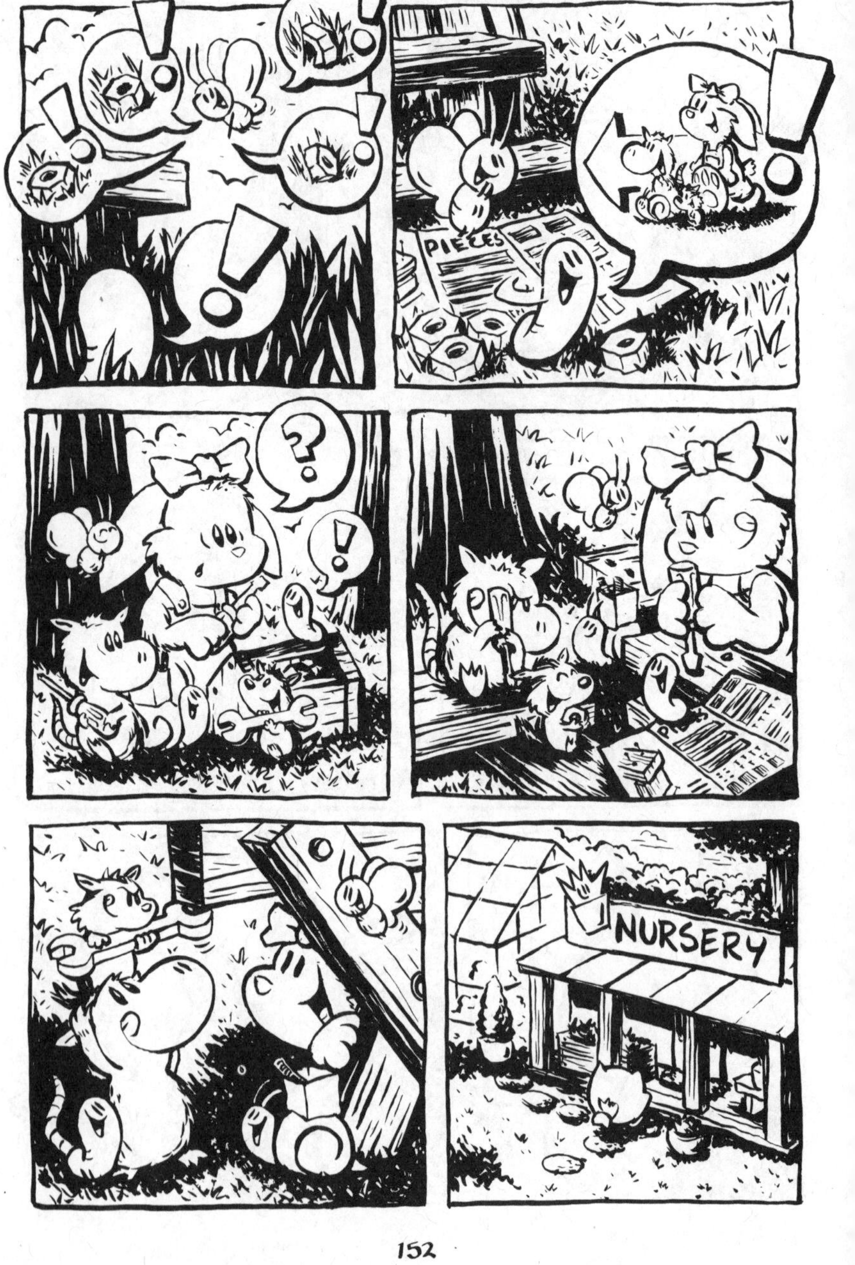
PIECES
NURSERY

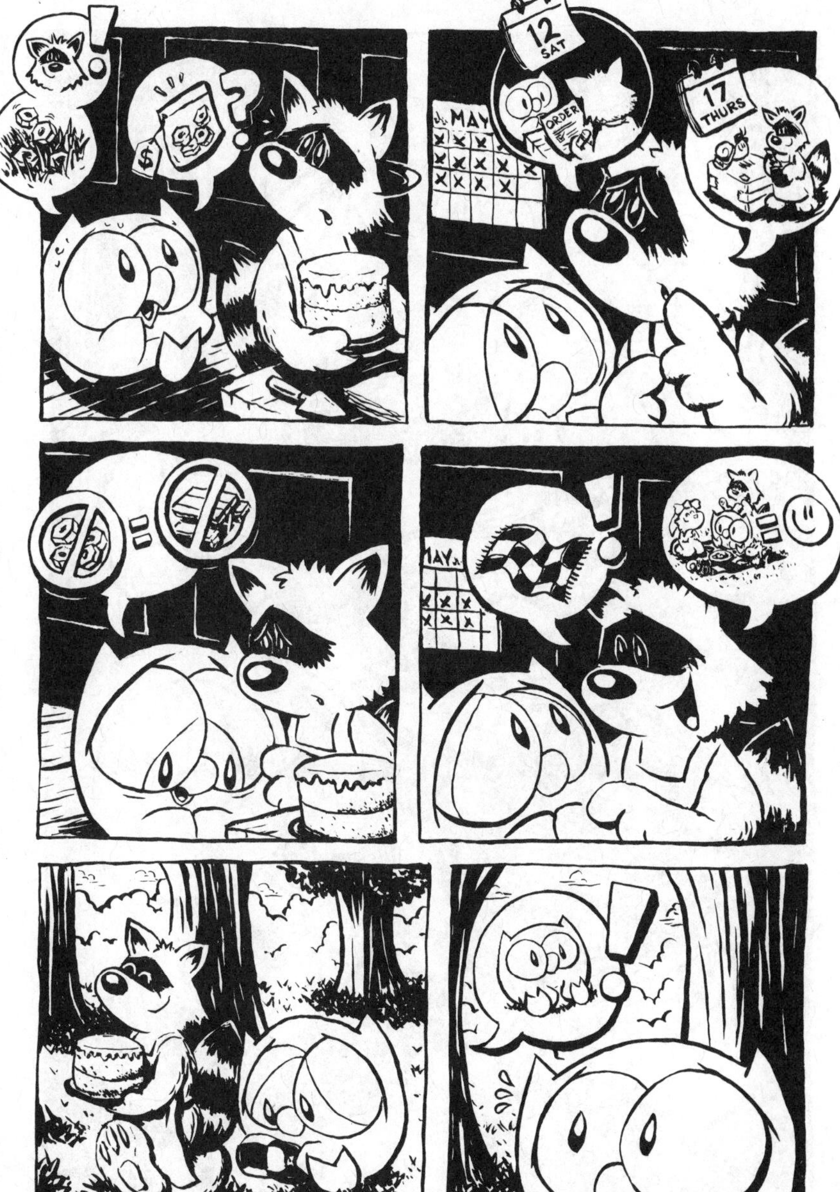

$
12 SAT
ORDER
MAY
17 THURS
MAY

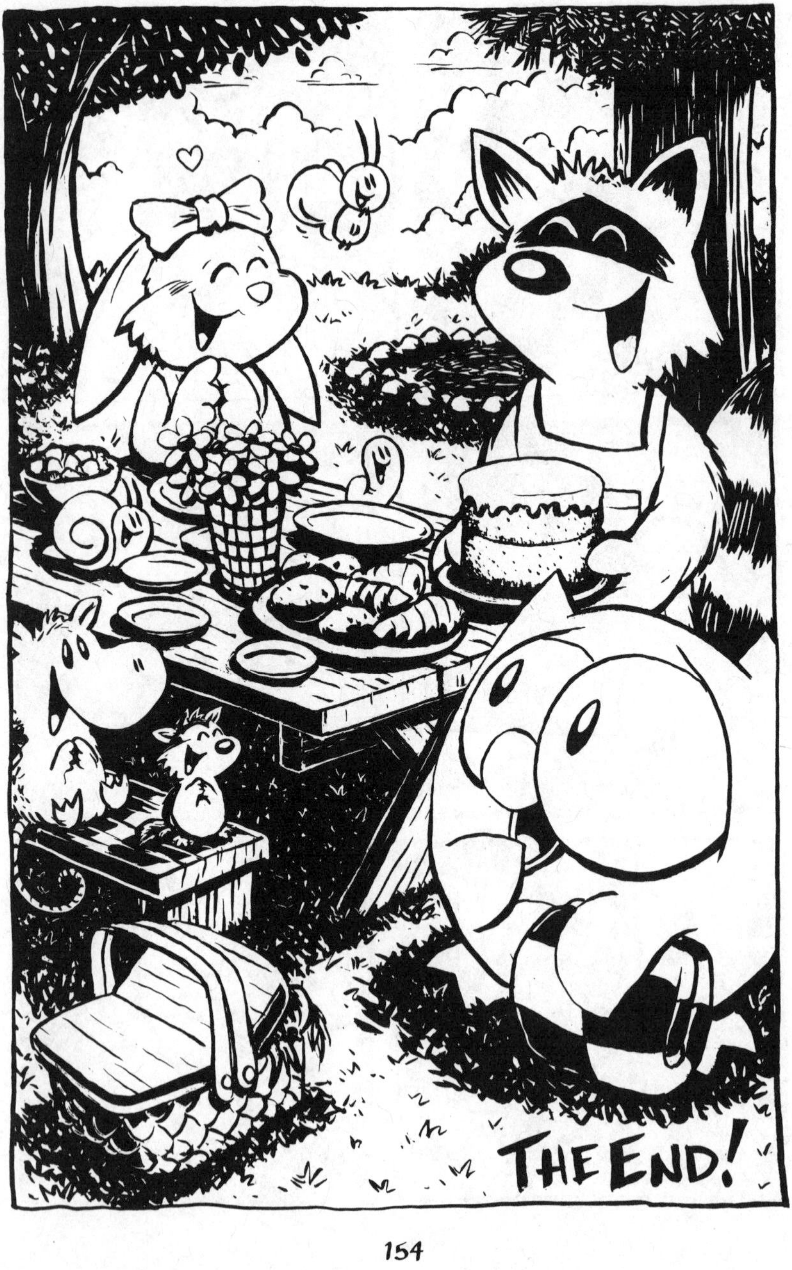
THE END!

EARLY OWLY ☺

WHERE OWLY CAME FROM...

I'VE ALWAYS LOVED TO DRAW BUT OWLY STARTED VERY SIMPLY AS A DOODLE ON A POST-IT NOTE. WHEN I WAS IN COLLEGE, I LIVED AT HOME, AND I WOULD STAY UP REALLY LATE WORKING ON DESIGN PROJECTS. I WOULD LEAVE SHORT NOTES FOR MY MOM AND LET HER KNOW WHAT TIME I WENT TO BED. IT WAS ALWAYS LATE, SO SHE BEGAN CALLING ME A LITTLE NIGHT OWL. SHE'S ALWAYS LOVED MY DRAWINGS - THE CUTER THE BETTER. SO ONE NIGHT, I DREW THIS LITTLE OWL ON THE NOTE TO MAKE HER SMILE. AFTER A WHILE HE SORT OF BECAME MY MASCOT. :)

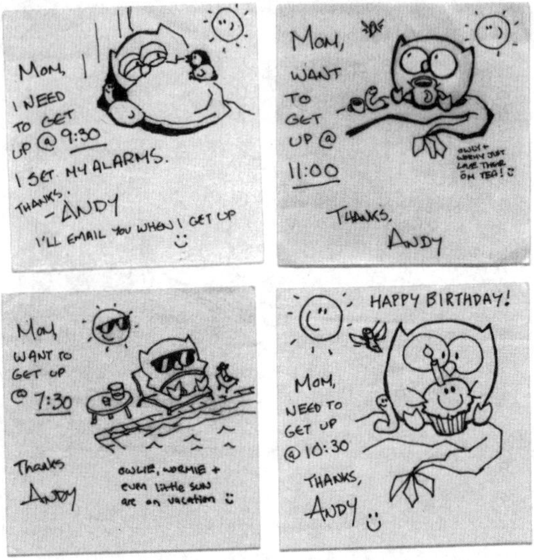
Mom,
I NEED TO GET UP @ 9:30
I SET MY ALARMS.
THANKS.
-ANDY
I'LL EMAIL YOU WHEN I GET UP
Mom,
WANT TO GET UP @ 11:00
THANKS,
ANDY
Mom
WANT TO GET UP @ 7:30
Thanks
Andy
owlie, wormie + even little sun are on vacation
HAPPY BIRTHDAY!
MOM,
NEED TO GET UP @ 10:30
THANKS,
ANDY

I DREW HIM TONS OF TIMES AND WORKED TO SIMPLIFY HIS DESIGN AND MAKE HIM MORE ICONIC.

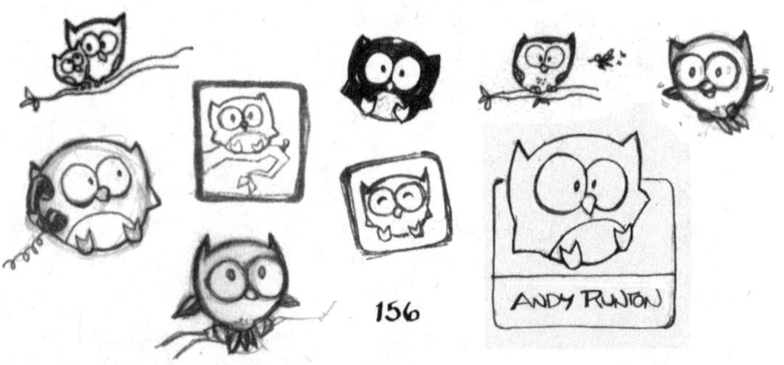
ANDY RUNTON

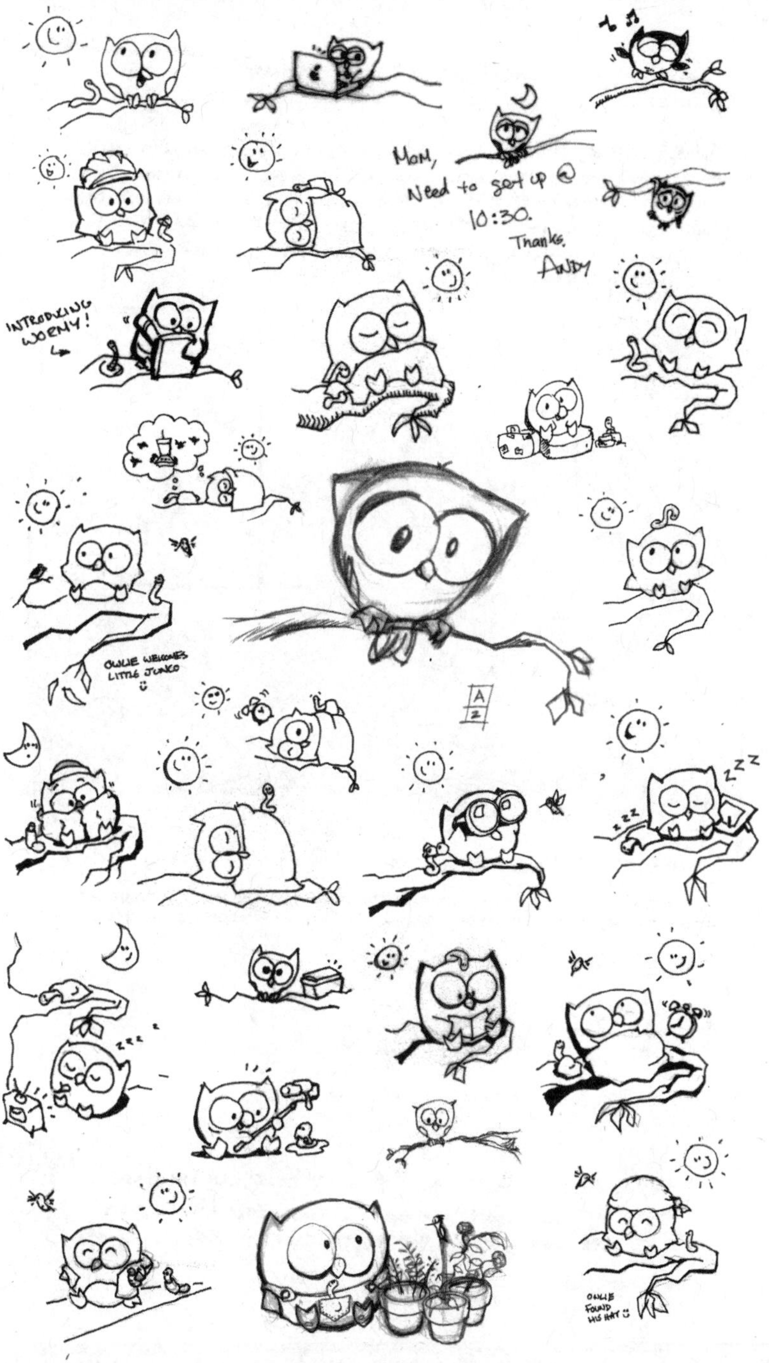
Mom,
Need to get up @
10:30.
Thanks,
Andy
INTRODUCING WORMY!
OWLIE WELCOMES LITTLE JUNKO
OWLIE FOUND HIS HAT

THE FIRST OWLY STORY

YEARS LATER, WHEN I WAS TRYING TO COME UP WITH A COMIC BOOK IDEA, I TRIED DRAGONS, ALIENS, NINJAS... BUT NOTHING WORKED. THEN ONE DAY, I LOOKED CLOSER AT MY LITTLE OWL. AND I DREW THIS... IT KINDA SUMMED UP WHAT I FELT. I WANTED TO DRAW COMICS ABOUT THIS LITTLE OWL. BUT I WAS AFRAID TO BE MYSELF.

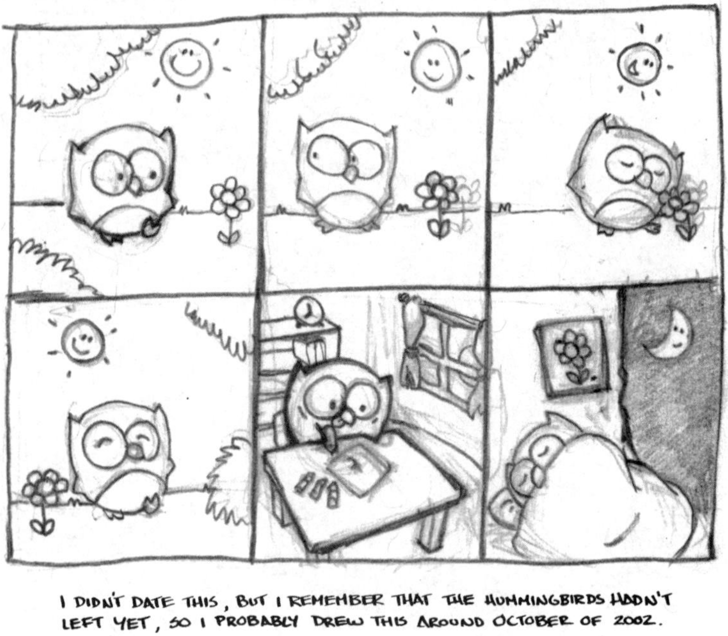

I DIDN'T DATE THIS, BUT I REMEMBER THAT THE HUMMINGBIRDS HADN'T LEFT YET, SO I PROBABLY DREW THIS AROUND OCTOBER OF 2002.

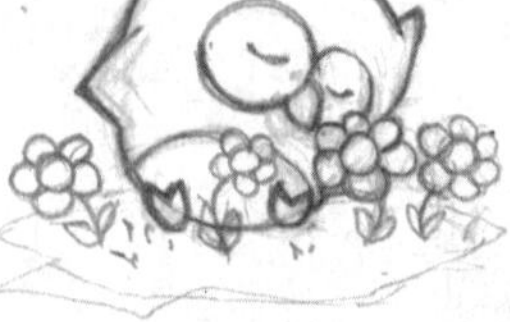

WITH THIS STORY I HAD FINALLY DROPPED MY GUARD, AND I ABSOLUTELY LOVED IT! THE STORY WAS VERY PERSONAL, WHICH MADE WRITING IT EASY.

EVENTUALLY I DECIDED TO POLISH UP THE STORY AND BUILD ON THE IDEA A BIT. I MODIFIED IT SOMEWHAT, AND ALTHOUGH YOU CAN SEE (BELOW) THAT THERE WAS A DRAFT WHERE OWLY TALKED IN WORDS, I DECIDED TO LEAVE THE DIALOGUE OUT OF THE FINAL VERSION BECAUSE I WAS UNSURE OF MY WRITING ABILITY. BUT I STARTED WRITING MORE AND MORE OWLY STORIES.

AFTER THAT, EVERYTHING JUST CLICKED. :)

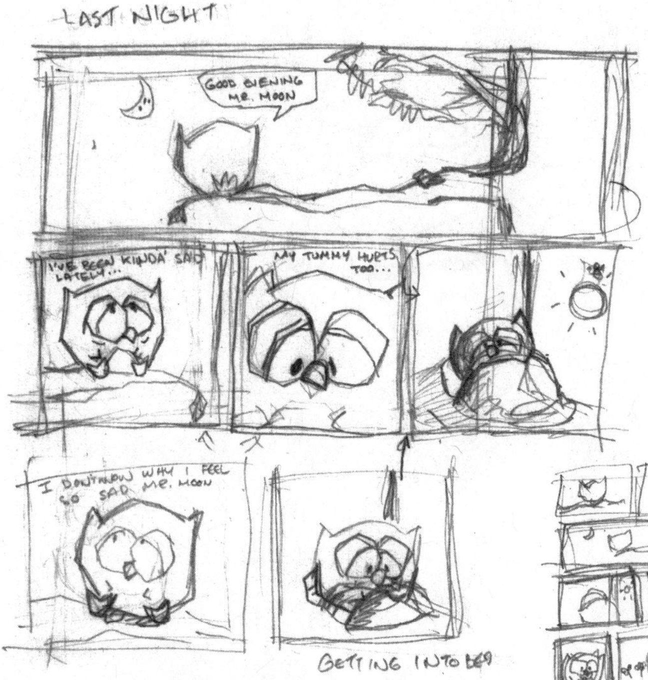
LAST NIGHT
GOOD EVENING MR. MOON
I'VE BEEN KINDA' SAD LATELY...
MY TUMMY HURTS TOO...
I DONTKNOW WHY I FEEL SO SAD MR. MOON
GETTING INTO BED
I, KNOW ITS EARLY BUT I'M JUST GOING TO GO TO BED. MAYBE I'LL FEEL BETTER TOMORROW NIGHT

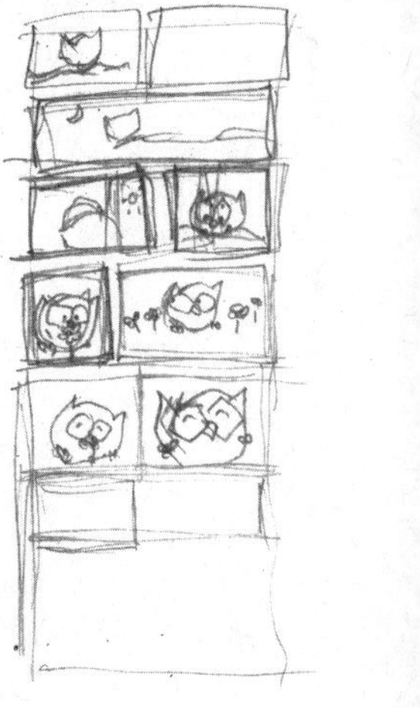

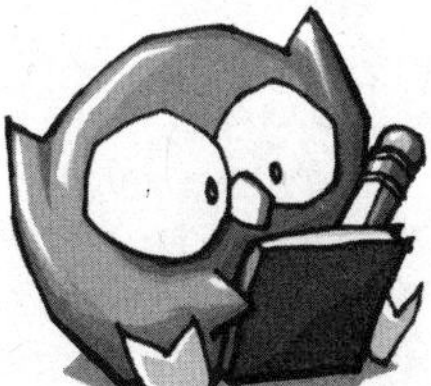

TABLE FOR ONE...

FEBRUARY - MARCH, 2003

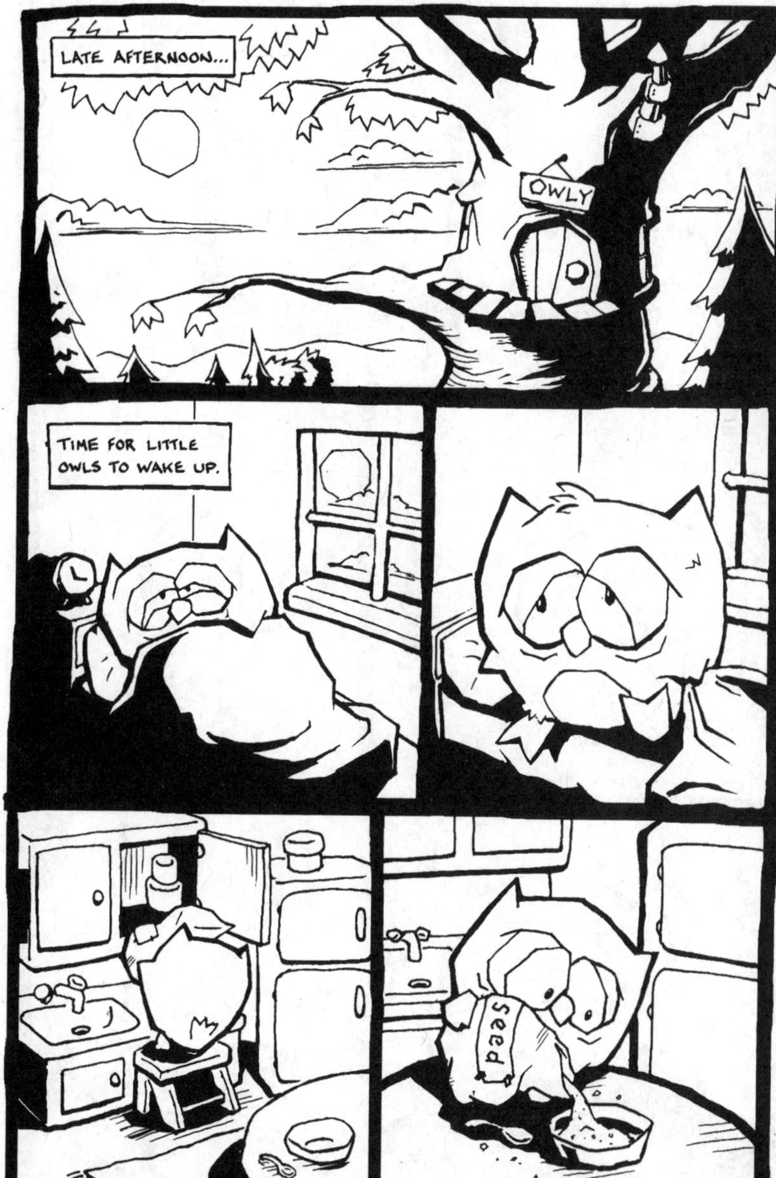
LATE AFTERNOON...
OWLY
TIME FOR LITTLE OWLS TO WAKE UP.
Seed

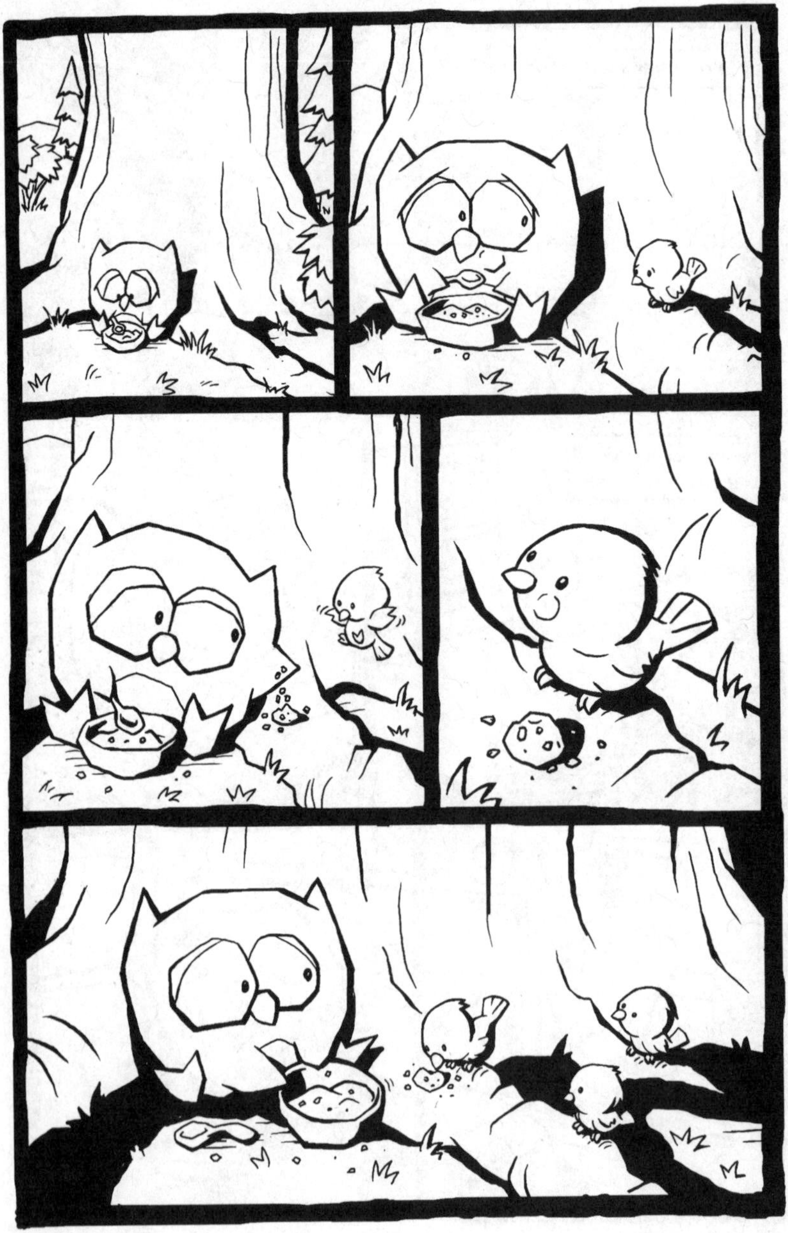

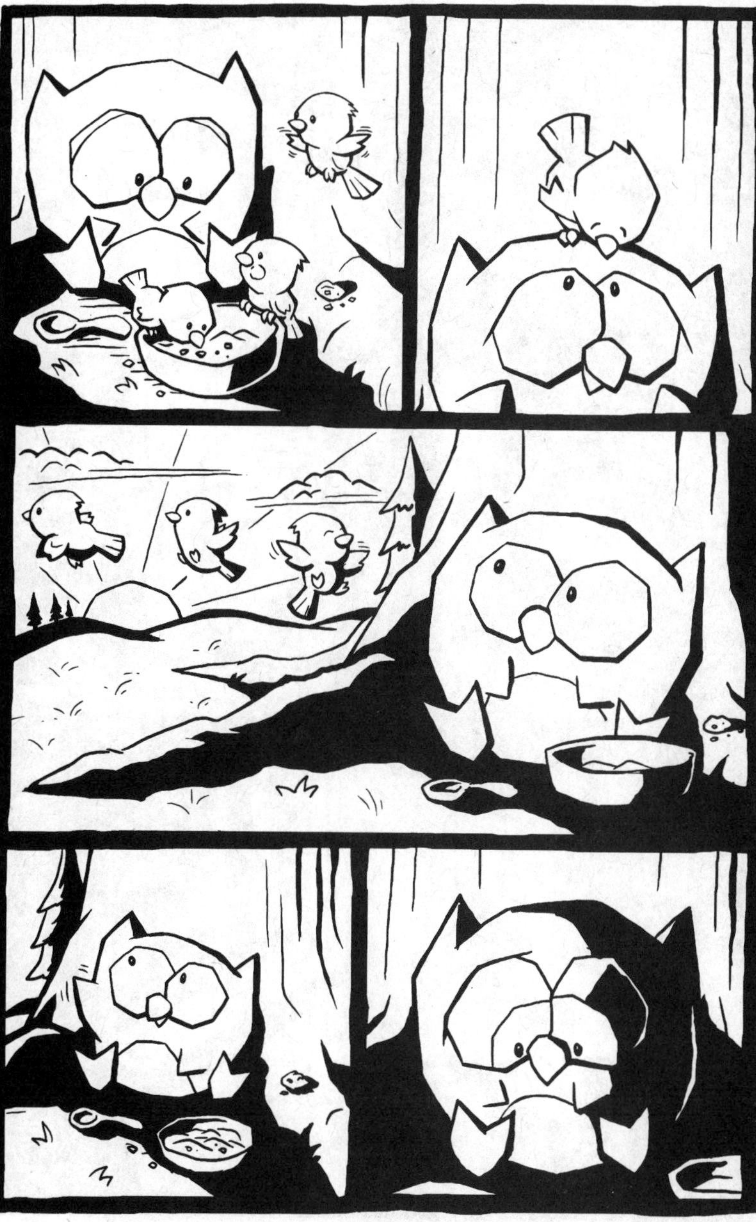

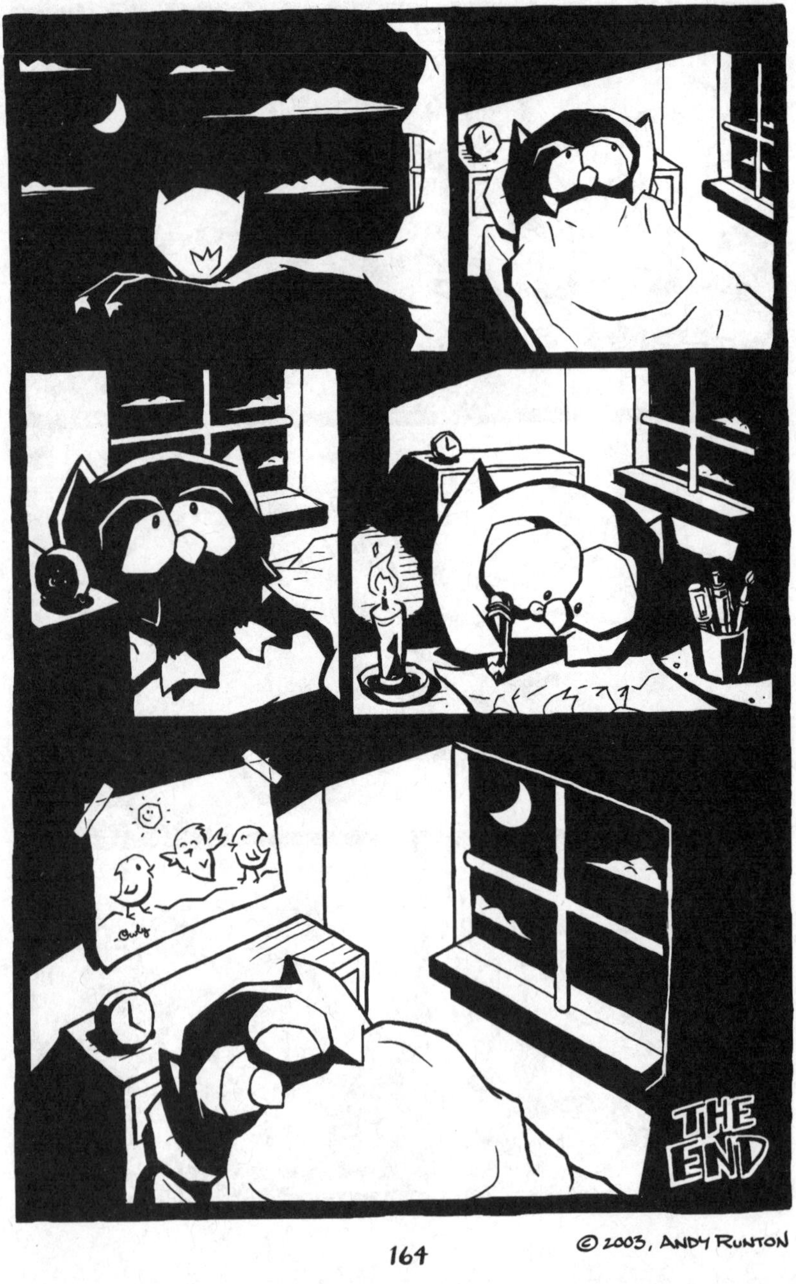
-Owly
THE END

CLEAN UP, AISLE TWO

☆ PLEASE NOTE: THIS STORY WAS INCREDIBLY IMPORTANT
TO OWLY'S DEVELOPMENT. IT WAS THE FIRST TIME I USED
SYMBOLS AND BALLOONS WITH OWLY. BUT IN THIS STORY, OWLY
GETS ... WELL, A LITTLE ... ANGRY. IT SEEMS INCREDIBLY OUT OF
CHARACTER NOW AND I ACTUALLY STRUGGLED WITH INCLUDING
THIS STORY. BUT, DEEP DOWN IT'S STILL OWLY AND IT SHOWS
A BIT OF HOW HE'S GROWN, SO ... ENJOY. ("

MARCH - APRIL, 2003

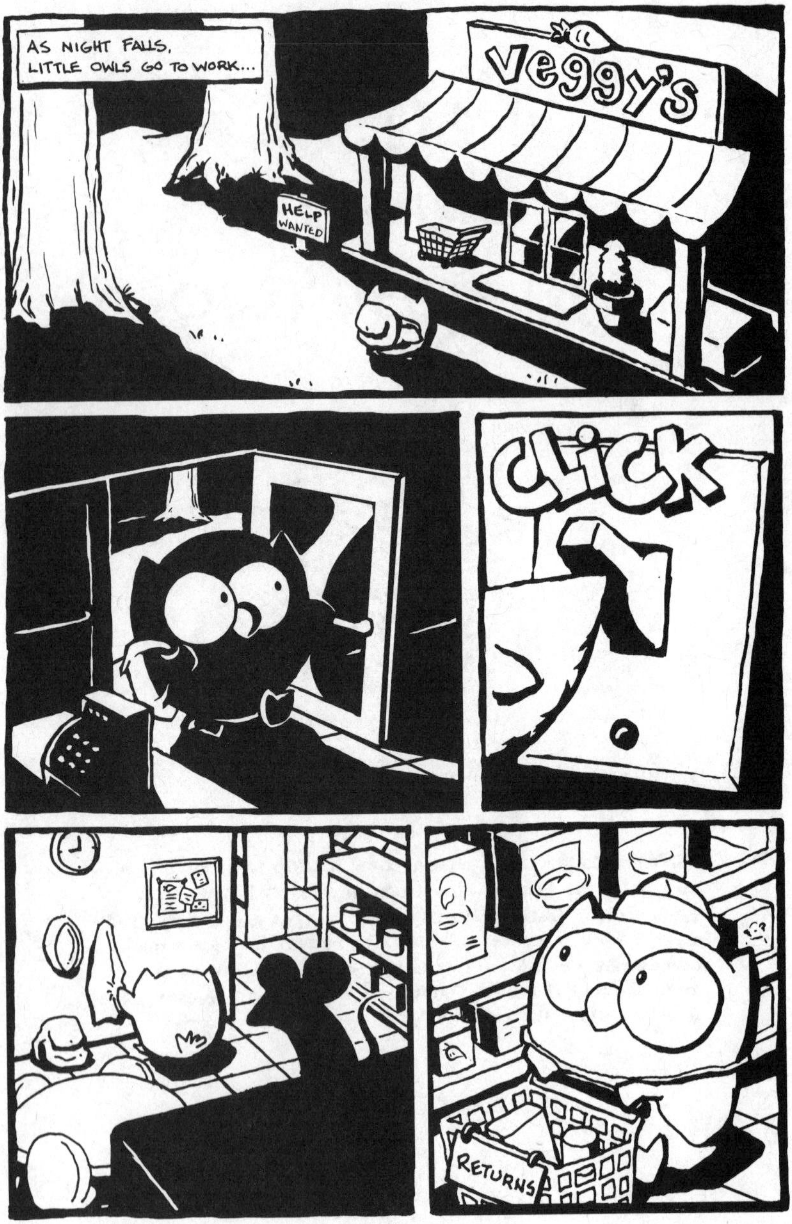
AS NIGHT FALLS,
LITTLE OWLS GO TO WORK...
veggy's
HELP WANTED
CLICK
RETURNS

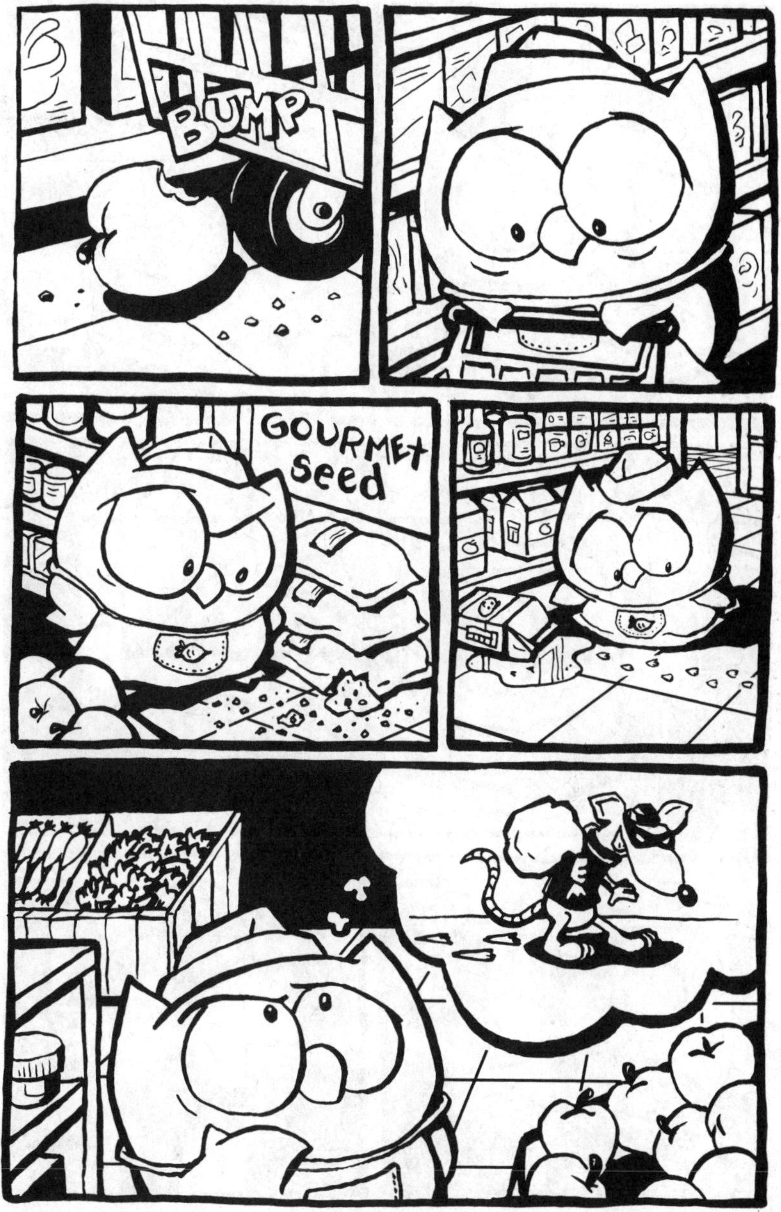
BUMP
GOURMET seed

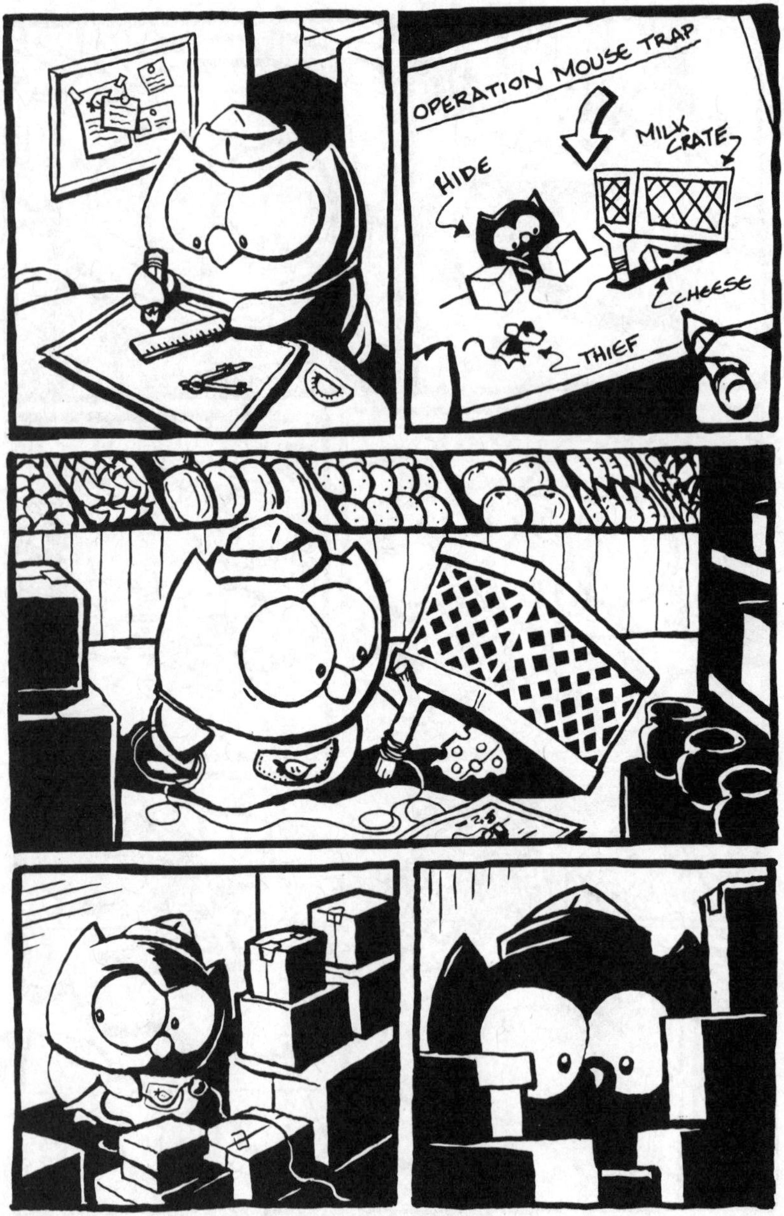
OPERATION MOUSE TRAP
MILK CRATE
HIDE
CHEESE
THIEF

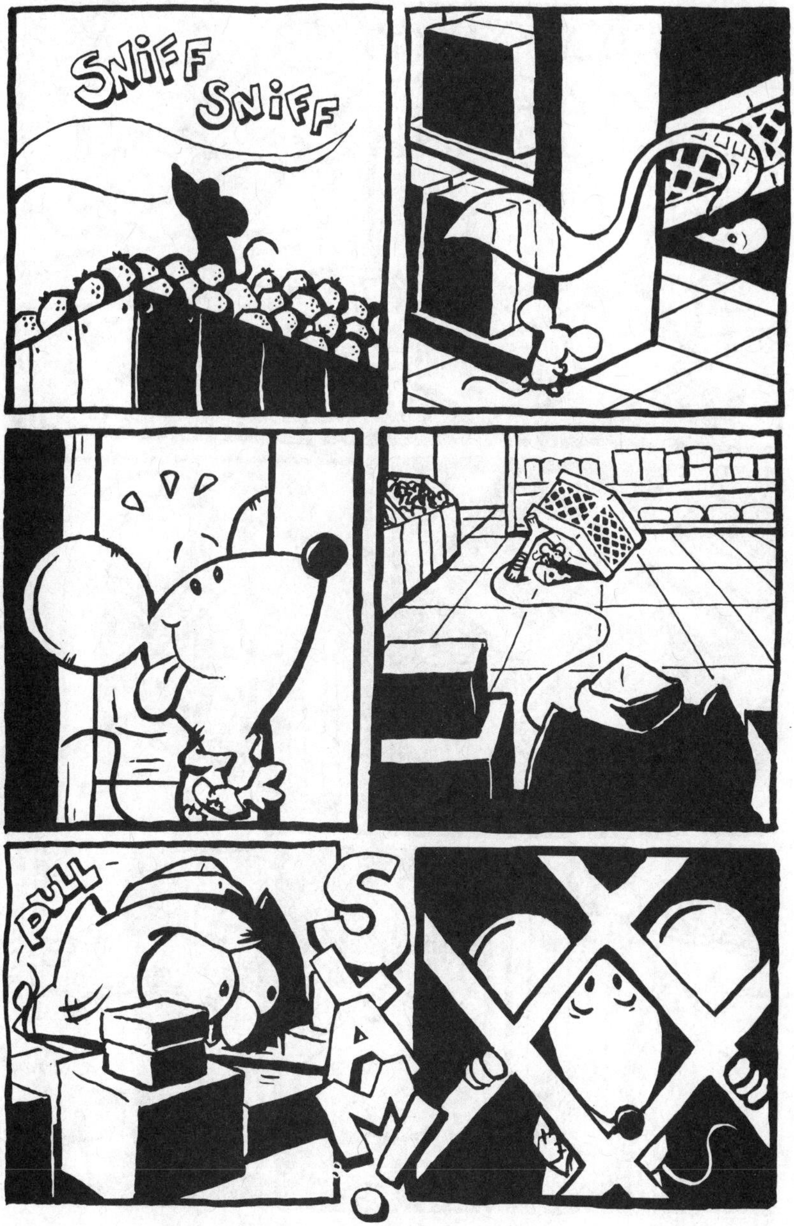
SNIFF SNIFF
PULL
SMACK!

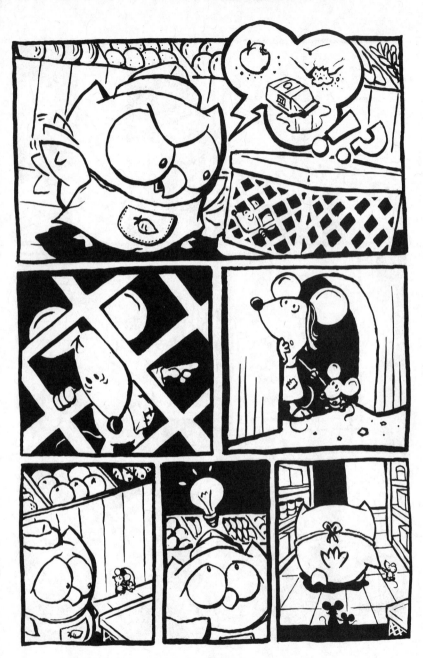

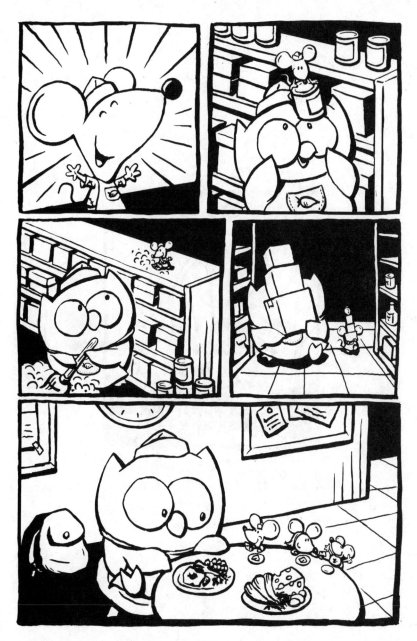

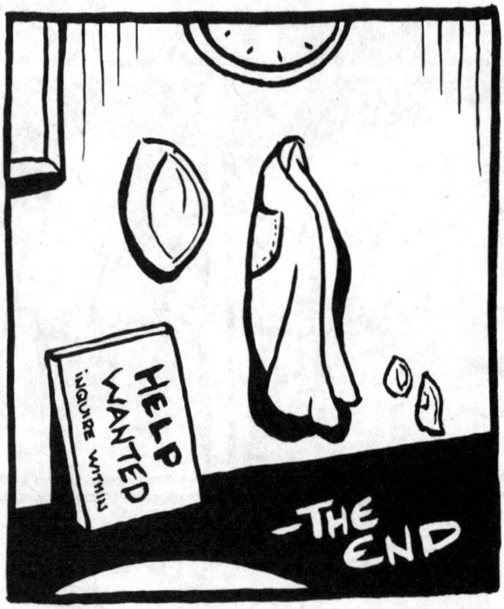
HELP
WANTED
INQUIRE WITHIN
-THE END

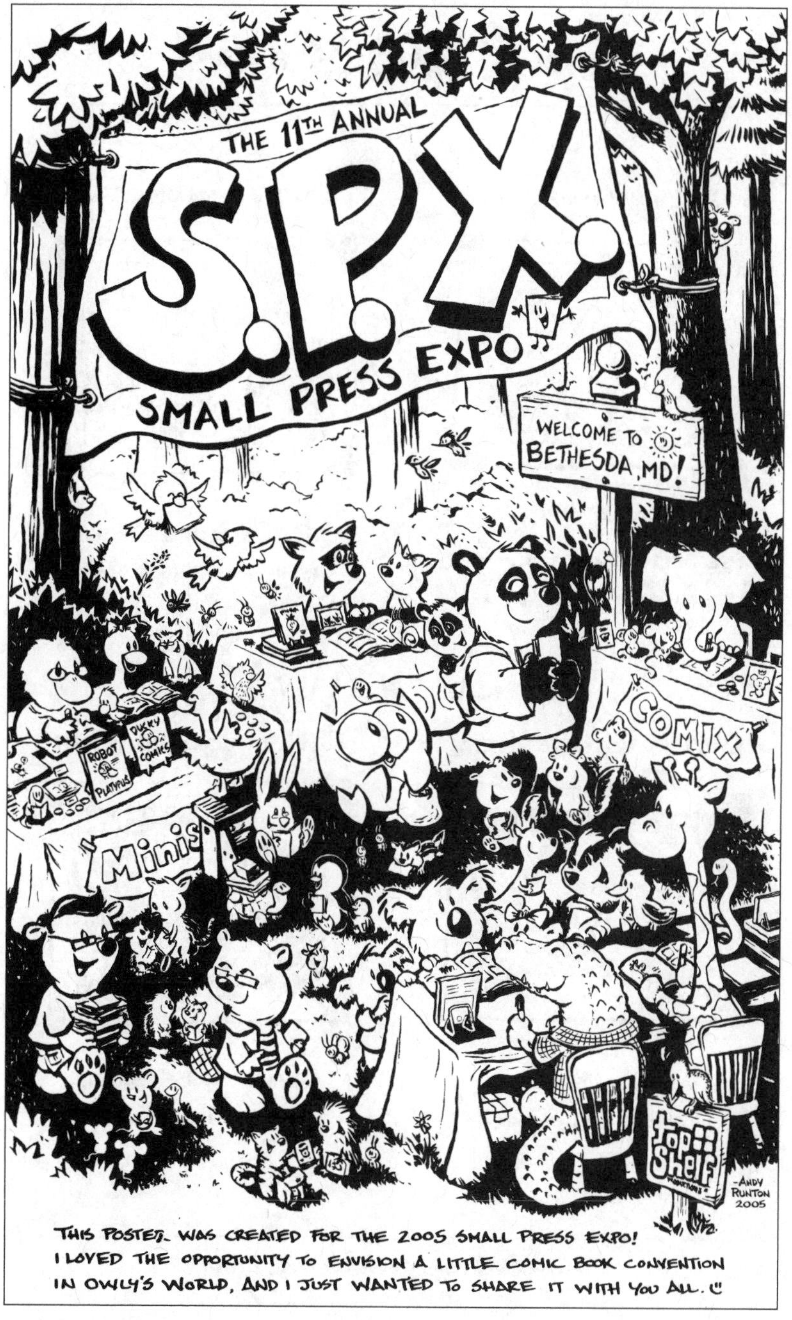
THE 11TH ANNUAL
S.P.X.
SMALL PRESS EXPO
WELCOME TO BETHESDA, MD!
ROBOT PLATYPUS
DUCKY COMICS
COMIX
Minis
top Shelf
-ANDY RUNTON 2005

THIS POSTER WAS CREATED FOR THE 2005 SMALL PRESS EXPO! I LOVED THE OPPORTUNITY TO ENVISION A LITTLE COMIC BOOK CONVENTION IN OWLY'S WORLD, AND I JUST WANTED TO SHARE IT WITH YOU ALL. :)

MORE OWLY BOOKS!

OWLY: VOLUME ONE

THE WAY HOME
&
THE BITTERSWEET SUMMER

ISBN: 978-1-891830-62-4

OWLY: VOLUME TWO

JUST A LITTLE BLUE

ISBN: 978-1-891830-64-8

OWLY: VOLUME THREE

FLYING LESSONS

ISBN: 978-1-891830-76-1

OWLY: VOLUME FOUR

A TIME TO BE BRAVE

ISBN: 978-1-891830-89-1

How to Draw OWLY!

by Andy Runton

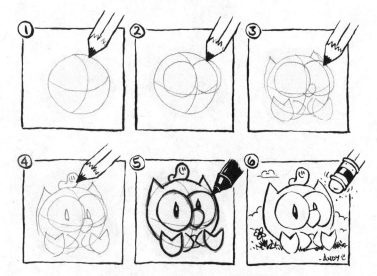

NOW USE YOUR PENCIL & PEN TO DRAW OWLY!
AND BE SURE TO SIGN YOUR DRAWING !

📷 : OWLY@ANDYRUNTON.COM

🐌 : OWLY & ANDY RUNTON
5502 EAST WIND DR.
LILBURN, GA 30047-6410
U.S.A.

WWW.ANDYRUNTON.COM

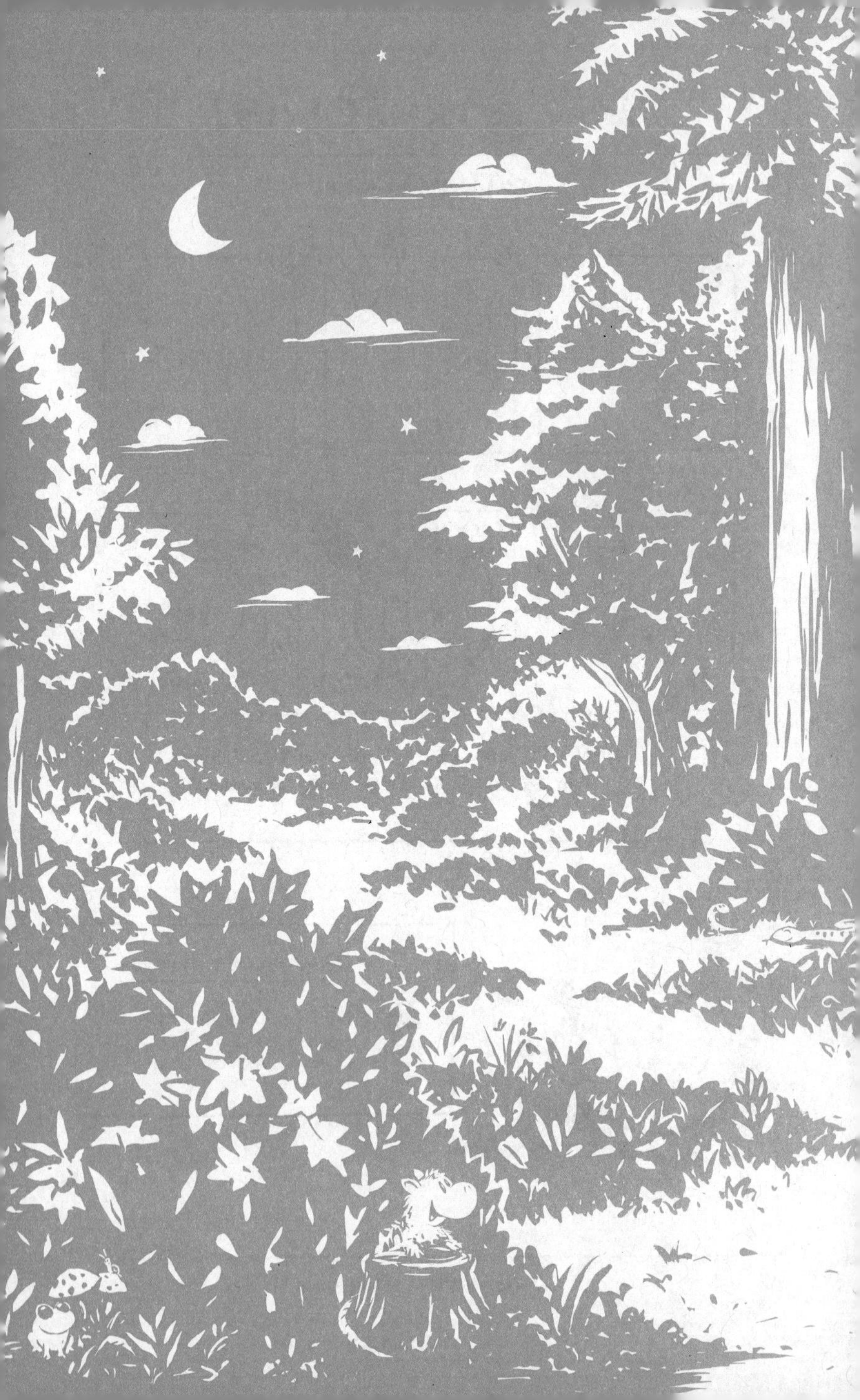